The Queen's Crown

LEAGUE OF RULERS, BOOK ONE

JENNIFER ANNE DAVIS

REIGN PUBLISHING

ISBN (paperback): 979-8-9864009-3-8
ISBN (ebook): 979-8-9864009-2-1

Library of Congress Control Number: 1-13052099481

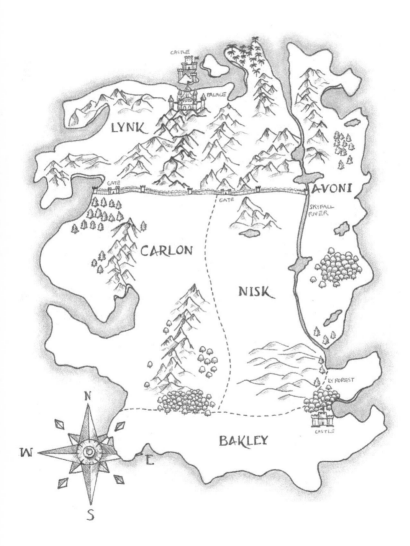

Chapter One

Sabine spotted her sister sitting on a bench under a sycamore tree, the man who'd been courting her on his knees before her. The exquisite sight made Sabine's heart leap. She quickly hid behind the trunk of the nearest tree so she wouldn't ruin their special moment. Excitement swirled within. It was about time Albert asked for Alina's hand in marriage—they'd been dancing around the topic for weeks.

After a minute, Albert and Alina stood. Albert took both her hands, kissing them, and then he hurried away.

Sabine ran to her sister. "Is that what I think it was?" she asked, trying not to jump and dance until she heard her sister say the words.

Alina smiled. "He proposed."

Sabine shrieked. "I'm so happy for you." She wrapped her sister in a hug.

Alina sighed, her face the perfect picture of bliss. "He went to go and speak with Father to ask his permission."

"It's about time, you old hag. I was beginning to think you'd never marry." Although she said it as a joke, Sabine had been concerned her sister wouldn't find someone worthy of her love, especially since she was already twenty-four years old. Most women her age had children by now.

Alina sat back on the bench. "I've finally found the perfect man."

Sabine plucked a flower from a nearby cherry tree and stuck it behind Alina's ear, pushing her long blonde hair away from her shoulder. "I am going to be your maid of honor." She sat beside her sister.

"I wouldn't have anyone else."

"This is going to be the most beautiful wedding." After watching her two eldest brothers marry, it was about time Alina would have the honor.

"I want to invite everyone to the celebration."

Sabine placed her head on Alina's shoulder. "No one deserves this more than you. Shall we go and tell Mother?"

"Yes. She's going to be so happy."

"Thankfully Albert lives nearby, so you won't be going far." She couldn't imagine Alina not living within walking distance. Albert and Alina truly made the perfect couple. They both had the same color hair, sparkling blue eyes, and they were tall.

"I'd never leave this countryside. It's too beautiful here." She stood and pulled Sabine up alongside her.

"You don't think Father will object to you marrying Albert since he's only a baron?" Their two eldest brothers had married daughters of prominent dukes.

"It shouldn't matter." The two sisters began walking toward the castle.

No, Sabine supposed it shouldn't. Not since Father had Karl as his heir, and Karl had two boys of his own. The royal line was well established, and Alina wouldn't have to worry about ever sitting on the throne. One of the perks of being born third, she supposed.

"Mother will be thrilled she'll have three of her six children married," Alina said.

Sabine rolled her eyes. "I don't see Otto, Viktor, or I marrying anytime soon, so don't you dare start on us."

Chuckling, Alina patted Sabine's arm. "I wouldn't dream of forcing you to do anything that wasn't your idea or you didn't agree with."

"What's that supposed to mean?" She nudged Alina in the side. "Are you implying I'm difficult?" As the youngest of six, she never bothered anyone. In fact, she'd say she was the easiest of her siblings and got along with everyone just fine.

"Never." Alina laughed.

"I am *not* difficult." She gathered her long, dark brown hair and twisted it into a knot atop her head.

"I didn't say you are," Alina said with a huge smile, implying otherwise.

They entered the castle and headed to the sitting room where they found the queen taking her afternoon tea.

"Just who I wanted to see," Elsa said, her blonde hair so like Alina's, perfectly braided atop her head. "Both of my daughters, together. Take a seat."

"Mother," Alina said, kissing the queen's cheek before sitting on the sofa across from her. "I have something to tell you."

Elsa turned toward Sabine. "Join us." It wasn't a question but a demand.

Sabine still stood in the doorway. She despised sitting around drinking tea. However, since this was a special occasion, she willingly entered the room. "I'd be delighted."

"Excuse me," Karl said as he stepped into the room behind Sabine.

"What a surprise," the queen said, a smile on her face. "Three of my children are here to join me for tea."

Karl looked at Alina. "Sister, Father needs to speak with you. I'll escort you there."

"I'm sure it can wait until after tea," Elsa said. "Come and sit with us, Karl."

"I'm sorry, Mother. This cannot wait." He stood with his hands clasped together, his dark hair combed back, impeccably dressed as always. As the crown prince, he took his position seriously.

Father probably wanted to speak with Alina before accepting Albert's proposal. Most likely he wanted to make sure it was what Alina wanted. Which meant Sabine would be stuck taking tea with her mother. Alone.

"Of course." Alina stood. "Mother, please excuse me." She turned to face Sabine and mouthed, "Don't say anything."

Sabine rolled her eyes. She wouldn't tell their mother about the engagement. If Alina wanted to be the one to share the news, she deserved to do so.

Karl and Alina exited the room.

"Sit up, dear," the queen said. "You're a princess, not a commoner. Act like one."

And this was why Sabine tended to wander out of doors and to avoid social engagements such as this one.

Three days passed and still no engagement had been announced. Every time Sabine tried speaking to Alina about it, her sister said she couldn't talk, and she'd hurry away. If anything, it seemed as if Alina was avoiding Sabine, which didn't make any sense. Besides being sisters, they were the best of friends and told one another everything.

Come to think of it, Sabine hadn't seen Albert since the proposal. This was supposed to be a joyous occasion, so she had no idea why all the closed-door meetings and secrecy was taking place.

Finally, on the fourth day, Sabine could take no more. She searched the castle for her sister only to discover she was with the king in his office. Again. Sabine paced before the office door, prepared to confront Alina about what was going on. However, Alina never left the room.

Instead of going to bed in her own room that evening, Sabine curled up on Alina's bed, waiting.

She awoke to darkness. "Alina?"

"Why are you in my room?" Alina whispered.

"I want to talk." Sabine scooted over on the bed, making room for her sister.

Alina crawled under the covers. "It's late. I'm tired and don't feel like talking."

Sabine slid her arm around her sister, hugging her. "Not even about the color of my dress for the wedding?"

Alina stiffened. "There's not going to be a wedding here in Bakley."

"What are you talking about?" There was nowhere else to have the wedding except here in Bakley.

"I'm not going to marry Albert," Alina whispered.

"Why not?" Her sister and Albert loved one another. Sabine was certain of it. "Did Father not approve? If not, I can talk to him. I'll tell him how Albert looks at you and that you're in love with him. He'll change his mind." It had to be that Albert was only a baron.

Alina didn't say anything.

"You deserve to marry and be happy."

"I *am* getting married," Alina whispered, a slight hitch to her voice.

"But I thought you said..."

"I'm marrying someone else."

There was no one else. Alina had never looked at any man the way she looked at Albert. "I don't understand."

"I've accepted the proposal of King Rainer Manfred of Lynk. I leave next week. The wedding will take place in his kingdom." She said it as if stating simple, undeniable facts.

Sabine laughed. "Don't joke about something like that."

"I'm not." Alina pushed Sabine's arm away. "I don't mean to be rude, but I'm exhausted and need to sleep. I don't want you in here tonight."

Sabine sat up, a stab of pain pressing on her heart. "What's going on?"

"Our kingdom will benefit greatly from an alliance with Lynk." Alina rolled over onto her side, away from Sabine.

"So you're going to sacrifice your own happiness?" None of this made any sense.

"I'm not sacrificing anything. I am a princess of Bakley, and I have a duty to our people."

"Our people?" Sabine crawled out of bed and began pacing. "Father is the king. Karl is the crown prince. Karl's two sons are his heirs. You're not going to sit on the Bakley throne. What you do doesn't matter."

"But I am a princess," Alina whispered. "And King Rainer needs to marry."

"Tell him to marry someone else!" Sabine yelled. "You're in love with Albert."

"Bakley is in trouble," Alina replied. "Lynk can help. By marrying King Rainer, I will be helping our people."

Sabine shook her head. "That's for Father to figure out, not you." This wasn't fair. Alina shouldn't have to fix their father's problems. He was the king, he made all the decisions, he could solve this mess without using his daughter as a bargaining chip.

"Sabine," Alina said, "I'm tired and wish to sleep. Leave me be. Please." Her voice wobbled, as if on the verge of tears.

"You're making a mistake."

"I only have a few days left here," Alina whispered. "I don't wish to waste it fighting with you."

"Then don't do this."

Silence filled the room.

"Fine." Sabine left Alina alone and returned to her own bedchamber. Tomorrow she would talk some sense into her sister.

When Sabine awoke the next morning, the castle was filled with activity. The servants were packing Alina's things, four seamstresses had arrived with yards and yards of material to make dresses fit for a queen, and a handful of sentries were being prepped to travel with Princess Alina to Lynk.

Sabine found her mother in the great hall, talking with the servants about how she wanted the room decorated for the ball that was going to be held in a few days to bid Alina farewell.

"Mother," Sabine said, "we need to speak."

The queen stepped away from the servants. "Honey, there is much to be done. If you wish to help, I can give you a job."

"No, I do not wish to help." She refused to aid in this madness. "Alina loves Albert."

"Hush, don't say such things." Elsa wound her arm around Sabine's, leading her out onto the balcony overlooking the large pasture behind the castle. "Watch what you say in front of the servants. They love to gossip."

"Mother." She slid her arm free. "What's going on?"

"Your sister is going to be a queen." She smiled. "I suggest you go to her and see what you can do to help her prepare." She turned and strode away from her daughter, going back into the great hall.

Standing there, dumbfounded, Sabine didn't know what to do to talk some sense into her family.

A thought occurred to her. Since her family wasn't seeing reason, she could talk to Albert and get him to help. She quickly made her way to the stables. Albert only lived a few miles away. She could ride her horse to his house and fix this mess.

Opening the door to her horse's stall, she heard someone walking toward her. She peered over her shoulder and found her brother, Rolf.

"What are you doing?" he demanded.

"Nothing," she replied, closing the door to the stall. "What are you doing?" Since his wife was pregnant, she expected him to be tending to her needs, not out here in the stables.

"I'm checking the carriage for the journey." He folded his arms across his wide chest. Like her father and other brothers, Rolf had dark hair and eyes. However, unlike them, he was far shorter at just five and a half feet. He also was on the stocky side, claiming it was all muscle. Sabine knew otherwise—he loved his ale a little too much and it showed around his stomach. "Where do you plan on going?" He tilted his chin toward her horse.

She folded her arms, mirroring him. They were the same height. "You're the commander of the army; don't you have someone else who can check the carriage?"

"I do. But Alina is my sister, and this is a dangerous journey. I trust something of this importance to no one else."

"If it's so dangerous, why let her go?"

"We need this alliance." He rubbed his face.

Now that Sabine was paying closer attention, she noticed the dark circles under his eyes. "What's going on?"

"Raiding parties from Carlon have been breaching our

border. They've been stealing food from our people. Last week, a couple dozen children were taken."

"What for?"

He shrugged. "No idea. But my army is spread too thin trying to protect our border. Father fears Carlon may try and overtake us."

Frustration built. Their father had always favored farming and agriculture over fighting. The result was that their army had too few men since the king didn't see the need to maintain a large standing army. "Can't we just recruit more people?"

His eyes narrowed. "Why do you think Alina is marrying King Rainer?"

It felt as if she'd stumbled into a fire. "She's marrying that man for his army?" She balled her hands into fists. Alina was choosing to marry a man she'd never met and didn't love just so their father could have access to the man's military might?

"It's more complicated than that, but yes, that's the gist of it."

Sabine stormed from the stables, heading back to the castle. She would talk some sense into her sister. There was no reason for Alina to give up on love because of their father's poor choices.

She found Alina standing in the middle of her bedchamber wearing a wedding gown, staring at herself in the mirror, her eyes filled with tears.

Sabine rushed to her sister, wrapping her in a hug. "You don't have to go through with it." Maybe if she held on and didn't let go, her sister wouldn't leave.

"I don't have to, but I want to." Alina hugged her back. "I thought I'd wear this to marry Albert."

"You still can marry him."

"Our kingdom needs me," Alina said.

"They do. You must stay here in Bakley. You can't go to Lynk." On the other side of the continent.

"Oh, honey," Alina said, squeezing Sabine and then releasing her. "We need this alliance. Please understand that I'm doing this for everyone, including me."

Tears involuntarily filled her eyes. "But why?" Her heart was breaking—for her sister, for herself, for love.

"Will you promise me something?"

"Anything."

"I want you to visit me when you can."

"Of course." Sabine couldn't imagine going a day without seeing her sister. Maybe she could go with her.

"And can you please give something to Albert for me?" She went over to her writing desk and withdrew a sealed letter, holding it out to Sabine.

"I will." She took the letter and tucked it into her dress.

"Please give it to him after I leave. It explains everything. I want him to understand."

Sabine didn't know how he was going to understand when she didn't understand it herself.

"I love you and I'm going to miss you." Alina held her arms out.

Sabine rushed over and hugged her sister again, the tears freely flowing. "Please don't go."

"I have to. One day you'll understand."

Chapter Two

S abine stood at the top of the staircase, leaning against the railing, observing the elegantly decorated great hall below. White wisteria hung on ribbons that stretched from one end of the room to the other. Hundreds of candles cast the area in a soft glow. A group of musicians played in one corner while dozens of couples danced. Scattered around the edges were people drinking and talking. A few couples hid in the shadows gossiping or perhaps even kissing. Sabine smiled at the thought of doing something so scandalous. At least everyone seemed to be enjoying themselves as they celebrated Alina's engagement and bid her farewell. Her hands tightened on the railing—she couldn't believe her sister was leaving tomorrow.

Viktor strode up the stairs carrying two goblets. "Mother and Father are wondering where you are." He handed her one of the drinks. "And Alina is asking for you. You're not going to sulk up here all night, are you?" He raised his dark eyebrows, awaiting her answer.

Sabine shrugged her delicate shoulders before taking a sip

of the strong wine, not quite ready to head downstairs and mingle yet. When she did decide to go down, she would have to be happy and cheerful for her sister. Right now, she felt like punching something. Or crying. Maybe both.

"I thought the drink might give you the courage you need to join everyone." Viktor moved to stand at the railing beside her.

Taking another sip of her wine, she let the warmth seep into her. "I still don't understand why our sister agreed to marry King Rainer," Sabine murmured. The entire situation irked her. Alina wasn't a cow to be sold off to the highest bidder, and that was what this marriage alliance felt like. A business deal. Sabine took another drink from her goblet as she watched the revelers dancing below. "Alina has never cared about something so trivial as her title."

"Says a princess who knows nothing of hardship," Viktor muttered.

"Excuse me?"

Viktor sighed. "You have to understand that Lynk is a large, powerful kingdom. Our sister is going to be its queen. I'd say it's an ideal situation for her. It puts her on equal footing with Father."

"But she's going to be all alone in a foreign kingdom, married to a man who's a stranger. She's not going to be happy." Alina hadn't even met the man, and she was going to be expected to sleep with him. The mere thought made Sabine nauseous.

"I didn't say it was perfect." Viktor nudged his shoulder against hers. "I only meant to explain how it's an appealing match. We should be happy and supportive of her."

Sabine understood that part of it and she really was trying. "I just wish Alina was marrying for love." Then she'd know her sister would be content, and she wouldn't have to worry about her. "I overheard Rolf and Otto talking. They said King Rainer must marry a woman who can produce an heir quickly and that his kingdom is in dire need of food. In exchange for him marrying Alina and receiving a sizable amount of grain every season, King Rainer will send five hundred soldiers to assist Father's army and secure our border." She finished off her wine and peered at her brother, wanting confirmation that what she'd heard was true.

"This is correct." He focused on the contents of his goblet, not looking her way.

Tears welled in her eyes. "How can you be okay with this?"

"I know you may not want to hear it right now, but Alina marrying such a powerful man is a good thing for our kingdom. I know you'll miss her, but she has to marry at some point. And now at least she can help make sure Bakley is secure, and our people are safe."

"But she loves Albert."

He chuckled; the sound harsh. "Albert is a nobody. A lowly baron. He's not an acceptable match for her. It would be a waste of a marriage."

Sabine didn't know how a marriage built on mutual love could be a waste. It wasn't fair that her brothers could remain here, not only in the kingdom but close to home, while her sister would be all alone, hundreds of miles away.

"Let's stop this sad talk and go join the party. Have you found your victim for the evening?" Viktor asked, nodding toward the guests below.

"No, and I have no intention of bothering with men tonight. I am here to celebrate my sister." And with that, she handed her goblet to Viktor and strode down the staircase, rolling her shoulders back and standing tall.

She ran her free hand along her silver dress, reveling in

the feel of the soft fabric. The color highlighted her gray eyes, making her face appear lively. Her brown hair had been braided and wound atop her head, exposing her long, elegant neck. She'd even managed to convince the seamstress to lower the neckline a few inches to showcase her diamond necklace. Even though her white gloves came up over her elbows, her mother would be furious once she saw Sabine, claiming the outfit revealed too much skin. She sighed. Her mother could be such a prude sometimes.

When she reached the bottom, she easily spotted her sister in the middle of the room dancing with their father. Alina's soft pink dress complemented her blonde hair and pale skin. She looked stunning—as she always did. The king twirled Alina around, and the song came to an end. As everyone clapped, Sabine wound her way through the people and to her sister.

"Sabine!" Alina said, her voice filled with joy. "You're here."

The king kissed Sabine's cheek. "Thank you for coming," he said. "Now if you'll both excuse me, I must find your mother."

"Shall we go and have a refreshment?" Alina asked.

The next song started. "No," Sabine said, taking her sister's hand. "Let's dance."

"But we're both women," Alina said with a laugh.

Sabine winked. "It'll be like old times." Like when Alina was twelve and Sabine six and the two of them would dance around the sitting room trying to hone their footwork. They'd imagine the day when they'd both be old enough to dance with men and marry. It seemed that day had finally come. "I'll lead." She knew all the male parts of the dances since Alina had always insisted Sabine play the part of the man when they danced.

The music sped up and Sabine took off, doing a basic three step, leading Alina around the dance floor. When Sabine went to turn, she almost spun Alina the wrong way, and she started laughing. Though they stumbled a few times, they both remained upright as they made their way across the dance floor, spinning as they went.

Alina bent her head back, laughing. "I haven't had this much fun in ages!"

Sabine started twirling her sister faster. The music came to an end, and everyone burst into thunderous applause. She hadn't realized everyone had stopped dancing to watch them. They each curtseyed.

"Thank you," Alina said, squeezing her sister's hand. "I'm going to miss you."

Sabine wrapped her sister in a hug. "It's not going to be the same without you."

"Wake up," Alina said, shaking Sabine.

Sabine reluctantly opened her eyes to find herself still in her party dress from the night before. She was sprawled on the sofa in the royal family's personal sitting room. Rubbing her eyes, she sat up. "I thought we were talking," Sabine mumbled. The last thing she remembered was her sister sitting on the sofa across from her.

Alina now stood before her dressed in a traveling cloak, looking put-together as always. "We did. You dozed off about an hour ago. I went and changed while you slept." She clutched a small satchel while shifting her weight from foot to foot.

Sabine didn't know how her sister could look so pretty, having not slept in the past twenty-four hours. "Where is everyone?" She stood and stretched, eyeing her sister's tight grip on her bag.

"Out front by the carriage. My things are being loaded."

The day Sabine had been dreading was finally here. Her sister was leaving. And by the looks of it, Alina was struggling to hold it together. "I don't want you to go," Sabine whispered, uttering the words she'd promised herself she wouldn't say.

"I know." Alina blinked several times as if trying to prevent herself from crying. "I never thought I'd leave our kingdom." She smiled, the action forced and not meeting her eyes. "But these are troubling times, and we must put others' needs before our own. That's what being a member of the royal family means. You understand, don't you?"

"Of course," Sabine said, surprised by the turn of the conversation. Last night they'd spoken of secret crushes, dreams, and what they wanted for the future. Sabine wrapped her arms around her sister, not wanting to let go. "I understand that you have to do what's best for our kingdom." Alina always put others first.

"I knew you'd understand." Alina held on to her tightly. "And now that I'm leaving, promise me you'll be there for Mother."

"I promise."

"There is a tremendous amount of pressure on her," Alina whispered. "She is very stressed from the current state of affairs. I need you to help by doing what's best for our kingdom. You'll be its only princess. Promise me."

"I will. I promise." Sabine tried not to roll her eyes. With a king, queen, and four princes all older than Sabine, she didn't think there was anything she had to worry about.

"It's time for me to go." Alina pulled away and headed to the door.

Sabine reluctantly followed her. At the front of the castle, the entire family stood waiting to see Alina off. Alina went over to Viktor, giving him a hug and mumbling something in his ear. He nodded. Then she moved to Otto, hugging him tightly. Next was Rolf who wrapped Alina in a hug while his pregnant wife waited demurely behind him. The last sibling to bid her farewell was Karl. The two of them spoke in hushed whispers a minute before Alina bid farewell to Karl's wife and two small children. Finally, the king and queen each gave Alina a kiss.

Alina wiped the tears from her cheeks before climbing into the carriage, not looking out the window at her family.

Tears filled Sabine's eyes. This would probably be the last time she saw her sister for at least a year or two. The castle would be so lonely without her.

The carriage pulled away with a jerk. A handful of mounted soldiers followed behind as the carriage headed away from the castle. It felt as if a part of Sabine were being pulled away from her body. Once the carriage was no longer in sight, emptiness filled her. Things would never be the same.

Sabine knocked on the door to Karl's wing with more force than necessary. She hoped to catch him before he went to the throne room to meet with some of the dukes from the kingdom. She was just about to knock again when the door swung open, revealing a disheveled Karl.

"I hope I'm not interrupting something," Sabine said, horrified that her brother might have been otherwise engaged with his wife, Jesamine.

He chuckled. "Just a lively game of tickle monster." He ushered her into his private sitting room where his two young boys, Haron and Beck, were running around squealing in delight. Karl dropped to his hands and knees, then roared and began chasing the boys.

"Honey," Jesamine said as she came into the room. "You're supposed to be meeting with your father and the dukes."

Karl rolled onto his back. Beck crawled onto his father and started tickling him.

"I know," Karl said. "It's just that I'd rather be here with my family than dealing with the kingdom's many issues. Sad of me to say, I know." He kissed Beck on the forehead before setting him aside and standing. Haron clutched onto his daddy's leg, trying to prevent him from leaving.

"You'll join me for some tea?" Jesamine asked Sabine.

She looked at her nephews, both red-faced and breathing hard. As cute as they were, she didn't know how her brother and sister-in-law had the energy to entertain them day in and day out. "I actually came to speak with my brother," she replied.

Karl straightened his shirt before sliding his jacket on. "Walk with me." He tilted his head to the side.

Sabine followed him out of the room. "I got your note."

He twisted his head, cracking his neck. "You were seen walking in the garden with Luther yesterday," he said once they were alone in the hallway.

"So?"

"He is not a suitable prospect for you to marry." They exited Karl's wing of the castle.

"You can't be serious." She would never consider marrying Luther. The man enjoyed gambling far too much for her taste. However, he was handsome, and she enjoyed looking at him. His snarky wit was also entertaining. They flirted with one another to be sure, but neither liked the other that way.

Karl pulled her into an alcove, out of sight. "You were alone with a man in the garden."

"It was *Luther*."

He raised his eyebrows, clearly not understanding.

"It was during the day, in view of the castle, and I've known Luther my entire life." She folded her arms, irritated. Her brother had never cared what she did before, so she had no idea why he was sticking his nose in her business now.

"It's not appropriate."

"Am I no longer allowed to have male friends?"

He put his hands on his hips, shaking his head. "Mother said you haven't been joining her for tea."

So that was what this was about. "I am." Just not every day. She shook her head and began walking away from her brother.

"Sabine," he called after her. "Now that Alina is gone, you have certain responsibilities."

She spun around to face him. "Alina being gone changes nothing."

"You can't be out gallivanting with a different gentleman each week. It's not appropriate."

Fury filled her and she clutched her hands together to keep her temper in check.

"You can no longer neglect your duties," he said.

She cocked her head to the side, trying to figure out what duties he was referring to. So long as she showed up for supper, her parents didn't care how she spent her days.

"You will take daily tea with Mother," Karl said. "You will attend all social functions being held at the castle."

She had to bite her tongue to prevent herself from saying a nasty retort. He was acting an awful lot like her father—which he was not. He needed to worry about his own children, not her.

He put his hands on her shoulders. "I don't want any

more reports of you out walking, riding, or attending any plays with a gentleman unless Father or I approve it beforehand. Do you understand?"

No, she did not understand, but instead of arguing with him, she simply nodded her head.

"Good." He released her and smiled. "I must be going. I'm glad we had this talk."

She cursed at his retreating back.

Sabine spent the next few weeks attending daily tea with her mother. Every afternoon there seemed to be a visitor or two of some importance. While the gentlemen would meet with the king, the ladies would take tea together. There was usually some idle talk about nothing of consequence, and then it would be over. Most days Sabine felt herself nodding off. How her mother managed to do this day in and day out, she had no idea.

Unable to handle another afternoon of complete boredom, she headed to the great hall, intending to exit through the back and sneak over to the stables. A ride through the countryside was exactly what she needed. The fresh air, the sun on her face. She'd finally be able to have a moment of peace to herself.

"What are you doing?" Karl asked, startling Sabine.

She turned in a slow circle until she spotted all four of her brothers coming out of the kitchen. "I'm just passing through."

"Just passing through, huh," Viktor said with a low chuckle. "Toward the back exit when the sitting room is the other way?"

She wanted to punch the smug expression off his face.

"Aren't you supposed to be at tea with Mother?" Karl asked.

Otto snorted. "Tea? She must be bored out of her mind doing that every day. No wonder she's running away."

Commotion came from the hallway to the right. A sentry came running through it, headed straight for Karl, yelling something as he approached.

Sabine couldn't make out what he was saying.

Karl took off running, Viktor and Otto right behind him. Rolf cursed and then ran after them as well.

Not knowing what else to do, Sabine sprinted after her brothers. They ran through the castle and to the main entrance. The doors were wide open, and the king and queen were standing outside on the top steps, watching something in the distance.

"Any idea who it is?" Karl asked no one in particular.

"No," the king answered. "A rider bearing the royal colors of Lynk has been spotted about a mile out accompanied by two of my soldiers."

Sabine squinted. She could just make out three people on horseback, dust floating in the air behind them. "They're traveling awfully fast. Do you think it's a message from Alina?"

The king and queen glanced at one another, and Sabine knew that that must not be the case.

"Maybe it's someone coming to let us know they're married, and King Rainer is sending soldiers?" Karl suggested.

The riders reached the gates. Sabine could see the sentries speaking with them. The gates immediately swung open, and the foreign rider continued racing toward the front of the castle flanked by the two Bakley soldiers.

The king moved to the bottom of the steps.

The Lynk rider stopped before him, half sliding, and half tumbling from his horse. "Your Majesty King Franz Ludwig?"

"Yes," the king said.

The rider heaved in a deep breath. "I am King Rainer Manfred's personal steward." His face was covered in dirt, his eyes red-rimmed. "I have been tasked with delivering a message." He glanced at everyone on the stairs before focusing back on the king. "I am sorry to inform you that Princess Alina Ludwig is dead."

Chapter Three

"What did you say?" the king asked, his voice laced with danger.

The steward glanced between the two Bakley soldiers on either side of him before responding. "I'm sorry to inform you that Princess Alina is dead. Her body is on its way here as we speak. King Rainer insisted I deliver the news on his behalf."

Sabine's world felt as if it tilted. This could not be happening.

"My daughter is dead?" The queen let out a wail before collapsing onto the steps.

"Careful," Viktor said as he slid his arm around Sabine's waist.

She hadn't even realized her knees had grown weak. A sick feeling took root in the pit of her stomach.

"Explain," the king demanded.

"Princess Alina's lady's maid went to wake her for breakfast," the steward replied. "When the princess didn't stir, the lady's maid shook her, finding her cold. The king came in with his doctor, and the princess was declared dead."

"Had she been ill?" the king asked, taking a step toward the steward.

"No," he replied. "She, uh, appeared to have been poisoned."

Sabine blinked, trying to look at the steward and make sense of all he said.

"Someone assassinated my daughter?" the king said, his voice a simmering rage about to blow over.

"We believe so." The steward handed the king a letter. "The details are in here. King Rainer is conducting a full investigation. The person responsible for her murder will be brought to justice."

The word *murder* sunk like a rock into Sabine's stomach.

"Easy," Viktor murmured in her ear, holding her upright.

"Someone in Lynk killed my sister?" Karl said as he moved to stand beside his father.

"We don't know what kingdom the murderer is from," the steward replied.

Murder. Alina was dead. Killed. In Lynk. A ringing noise sounded in Sabine's ears, and she no longer heard what anyone else said. Her entire body shook. This could not be happening. It had to be an error. No, a nightmare. One she needed to wake up from. Her sister couldn't be dead. Alina didn't deserve this.

Sabine vomited.

"Get the queen and princess inside," the king demanded. "Have the Lynk steward escorted to the throne room. Karl, Rolf, Otto, and Viktor, you're with me."

A Bakley soldier rushed over to Sabine, taking hold of her arm, and ushering her inside.

Her body felt numb. Tears streamed down her face and her head began to pound. This could not be happening. Alina couldn't be dead. It was just a nightmare. Or some sick and twisted joke.

The soldier took Sabine to her bedchamber where a servant helped her sit on the chair near the window.

Sabine couldn't move. It felt as if worms were burrowing into her body.

The queen's screams pierced the silence of the castle.

She wished for darkness to swallow her whole.

Sabine didn't leave her bedchamber for three days. Her stomach felt too queasy to consider eating. Besides, there was no reason to be around anyone else. Her grief was impossible to handle, nearly unbearable, so there was no way she could see her own pain mirrored in her family members. Standing at her window, she maintained watch of the road leading to the castle, knowing her sister's body was on its way. She prayed that when it arrived, Alina would be alive and well. That this entire thing had been a terrible misunderstanding. That Alina was simply in some sort of deep sleep. Not dead. Not *murdered*.

Someone knocked on her door. "Come in," she whispered, unable to speak any louder.

"Sabine," Karl said as he stepped into her room. His eyes were red, his hair disheveled, his clothes wrinkled. It looked as if he hadn't slept in days. "I need you to go see Mother. She hasn't gotten out of bed or eaten in three days."

Sabine was in no position to help. She didn't know how to comfort someone else when she felt the same. She turned away from Karl, not wanting to see his grief, and instead focused again on the road outside. "Is there any new information?" she asked, placing her palm on the glass. It was cold. She removed it, surprised she could feel anything at all.

"No. We're hoping once the rest of our soldiers return

that they'll have more details." Karl came to stand at the window beside her. "Father thinks someone from Carlon did this."

"Why?" She thought the same thing since raiding parties from Carlon were coming into their kingdom to steal food and kidnapping their children. But she wanted Karl to explain it to see if he had any additional insight as to why they might be doing this to them.

Karl peered at her. "I think King Rainer did it."

That didn't make sense. "Doesn't he need an heir and our food? Why destroy an alliance that benefits him so greatly?" And from what she'd gathered from Alina, Rainer had been the one to reach out to them with the proposal.

"Carlon could have killed Alina on her journey to Lynk," Karl said. "It would have been much easier to attack a carriage with only a dozen soldiers than it would be to sneak into a fortified palace and poison someone. She was killed in Rainer's home. It had to be an inside job, so if it wasn't Rainer, then it had to have been someone from his kingdom."

"Or Carlon wants to place the blame on King Rainer."

He shook his head. "You don't understand. The kingdom of Lynk is nearly impossible to get into."

Sabine had never been to any of the other kingdoms, so she had no idea how difficult it might be to get into Lynk. However, she assumed that someone trained in the art of killing would be able to find a way in.

Karl turned and sat against the window ledge. "This is a disaster."

She tilted her head to the side, observing her brother. "The death of our sister is a tragedy. That is the *only* thing I'm focused on right now. If you're upset over losing this treaty with Lynk, I suggest you leave my room before I say something I'll regret." She hadn't meant to speak so harshly, but anger started to worm its way into her heart, replacing the grief. Somehow anger was easier to deal with than horrific sadness.

"If we go to war, we're going to lose a lot more than just our sister. We'll be lucky if any of us make it out alive."

His words sent a chill through her body. "War?"

"If Carlon is truly behind this like Father thinks they are, he'll either strike against them for murdering Alina, or Carlon will eventually invade us—which is what he has been expecting based upon the raids and kidnappings. Either way, we'll be at war with them. Or, if Lynk is responsible for our sister's death, then we'll be at war with *them*." Karl pushed away from the window ledge, folding his arms. He began pacing in the middle of the room.

"But our army is..." Barely an army. They had limited resources and couldn't afford to go to war.

"If we go to war, we lose." He closed his eyes. "My wife, boys..." When he opened his eyes, he looked right at Sabine. "I don't want those I love to suffer. Or die."

They needed a stronger army. They needed more soldiers. And then she remembered why her sister had agreed to marry King Rainer in the first place. "Without a wedding, there's no soldiers coming to our aid," she said out loud, the realization only now dawning on her. There would be no stopping Carlon.

"Our kingdom is not in a good place. I fear for what's to come." Karl ran a hand over his tired face.

Sabine couldn't lose anyone else she loved.

"I need you to go see Mother. Please." His soft voice hinted at the grief he barely had under control.

She nodded. As a member of this family, she would do her part. Karl was clearly doing his right now, trying to hold the family together. Her parents' grief had to be unimaginable. If her brother needed her to be there for their mother, she would. As much as she could be.

"Thank you." He kissed the top of her head then left.

Sabine resumed staring out the window, waiting for Alina's body to arrive. Her dear sister had been alone in a foreign kingdom when she was killed. *Murdered.* Did Alina know she'd been poisoned when she was dying? Or had she passed in her sleep? It wasn't fair that the sun shone outside, bathing the land in warmth. It should be dark, cloudy, and raining. Like the inside of her mind right now. The world shouldn't be beautiful and going on as if nothing had changed. As if Alina hadn't died. Tears slid down her cheeks.

Dear, sweet Alina had gone to Lynk to protect Bakley. Now it seemed as if it had all been for nothing. If she hadn't gone, she'd be alive. They'd be in the same position they were currently in—threatened by Carlon. If Carlon was responsible for Alina's death, they had to pay. Their father had no choice but to defend their kingdom and go to war. But Bakley's army was severely lacking. Without Alina's marriage to King Rainer, there would be no additional soldiers coming to help. The only way to secure those soldiers would be if someone from Bakley took Alina's place and married the king of Lynk thus fulfilling the contract—assuming King Rainer wasn't responsible for Alina's death. However, since he needed Bakley's food so badly, she doubted he'd sabotage the union. It had to be Carlon.

A thought suddenly occurred to Sabine. She was eighteen and of marriageable age. If she took her sister's place and married King Rainer, the contract could still proceed as negotiated. Her kingdom would have the protection it needed while Lynk received the food they desired. And, the best part, Sabine could hunt down the person who'd murdered her sister. Instead of relying on King Rainer to investigate when he had a million other things to worry about, Sabine could be the one to do it.

And when she found the murderer, she'd kill him for

taking her sister's life. A life for a life. It seemed fair. Justified. Now all she had to do was convince her family to let her go in Alina's place.

Sabine stepped into the queen's bedchamber. The curtains around the bed had been drawn shut. She stood beside the bed, not daring to part the curtains and intrude into her mother's personal space. The queen would come out when she was ready.

She didn't know why Karl had asked her to come and not one of their other siblings. Probably because she was the only daughter left and somehow, being a woman meant she was more equipped to deal with grief than a man.

"I know you're in there," Sabine said, her voice soft so as not to startle the queen. "I've been hiding in my room as well." She clasped her hands together, fidgeting with her fingers as she tried to find the words to say. "I know it hurts." Her voice cracked. She closed her eyes and took a deep breath, letting it out slowly. To survive, she had to cling to her anger and the plan she'd formed. It was the only thing pulling her out of the black hole she'd fallen into. The only thing giving her comfort and purpose. "I'm going to find who did this and make him pay. I promise."

The queen didn't respond.

"I love you," Sabine whispered.

Not knowing what else to do to comfort her mother, she left the room. As she walked through the halls of the castle, her hand trailing along the stone walls, she considered how best to implement her plan. If she went to her father, he'd dismiss her without even considering it. Karl seemed to be in a rather emotional state at the moment. His thoughts were too focused on his fear of losing another person he loved.

Otto and Viktor held no sway with the king, and both tended to be far too overprotective of her. Rolf tended to be the most sensible of her brothers and was the only one who'd objectively consider her plan.

Since Rolf liked to spend his mornings with his soldiers, he usually reserved the afternoons for working in his office. She headed that way, hoping to find him alone and not in a heated meeting with his generals. When she neared the door to his office, she slowed and listened for voices. Not hearing any, she knocked.

"Come in," Rolf called out.

Sabine entered, closing the door behind her.

He raised his eyebrows. "I didn't expect to see you today." He gestured for her to take a seat across from him.

She sat, looking at his disorganized space. Stacks of papers were strewn over his desk, books were shoved on the bookshelves instead of being lined up and orderly, swords were piled in one of the corners, and a pillow and blanket were on the floor.

He scooted his chair back, stretching out his legs and crossing them at his ankles. "Sarah isn't sleeping well at night," he said, pointing to the pillow and blanket. "Sometimes this is the only place I can catch a few hours of uninterrupted sleep."

"Her stomach is rather large," she replied, assuming that was the reason for Sarah's tossing and turning and not the death of Alina. "How many weeks until she delivers?"

"The doctor thinks it'll be within the next two to three weeks."

She nodded. One of the things she loved about Rolf was that he didn't pry. He didn't ask her how she was doing, how she was feeling, or if she was well enough to be up and about the castle. "I want to discuss something with you."

"I figured as much."

Suddenly, the right words eluded her, and she didn't know where to begin. "I want to help."

Rolf steepled his fingers together. "I know our army is in desperate need of able-bodied fighters, but you can't join us. You're no match for a man when it comes to fighting."

She snorted. "I know that." She could barely lift a sword since the thing was so heavy. "I don't want to fight." At least not with a sword. "I want to help prevent a war from happening in the first place."

He shrugged. "How?"

At least he didn't laugh. Granted, he wouldn't like what she was about to say, but he would at least consider it. If he managed to see value in it, he'd discuss the matter with their father. She just needed to choose her words carefully, so he'd understand her reasoning and agree with her. "Our sister decided to marry King Rainer for the betterment of our kingdom. Specifically, to garner Lynk's soldiers to help protect our border."

He uncrossed his ankles and scooted his chair forward, folding his hands together atop his desk. "What are you getting at?"

"We need Lynk's soldiers because we can't fight Carlon without them. And we need to find Alina's killer."

His focus shifted to the window as he gazed outside. "When did you become so well versed in politics? I thought you hated this sort of thing and that's why you're always running wild."

"I do not run wild." She folded her arms, irritated at the implication.

He chuckled and looked at her. "As a child, you were always outdoors riding or swimming in the pond. Nowadays, you're usually to be found flirting with some unsuspecting man."

"Rolf!" She'd come there hoping to be taken seriously, not be chided for her behavior.

He watched her for a minute. "How do you propose we find Alina's killer? King Rainer said he was investigating."

"To find the killer, we need someone on the inside."

"And how do you propose we get a man in the Lynk palace? I don't employ assassins. And even if I did, they'd never get into Lynk. The kingdom is walled off. No one gets in or out unless the king wills it."

"I have an idea for that."

"I'm dying to hear it."

"And...I have an idea on how Bakley can still get Lynk's soldiers." The thought of anyone else she loved dying was too much to bear. "You have a baby on the way," she continued, as if that explained everything. "If you died, you'd leave Sarah all alone. Your child wouldn't even know his or her father."

Rolf's jawline tensed. "You're not telling me anything I don't already know."

"I can help our family."

"There's nothing you can do."

She wiped her sweaty palms on her skirt. "I can take Alina's place." She forced herself to maintain eye contact with Rolf so he'd know how serious she was.

He shook his head.

"I'll marry the king of Lynk and fulfill Bakley's end of the contract."

"You can't, Sabine." He leaned back in his chair and rubbed his face. "You're woefully unprepared for something like that."

While she happened to agree with him, she wouldn't let him know that. "You have to consider what I'm offering. I will take Alina's place and marry King Rainer. Lynk will receive their promised food, so they'll agree to it, and we'll get their soldiers."

"I know you," Rolf said as he stood. "You're not selfless like Alina." He rounded the desk and sat on the edge of it before Sabine. "You have an ulterior motive."

"I think preventing a war is motive enough, don't you?"

He chuckled; the sound humorless. "You think you can hunt down the killer yourself?"

"Think about it." She scooted to the edge of her seat, closer to Rolf. "If I marry King Rainer, not only will it prevent a war against Carlon, but it'll get me into Lynk. Inside the king's palace where I can investigate."

"And what if you discover it's someone from Lynk who murdered Alina? Then what?"

"If I'm married to the king and one of his subjects killed my sister, I will be able to seek justice."

"You do understand this means you'll be *married*."

"If it means saving the lives of the rest of my family, if it means Alina's death wasn't in vain, then it'll be worth it." Truthfully, the idea of marriage terrified her. But he didn't need to know that. She'd figure that part out later, after she discovered the killer.

He reached forward, placing a hand on her shoulder. "And what if the killer comes after you?"

She hadn't considered that part. "Then I suppose you better prepare me to face such a situation."

He nodded and stood.

"Does that mean you'll let me do it?" Her heart pounded.

"No. It means I'll mull it over and discuss it with Karl."

"And what about Father?"

"Don't get ahead of yourself."

Sabine stood in the garden cutting lavender and placing it in the basket hanging from her arm. She thought being outside, in the warm sun, would calm her. However, her hands still shook. Watching her sister's casket be buried yesterday had been harder than she thought it would be.

"I figured I'd find you out here," the king said by way of greeting.

She looked up and spotted her father entering the garden from the west side.

"What are you doing out here all alone?" he asked when he reached her.

"This is Alina's favorite flower." She planned to make an arrangement for her sister's grave.

"Rolf told me your proposal." He gazed at the farmland in the distance.

It had been almost a week since she'd gone to Rolf and offered to take Alina's place. No one had said a word to her about it, so she'd assumed it wasn't being considered.

"I don't want to lose another daughter. Hell, I don't want to lose another child. But it seems to me," he continued, "that I don't have a lot of options. Do I risk your life to prevent a war? Or to get the troops necessary to go to war well-prepared? Do I risk your life for the betterment of my kingdom?" He shook his head. "If you die, too, it will all have been for nothing. I'll lose not only you, but possibly my entire family and kingdom."

Shock filled her. He hadn't downright dismissed the idea —which meant he was considering it. "If you don't send me, you're guaranteed to lose it all."

"You're asking me to take a huge gamble with your life."

"I'll be better prepared than Alina." And Rolf could help train her to get ready for the perils she'd face.

"True. But like I said, I don't have many options. As king, I swore an oath and must do what's best for my kingdom."

She set her basket on the ground, wondering what he was getting at.

"I sent word with King Rainer's squire stating that you will take Alina's place. The contract will be fulfilled on our end. You leave in a fortnight."

"You're letting me go?" she asked, unable to believe it.

"I have little choice."

Emotions overwhelmed her—so many that she had trouble deciphering and understanding them all. She forced herself to focus on what really mattered—finding the person responsible for murdering her sister.

"There is much to go over before you leave," the king continued. "You must learn about Lynk and what will be expected of you as its queen. You must learn about its ruler, though there is little known about him since he's only been on the throne for a short while. And I'll feel better if you have a dagger and know how to use it. I'm going to talk to Rolf now and charge him with preparing you to defend yourself. Alina was woefully unprepared." He shook his head, still focused on the farmland in the distance. "And since you are going to be married, your mother will need to prepare you for that." He finally turned to face her. "Of course, I won't force you to go in your sister's stead if you don't want to, but Karl said you'd offered. We really do need this union."

"I'll go," she said, the words coming out softer than she'd anticipated. Somehow, she'd been so wrapped up in seeking revenge for her sister's murder, that she'd forgotten about having to perform marital duties. Not only that, but she was going to be the queen of Lynk; a role she never thought she'd have. Not wanting to dwell on that, she picked up the basket again, clutching the handle and forcing herself to focus on helping her kingdom and bringing about justice for Alina's death. That was all that mattered.

The king patted his daughter on her back before turning and leaving her alone in the garden.

Once her father was no longer in sight, Sabine headed over to the royal family's cemetery. When she reached Alina's grave, she knelt next to the freshly packed dirt. After running her hand lightly over the surface, she withdrew some of the lavender from her basket, setting it atop the grave.

Her tears dropped onto the chocolate-colored dirt, making a soft patter sound.

She squeezed her eyes shut. Alina didn't deserve to die. She should have lived to be the queen of Lynk. She deserved the title, she deserved to have children of her own as she'd always wanted, and she deserved to be happy. How anyone could have killed her was beyond Sabine. Alina was the kindest, gentlest, and most wonderful person she'd ever known. All Sabine had ever cared about was herself. She should be dead, not Alina.

She laid a few more pieces of lavender on the grave. Since the day she'd learned of her sister's death, there'd been a sick feeling in her stomach. A feeling of wrongness. If only she could find a way to undo what had been done. Oftentimes, it still didn't feel real. It seemed as if Alina was in Lynk where she was supposed to be. Not dead.

She wiped her tears, wishing she could hold her sister one last time. Dance with her sister one last time. Laugh with her so hard they started crying happy tears. Heck, she'd even have an argument with Alina if it meant getting her back.

The wind blew softly. Sabine stared at the dirt, as if she could somehow see her sister lying below. "I swear to you I'll discover who did this," she whispered. "The person who killed you will be brought to justice." Taking one of the white roses her mother had left on the grave, Sabine slid a thorn across her wrist, drawing blood. She let the blood drip onto the dirt. "With my blood, I promise to avenge your death."

Chapter Four

S abine sat at the table, six small mixing bowls before
  her. For the past hour, she'd been smelling their
  contents, trying to differentiate them. So far, she
hadn't managed to properly identify a single one. She let out
a frustrated sigh.

"These are the most basic poisons," Rolf chided her. "You
have to know them."

"I can't figure out what I'm supposed to be smelling in
the first place." Leaning back in the chair, she stared up at
the ceiling, wondering what poison had been used on her
sister. Something could have been slipped in her drink, over
her food, or even in the water she bathed in.

"Maybe I can help," Queen Elsa said as she came into the
room.

Sabine straightened. This was the first time she'd seen
her mother since the day they buried Alina.

"Excellent timing," Rolf said as he stood, placing a kiss on
the queen's cheek. "I have to meet with the soldiers who will
be accompanying Sabine to Lynk. Given what happened with

Alina, I am putting additional safety measures and protocols in place."

"I think that is a wise idea." The queen clutched her hands together.

Rolf left the room.

"How are you doing?" Sabine asked. Her mother's face looked pale and her eyes bloodshot. She wore a demure black dress and her hair had been braided and wound atop her head.

"Your father told me you offered to go in Alina's place to save the alliance," she said instead of answering.

"I have."

The queen nodded. "Good." She approached the table and observed each of the bowls. She lowered her voice and said, "While you're there, I want you to always keep your ears and eyes open. If you hear anything about the person who killed Alina, I want to know."

Sabine's heartbeat sped up. "That's what I intend to do. I plan on finding the person responsible for her death and making them pay."

The queen nodded as she sat on the chair beside Sabine, looking in her eyes for a full minute before responding. "You are not in a position to seek justice on your own."

She thought they both wanted the same thing—the killer found. "I don't understand."

"I don't want two dead daughters," Elsa answered. "You are to act as a spy on Bakley's behalf, but you will not execute anything. Any information you glean will be given to me, and I will make sure Rolf gets it. He will put a plan into place to make sure we capture the murderer."

"Why don't I just send any information directly to Rolf?"

"They might expect that, or someone could be reading your letters to him. However, correspondence between a mother and daughter is different. You can be discreet.

Others won't know what you're saying or implying, but I will."

Sabine nodded. "The person may very well be from King Rainer's own court." Though she didn't think it likely.

"I believe someone in Lynk's court knows or saw something that can lead us to the killer. Maybe there's a mole. Someone who helped the assassin gain access to the palace in the first place." She glanced over her shoulder at the door. "When you're there, don't trust anyone."

"I won't." She reached out and took hold of her mother's hand, squeezing it.

"Good. But to ensure your safety," Elsa said, "you need to be prepared. Alina knew her wifely duties and what was expected of her as the future queen of Lynk. However, she couldn't defend herself or navigate the politics of the kingdom. Her death proves that. You will be ready." She released her daughter's hand. "You must be able to identify each of these poisons."

Sabine nodded, ready to try again with renewed vigor.

"Most poisons are made from plants. Each has a slight trace of that plant. If you know which one, you'll recognize the poison."

That made sense. As to why Rolf hadn't just said so, Sabine didn't know.

"Your brother has collected the most commonly used poisons." Elsa pulled the first bowl toward Sabine. "What do you notice about this one?"

"It's a yellow powder." She didn't smell anything pungent, but she didn't want to stick her nose in it either.

"It's the center of a yellow makey flower. Because it can be ground up without losing potency, it's usually sprinkled over food. One bite and you'll be dead."

Sabine pushed the bowl a little farther away.

"It does no good learning the smell of this one since the

food can mask the smell. If you taste it, it's already too late because you'll be dead in thirty seconds."

"What do you recommend then?" Sabine asked, horror filling her. She'd never be able to eat food again and enjoy it. Every time she took a bite, she'd be wondering if it was her last.

"When your plate is set before you, take a moment to look at your food. If you notice anything with yellow powder on it, don't touch it. This poison won't melt or change properties, so you should see it if you're paying attention."

She nodded her head, trying to remember everything her mother said.

"The king should provide a food taster, especially after what happened to Alina; however, I don't know how good the person will be. Also, the best chance of killing you via poison will be when food comes from the kitchen to your chambers in the morning. I recommend you not take food in your room. Try to eat with the king as much as possible to ensure the meal isn't tampered with on its way to you."

Sabine swallowed, her stomach feeling sick with all this information. The idea of going to Lynk was becoming overwhelming. Dangerous. A stupid idea. Here in Bakley, she had guards and servants who were loyal and protected her. When she reached Lynk, she'd be truly alone with only herself for protection.

She rubbed her temples and looked at the next bowl. "What about this one?" She pulled it closer, noticing it was a light green liquid and had a funny smell that made her eyes water. It kind of reminded her of rotting eggs.

"That's giplig. It won't kill you, but I consider it to be the most dangerous of all the poisons here."

"How can that be if it's not lethal?"

"If this is placed on a piece of cloth and held over your mouth and nose for a mere five seconds, you'll fall asleep."

That didn't sound too bad. "At least I won't be dead."

The queen raised her eyebrows and placed her hand on Sabine's arm. "The purpose of this one is to kidnap you. Who knows where you'll wake up and what state you'll be in. I'd rather die than be at the mercy of my enemy. I pray you never find yourself in that situation. It is a fate worse than death."

Her stomach rolled with nausea.

"Are you okay?" Elsa asked.

"Maybe this isn't a good idea," Sabine whispered. "There are so many dangers."

"And you don't think we have the same dangers here?"

She looked at her mother, confused. "No. It's safe here. We have nothing to worry about." They didn't even have that many sentries guarding the property.

A small smile graced the queen's lips. "I wish that was the case, but it's not. You're sheltered and unaware of the dangers lurking here in your own home. An assassin can come at any one of us at any time."

Cold fear coated Sabine's clammy skin. "Why haven't I been trained to use a weapon or sniff out poisons before?"

"You've never taken an interest. Besides, your father believes his men are loyal and will protect us. However, the only person I trust completely to keep myself alive is me. You must think the same way."

How Sabine had managed to live eighteen years without knowing or understanding any of this was beyond her.

The queen patted Sabine's hand. "Don't worry," she said. "You're rectifying it now. Are you ready for the next one?"

Sabine nodded.

Elsa then went on to describe a single, unique trait for each of the poisons. Sabine spent the next several hours with her mother, committing each one to memory.

The following days passed in a blur. The king insisted Sabine spend the mornings with her mother going over basic royal etiquette. Even though she hadn't learned the duties of a queen in any formal capacity since she was the sixth born child, she watched her mother on a daily basis and knew what was expected of her. In the afternoons, she trained with Rolf learning simple self-defense moves along with how to wield a dagger. He taught her how to hold the weapon and what would happen if she had to stab someone with it. Hopefully it would never come to that.

Late at night when she climbed into bed, exhaustion consumed her. At least the physical toll from her daily work kept her mind focused on the tasks at hand. It helped keep her grief for Alina somewhat manageable. However, sometimes late at night, she'd wake up thinking about her sister. It was in those quiet hours that her thoughts turned to darker matters. Things like revenge would consume her.

Every so often she'd awake in a sweat. It was as if she could hear Alina's screams, pleading with her killer to spare her. All the reports they'd received from their soldiers had agreed with the story the Lynk steward conveyed—that Alina had died in her sleep, poisoned by something. Sabine liked to think that her sister didn't suffer. Her body had no signs of trauma. If it hadn't been for the oddly colored drool running from the corner of her mouth to her neck, they never would have known she'd died from poison. Regardless, those were the days she'd wake up early, eager to begin her training.

On her last night at home, her family held a private farewell supper. The entire family came, even the children. Roasted turkey, boiled potatoes, and carrots were served. The servants baked bread with rosemary—Sabine's favorite.

When they finished eating, the king leaned back in his chair and said, "You always were a wild child. You loved to chase after your brothers, swim in the nearby lake, and ride a horse like a boy. It's about time you settle down."

Sabine rolled her eyes. Growing up, her father had always been busy with Karl and Rolf while her mother entertained other ladies. No one had ever cared what she did so long as she didn't get in the way or bother anyone.

Karl laughed. "I remember when I found you hiding under my bed one night because you didn't want to go to sleep in your own room. You said something about the lightning bothering you. I had to drag you out of my room by your legs. You screamed and cursed at me."

"You've always had a foul mouth," Viktor said, chuckling.

"I do not," Sabine said, horrified her brother had said something like that in front of their parents. She was going to have to smack him upside his head when they were alone.

"The first time I met you," Jesamine said, "you were running through the castle and screaming about some boy. You had mud all over your boots and you were making such a mess. I think you were thirteen."

Everyone laughed.

Sabine folded her arms, irritated that even Karl's wife was ganging up on her.

"Remember when she didn't want us to slaughter and eat that cow for the spring festival?" Otto asked.

Rolf laughed. "She tied herself to the cow thinking she could save it."

"But she tied the knots so badly she couldn't get them off," Otto said. "When she got hungry, she was ready to slaughter the cow herself."

"I remember the first time I had her attend a tea party with all of the duchesses," the queen said. "She poured all of the tea into my potted plant thinking she could leave if there wasn't any left to drink."

"Oh, not you too, Mother," Sabine groaned. It was her last

night at home in the castle. She didn't need them all telling these embarrassing stories.

A soldier rushed into the great hall, carrying a letter. He approached the king, bowing before handing it over.

The king picked up his dinner knife, using it to slice the seal open. The room remained quiet as he read its contents. When he finished, he folded it up and slid it into the pocket of his tunic. "I want to thank my family for being here tonight," he said. "Even my grandchildren." He raised his goblet. "A toast to Sabine. May your journey be safe, your marriage blessed with children, and your life in Lynk happy."

"Here, here!" everyone said before taking a drink.

"I hate to end this early, but I must speak with Karl, Rolf, and Otto in my office. Immediately." The king pushed his chair back and stood.

"That works out quite well since I must talk to Sabine about the wedding night," the queen said.

"Everyone is leaving except for me?" Viktor asked, folding his hands behind his head. "That's brilliant."

"It's late, Father," Rolf said. "I'd like to escort my wife to our rooms."

"It'll have to wait," the king replied. "I've received word from the League. There's an issue we need to address. Now."

Without another word, Karl, Rolf, and Otto followed their father from the room.

"You're not going to talk to me here in front of Viktor, are you?" Sabine asked.

"No. Let's retire to your bedchamber." The queen stood.

Sabine took one last drink before asking Viktor, "Do you know what the League is?"

He shrugged. "No idea. I've never bothered to ask because I'd rather not be involved in anything. The less I know, the better."

Sabine glared at him. So typical. Whenever it came to

politics or anything regarding the kingdom, he acted as if he knew nothing and didn't care.

"Come," the queen commanded. "You don't need to concern yourself with the League."

Sabine followed her mother down the hallway, up the stairs, and to her bedchamber. This would be her last night in her home. Sadness filled her.

Elsa closed the door. "I can't believe my baby is leaving tomorrow."

While Sabine was hardly a child, she understood her going away would be hard on her mother. She had no idea when she'd see her family again.

"We must discuss what will happen on your wedding night."

Sabine rubbed her temples. All thoughts of being wed to King Rainer and all that it entailed she'd managed to block from her mind. If she allowed herself to think about getting married, it became overwhelming. She'd once chided her sister for agreeing to wed a stranger and here she was, taking her sister's place and doing the same thing.

Once Alina got the justice she deserved, Sabine would deal with being a wife and queen. Somehow that part didn't seem real to her. Her breathing sped up.

Elsa sat on the bed, patting the spot next to her.

Sabine went over and sat next to her mother.

"We must discuss the bedroom duties you will be expected to perform with your husband-to-be."

Horror filled her. "Bedroom duties?" If this had to do with making babies, she didn't want to know. She'd seen enough animals procreate that she knew the general gist. Having her mother go into detail would only cause her more panic and foreboding, and she already had enough to deal with.

"The night of your marriage, you will be expected to let your husband have his way with you. Once he is finished, you will remain lying there on your back so that someone can confirm the deed is done. After this person verifies the two of you have consummated the marriage, you may go to your own bed."

"I don't want to talk about this." Although she didn't understand why anyone would need to check her to verify that she'd been with her husband. The idea of taking her sister's place seemed like the worst thing possible.

"You need to understand that the marriage isn't official until it's consummated. This way, it isn't your husband's word against yours. There will be proof. You must not leave the bed until you've been checked. Do you understand?"

Her mother must be saying this from personal experience. Sabine couldn't imagine allowing King Rainer to have his way with her before letting someone else see her naked to make sure she'd done her duty as a wife. The room felt hot and stuffy, as if there wasn't enough air to breathe. She stood and started pacing. "Is that all you wish to discuss?" She hoped it was since she felt a headache starting.

"Yes, that's it." Elsa stood. "Please remember everything we've taught you. If you come across as calm and demure, no one will feel threatened by you. That means you must keep your temper in check. Make friends with your lady's maid. She'll hear a lot of the servants talking and can provide you with some useful insight." She placed her hands on Sabine's shoulders. "Most of all, be careful, watch your back, and trust no one."

"I will. I promise."

"I can't stand the thought of losing another daughter. I need you to be strong so you can survive this."

Sabine nodded, tears filling her eyes. She would miss her mother terribly.

"You're doing the right thing," the queen said, reassuring her. With her pointer finger, she tilted Sabine's chin up, so they were looking into each other's eyes. "Bakley needs King Rainer's soldiers. His people need our food. You're saving lives."

Knowing she was doing the right thing didn't make it any easier.

Chapter Five

Standing on the front steps of the castle, an eerie sensation filled Sabine as she bid her family goodbye. Alina had done this exact thing only weeks ago. She couldn't let the similarities get to her.

"Keep your wits about you," the king said as he hugged his daughter. "Don't get distracted by court finery. Remember everything your mother taught you. You will be the queen of Lynk—make us proud."

Sabine kissed his cheek. "I will."

"You can do this," Karl said as he moved to hug her. "You know what needs to be done and what's at stake."

She squeezed Karl. "Subtlety has never been your strong suit," she whispered as she released him. "But I get it. I won't screw up. I promise."

"How about you just stay alive," Rolf said as he kissed Sabine's cheek. "You have the dagger I gave you?"

She nodded.

"I can't believe you're getting married before me," Otto teased her. "I honestly thought you'd never marry. I thought you'd be a spinster doting on your nieces and nephews."

She would have liked to have seen her brothers' children grow up. After hugging Otto, she moved to stand before Viktor.

"Just remember, don't get distracted by all of the men—I mean court finery," Viktor said with a chuckle.

Sabine hit his arm. He loved to irritate her. Somehow, she'd miss his banter. "If something happens to me, remember those were your last words."

He kissed her cheek. "I'll miss you."

"My turn," the queen said.

Sabine hugged her mother tightly. "I love you."

"And I love you. Please be careful. Your life is more important than finding the murderer."

"I'll be careful. I promise." She let go and then climbed into the carriage. When the door closed, she waved goodbye to her family.

The driver expertly guided the carriage out of the courtyard and down the road, leading away from the castle. At the gatehouse, eight mounted soldiers surrounded the carriage. These men were tasked with keeping her safe during the long trip north to Lynk.

Her hands began to shake as terror squeezed her heart, making her want to vomit. What had she done? She was neither ready to marry nor was she the most qualified person to be searching for a trained killer. Sweat broke out over her forehead. This entire plan was stupid. Balling her hands into fists, she took a deep breath and remembered that her kingdom needed protection. Marrying King Rainer would guarantee it. She had to keep that in mind. Otherwise, her sister had died for nothing.

One of the soldiers knocked on her window. "Your Highness, I'm Lieutenant Markis Belle," he said, loud enough for her to hear through the glass. "If you need anything, please let me know."

She nodded.

"Please pull the curtains closed as we travel. We don't plan on stopping until it's dark. There's food under your bench seat."

She did as he said, upset she wouldn't be able to see the countryside.

Sabine remained this way—traveling in the carriage with the curtains closed—for two weeks. The only time she was permitted to leave the carriage was once in the morning and evening to relieve herself. Otherwise, she slept, ate, and rode inside with no one to talk to and nothing to see.

She'd been told they'd reach Lynk tomorrow. With her boots off, she curled up on the bench seat, reading her book, trying to pass the time.

The carriage abruptly halted, and Sabine almost toppled off the seat. She peered around the curtain to see what was going on. It was only midday—not time to stop for the night yet. The soldiers accompanying her remained on horseback, moving so they faced away from the carriage. Each man withdrew his sword.

Shouts rang out as men rushed toward them. Fear shot through Sabine, and she quickly backed away from the window. A thud sounded to her right and she looked that way, spotting an axe sticking into the side of her carriage, level with her head. Her heart pounded and she immediately rolled onto the floor, flattening herself against it. She could not believe they were under attack.

"Do not pursue them," Markis shouted. "Hold your position."

Steel clanked and men grunted as fighting took place outside the carriage, mere feet from Sabine. With sweaty hands, she reached into her bag, fumbling around until her fingers came across the hilt of her dagger. Pulling the weapon out, she clutched onto it, ready to do her part if someone came at her.

If whoever was attacking managed to kill her soldiers or get past them, they'd come for her. And there she was, lying on the floor of the carriage, unable to hold her dagger steady because she was shaking so badly. She had no idea how many people were out there, or how the fight was going. It would be horrible if she died before she even reached Lynk. She should never have taken her sister's place.

The door by her feet opened. Sabine glanced that way and saw a large, beefy hand reach in, grabbing hold of her ankle. She squealed and started kicking the man's arm with her other foot.

The owner of that arm stuck his bearded face in her carriage. "You the princess?" he asked, looking her over.

"Who are you?" she countered.

He yanked her toward him.

She kicked the man's chin, knocking his head back.

He snarled and glared at her, hatred gleaming in his eyes. "I'll just kill you here. The sooner you're dead, the better." He withdrew a knife from his belt.

Sabine tried kicking his face again; however, he twisted her leg so her body was now on its side and she could no longer reach him. Still holding her dagger, she angled the blade toward her feet. When the man pulled her closer to him, she aimed for his stomach and tried impaling it into him. She missed, striking his arm instead. She managed to catch him off-guard long enough to ram her dagger into his shoulder though she'd been aiming for his neck.

He released her, and she immediately scooted away from him.

"Zounds!" The man stood there, his eyes narrowing and

his face contorting with rage. Not even bothering to pull her dagger free, he lifted his own knife, about to hurl it at her, when his body flew forward, his head smacking the floor of the carriage a mere foot from Sabine, a sword protruding from his back.

Markis stood behind the man, heaving deep breaths. He yanked his sword free, grabbed the back of the man's tunic, and hauled the body out of the carriage.

"Are you okay?" Markis asked, his left cheek splattered with blood.

She nodded, unable to speak. Everything had happened so quickly. She thought she might be sick.

"Let's go." He waved her toward him.

Sabine grabbed her boots, shoving her feet into them before climbing out of the carriage. Outside, bodies littered the ground. Sabine bent over and gagged. There were a dozen dead men. Nine wore plain clothing; the other three were Bakley soldiers. She'd lost three of her men.

"Why is there blood on your hands?" Markis demanded, grabbing her wrists to inspect her, and forcing her attention away from the bodies.

She looked at him and blinked, trying to comprehend what he'd just asked.

"Princess Sabine," Markis said, his voice softer. "Are you injured?"

"No." She pulled her hands free, looking at the blood on them. "I..." She pointed at the man on the ground.

Markis rolled him over, revealing her dagger embedded in the man's shoulder. Markis yanked the weapon free, wiping the blood on the dead man's pants before handing it back to her. "We need to get moving." He scanned the surrounding area.

Sabine clutched her dagger, not wanting to be without it.

"These men are dressed like Nisk mercenaries," one of

her soldiers said. "But it seems too convenient since we're traveling through Nisk."

"I agree," Markis said.

"The man I encountered used the word zounds," Sabine said. "Isn't that a slang word used in Carlon?" She recalled when a group of courtiers from Carlon visited her castle. She'd danced with one of the young men before having a drink with him in a dark corner. She remembered him using that word when her brother found the two of them alone and threatened to kill him.

"It is," Markis murmured. He scratched the side of his chin, looking at the men sprawled on the ground. "Their skin is a bit light for them to be from Nisk."

"What are your orders?" one of the soldiers asked Markis.

Markis sheathed his sword. "Princess Sabine," he turned to face her, "please clean the blood from your hands."

She nodded and reached inside the carriage, grabbing the blanket from the bench seat and her pouch of drinking water.

Markis started barking out orders, but Sabine didn't pay any attention. Her focus went to trying to scrub away all traces of the man's blood that was on her skin. Her hands shook. She'd stabbed a man with her dagger. That man would've killed her if Markis hadn't gotten there in time.

"Your hands are clean," Markis said, taking the water and blanket from her. "Now I need you to change."

Another soldier handed her a bundle of clothes. She nodded and took them. Going into the carriage, she quickly removed her dress and put on the navy-blue pants and tunic. Once dressed as a soldier, she exited the carriage.

Markis handed her a cap. "Put all your hair up under this so it's hidden."

She did as he said, surprised by how informally he spoke to her.

"Let's go." Markis took hold of her elbow, steering her over to where a soldier stood with two skittish horses.

She took the reins of one, and Markis helped her mount.

He climbed onto the other animal. "The two of us are going to continue north. The rest of your soldiers will remain with the carriage."

"I don't understand," she said, still trying to comprehend all that had just happened. It frightened her that someone wanted her dead and was willing to go to such lengths to kill her.

"The two of us will be able to travel faster without the carriage. We'll also be able to be anonymous on our own."

"But all of my things are in there." All the dresses her mother had commissioned for her.

"The soldiers will continue with the carriage. It'll just arrive a few days after us."

The soldiers began pulling the dead bodies away from the road and into the cover of the surrounding forest.

"We need to get as far away from here as quickly as possible in case more men come," Markis said. "Are you able to ride on your own?"

"Yes." Sabine urged her horse onward, and they set out. Karl had taught her to ride when she was only four years old. Riding came naturally to her.

After about a half mile, her heart rate returned to normal and she began to calm down. The fresh air filled her lungs, the sun warmed her skin, and she could almost forget about what had transpired a mere hour ago.

Sabine glanced sidelong at Markis. He had tanned skin and a light dusting of freckles across his nose. Dark blond hair stuck out from beneath his cap. She guessed his age to be around twenty-six. A little young to oversee not only her safety but the other soldiers as well. She wondered how he'd gotten a prestigious position at such a young age.

They rode in silence for a few minutes. The entire time, Markis scanned their surroundings as if he expected someone to attack them at any moment. A crow flew overhead but other than that, Sabine saw no forms of life anywhere nearby.

Reaching down, she felt her dagger tucked under the waist of her pants. Hopefully she wouldn't need it again. "Thank you for saving my life back there."

"I was just doing my job," Markis said.

Something about his words deflated Sabine. She was a job, nothing more. Markis held no loyalty to her—it was the crown he served. She wanted to change the topic. "When will we stop for the night?"

"As soon as the Lynk border is in sight. Probably in a couple of hours. It'll be well before dark if that's what you're concerned about."

His words sent a chill down her spine. She'd forgotten they were due to arrive in Lynk tomorrow. "You plan on escorting me to the palace, correct?" Not leaving her to fend for herself. The mere thought terrified her.

"Your father tasked me with delivering you safely to King Rainer's palace, and that is what I will do."

"Once we're there, will you serve as the head of my security?" If soldiers from Lynk were assigned to protect her, she had no idea if they'd be loyal or if she could even trust them. No, she needed her own men to feel safe and secure. Since three had been killed in the ambush, that left Markis and four additional soldiers. Five should be adequate.

"I will remain at your side unless King Rainer orders me to return home." He gripped the reins of his horse tighter, the movement slight, but Sabine noticed.

"Surely he wouldn't do that." Especially if she wanted Markis to remain with her. As a princess and the future queen of Lynk, she had to have some say in what happened.

"I'm not sure King Rainer will want foreigners he doesn't know or trust in his home."

"I will vouch for you," she replied. "That should be enough."

"What do you know about King Rainer?" he asked.

"Not much, but that doesn't matter. Our kingdom needs this alliance. If my sister could agree to marry a man she knew nothing about, I can do so as well."

"One of your brothers told me the princess and king had been exchanging letters for some time."

That was new information to her. None of her brothers had said a word to her about Alina and Rainer corresponding. "My brother told you that?"

"Prince Rolf wants me to look for the letters when I'm there. Since leaving Bakley, the princess's things hadn't been returned. We don't know if she kept the letters, but your brother believes she did. He thinks they are probably with her personal items."

"What does he hope to glean from them?" she asked, her thoughts drifting to the idea that her sister's belongings might still be at the palace. If she could smell her sister's sweet scent one more time...tears welled in her eyes at the mere thought.

"Your brother is simply looking for suspects and motives."

Sabine nodded as if all of this made sense. It hurt her that her sister hadn't confided in her. All this time, she thought Alina was going to marry a man she knew nothing about. However, that was not the case. Her sister had been corresponding with him. Which meant he had to be a decent person or else Alina wouldn't have agreed to go through with it.

"I understand people of royal breeding have certain

duties," Markis said, "but I can't imagine being in your situation."

"It is a bit daunting to be on my way to marry a man I haven't even met." All she'd been told about King Rainer was that his father had recently died so he'd inherited the throne at the young age of twenty-four. The king had three siblings, twin brothers who were twenty-two and a younger sister who was twenty. She'd also been told that for Rainer to maintain the throne, he had to marry and produce an heir—which was one of the reasons he needed to wed quickly. "What about you?" she asked. "Are you married?"

"I am. I've been married for three years. We have…"

"You have?" she prompted.

He glanced at her. "One daughter. We lost our son." He didn't extrapolate.

"I'm sorry," she said, not knowing what else to say. She shouldn't have pried. Perhaps he'd chosen to be a soldier to get away from his house where the memories were. Losing a loved one was never easy. That was why she dove headfirst into taking Alina's place. Focusing on training and preparing for this journey made it easier to deal with her sister's death. Markis could be doing the very same thing.

"One of the reasons I asked Prince Rolf if I could accompany you on this trip is because I know what you're going through."

Surprise filled her. She'd had no idea he'd volunteered for this.

"Losing someone is never easy," he continued. "Sometimes it makes us do rash things." He looked pointedly at her.

Her face heated up at his implication. Taking her sister's place wasn't rash—it was heroic. She was saving her kingdom. But that little voice in the back of her mind also reminded her she was doing this for a very selfish reason. She wanted to find her sister's killer. Instead of admitting that, she asked, "Did you behave rashly after the death of your son?"

He focused on the road straight ahead. "I lashed out at those trying to help and console me. Watching my wife suffer was unbearable, so I took on dangerous missions just to feel alive and not be consumed by the pain."

That was something Sabine understood. She'd thrown herself into training with her mother and Rolf to avoid the pain.

"That's the wall up ahead. Let's stop and make camp just off the road."

"Wall?" Sabine said as she steered her horse after Markis.

He glanced over his shoulder at her. "It's just over twenty feet tall and made entirely from stone."

Sabine squinted, trying to see it from where she was. "Does it go from one end of the kingdom to the other?" She had no idea how the Lynk people could have made something so large.

"It does. It even goes into the mountains." He led them to the cover of a nearby patch of trees.

"Interesting," she mused. "So, in theory, no one from another kingdom should be able to sneak in?" Which meant her sister's killer had to be from Lynk.

"Not necessarily. Someone could take a boat and get around the wall that way, entering Lynk from the ocean. I also believe there isn't a wall separating Lynk from Avoni, but that hasn't been confirmed."

"I wonder why they didn't build a wall around their entire kingdom." If they went through so much trouble to close themselves off from Carlon and Nisk, it seemed they should have extended the same to Avoni.

"There's a large river which separates Lynk from Avoni which is why I believe there isn't a wall there. Also, all their trade is done via ships since it's the easiest way to get supplies in and out. And, if they needed to, they could get their army on the coastline of any kingdom on the continent. If they attacked by land and sea, they could almost surround another kingdom, ensuring total victory."

"Couldn't another kingdom attack them from the ocean?"

Markis smiled. "No. It would be suicide."

Sabine was beginning to think this entire mission was suicide. She should never have offered to take her sister's place.

Chapter Six

S abine and Markis awoke early. They set out, only having a mile or so to go until they reached the border. Now that they were back on the main road, she could easily see the large, imposing wall directly ahead. It had to have taken an enormous amount of effort and resources to build something of that magnitude.

"Impressive, isn't it?" Markis said.

Sabine nodded.

"With an army as large as theirs, I'm surprised they bothered with the wall." Markis shrugged. "At the very least, it keeps unwanted intruders out."

She'd learned that the previous Lynk kings had prided themselves on having a large army. However, a thought occurred to her. "Are we sure their army is as strong as they claim it to be?" Perhaps the wall was meant to mask an illusion.

"Unfortunately, yes. Every so often they'll do something to show their power and to remind the other kingdoms that they aren't to be messed with."

"Like what?" she asked, wondering if they were simply putting on a show to scare others away.

Markis sighed. "Do you really want to know? It's pretty brutal, and you are marrying the leader of the Lynk army."

Until now, Sabine hadn't thought much about her future husband. It was easier to go through with this stupid plan of hers if she didn't consider the man she was going to marry. Pure terror filled her. As the leader of such a powerful military, King Rainer had to be rough and commanding—not at all like her father or brothers.

She suddenly felt like a pig being led to her slaughter. "I want to go home." She pulled on her horse's reins to turn around. Maybe her sister had killed herself rather than be married to the king of Lynk.

Markis reached out and grabbed hold of the reins, stopping her. "Look at me," he demanded, his voice strong and steady.

Instead of doing as he said, she looked south, at the road she wanted to be traveling on back to the people she loved. She was the princess of Bakley and Markis her guard. She could order him to escort her home. Unwanted tears filled her eyes, making her feel weak and out of control. She was better than this. Whenever a challenge had presented itself, she'd always run headfirst toward it. She prided herself on being fearless and pushing the boundaries. But this, this she couldn't do.

"I know the task before you is daunting," Markis said, his voice calm and reassuring. "But you can do this. I wouldn't have agreed to accompany you otherwise. Please know that I'm here with you, and I won't let anything happen to you. I promise."

"This is the worst idea I've ever had." She shouldn't have asked to take her sister's place without fully understanding what she was getting herself into. She'd been so blinded by seeking revenge that she hadn't stopped to consider what this might do to her.

"I don't think wanting to protect your kingdom is a bad idea," he replied. "When you marry King Rainer and fulfill Bakley's end of the contract, he'll send soldiers to secure our border which will in turn protect our children. You're saving countless lives."

She knew they needed this alliance. "You said the Lynk army is vicious. What if King Rainer is a monster?" Her voice came out like a soft whisper.

Markis released her reins and rubbed his eyes. "I don't know. If he's that bad, I'll get you out of there."

Knowing Markis was going to be with her offered some comfort. She'd seen him in action and trusted his skills to keep her safe. A thought suddenly occurred to her. "What if King Rainer killed my sister?" Her stomach twisted with nausea.

"The king penned letters to Princess Alina before they drew up the marriage contract."

He'd mentioned that once before. "What does that have to do with anything?"

"I don't think an evil man would have bothered writing letters to Alina to try to get to know her."

When he put it that way, she didn't think so either.

"And his kingdom needs Bakley's food. If something happens to you, your father isn't going to send the shipments."

Now that Markis was stating the facts and forcing her to think clearly, she was beginning to calm down and see reason.

"And don't forget, he must have a titled wife who can give him an heir. He's not going to hurt you when he needs you to keep his throne."

That point she could have done without. She didn't

particularly want to think about breeding to fulfill her end of the bargain.

"Granted, none of this means he's going to be the man you'd choose to marry if you didn't have responsibilities." He looked pointedly at her.

She knew he'd picked his words carefully, adding that part about her having a responsibility to her kingdom. She sucked in a deep breath, letting it out slowly.

"Rainer is a king who controls a mighty army. We need this alliance. Most likely, he'll leave you alone to do as you please. You're a foreigner, so I can't imagine him relying on you for much else besides producing an heir. You have nothing to worry about."

"You're right," she said, rolling her shoulders back. This was simply another challenge she needed to tackle. "The sight of the wall just frightened me." When she had first seen it, it had felt as if she were about to enter a prison from which there would be no escaping. Now she understood she was choosing this. And she would survive.

"Let's get going before the Lynk soldiers guarding the wall start to wonder why we're stopped in the middle of the road." Markis nudged his horse and began heading north once again.

Taking a deep breath, Sabine steered her horse after Markis. As they neared the wall, she noticed there were not only guards standing in front of a large gate, but also sentries patrolling the top of the wall. If Bakley had enough soldiers to monitor their border, their children wouldn't have been kidnapped. Envy filled her—these soldiers were protecting the Lynk people. If her father had been more careful with his army, she wouldn't be in this predicament. Regardless, she would fix the matter and secure the Bakley border for her father and his subjects.

When they were about fifteen feet from the gate, one of

the soldiers called out for them to halt. Sabine did as instructed, scanning the men. Each one had a sword strapped to his waist. Several held long poles with spikes at the tip. She reached forward, stroking her horse's neck to keep the animal calm.

"State your business," one of the soldiers commanded.

"My name is Lieutenant Markis Belle, and I am from the kingdom of Bakley. I am tasked with escorting Princess Sabine Ludwig to His Majesty King Rainer. I have a sealed letter from my king, along with a letter from King Rainer's personal steward, Gunther." He reached under his tunic, producing two letters.

"Where's the princess?" the soldier asked.

"This is Her Highness Princess Sabine." Markis gestured toward her. "We were attacked on our way to Lynk. We left the carriage behind to travel anonymously."

Reaching up, Sabine removed her cap, allowing her hair to cascade down so they could see she was a woman.

One of the soldiers neared, his hand on his sword. "I'll take a look at those letters."

Markis handed them over.

The soldier took the letters and returned to the gate, speaking with one of the other soldiers. A moment later, he approached them again. "You are granted entrance. I have two men who will escort you to the palace."

Sabine nudged her horse forward. Embedded in the wall, an iron gate swung open, granting them entrance. As she passed through the wall, she marveled at how thick it was—at least ten feet. She had no idea how such a thing had been built.

As soon as she cleared the wall, the gate swung shut, closing with a bang.

Two mounted Lynk soldiers approached. "Follow me," the

one on the right said. He steered his horse north, and Markis went after him.

"I'll bring up the rear," the other soldier said with a wink, gesturing for Sabine to go before him.

They traveled single file along a narrow valley between two steep mountain ranges covered with black rocks and bright green plants. Sabine had never seen anything so strange in all her life. It felt as if she were on a different continent altogether and not simply a different kingdom. Examining the two soldiers in greater detail, she observed that their skin was slightly darker than hers, somehow creamier and more beautiful. Both men had black hair and dark eyes.

"Are you doing okay?" Markis mumbled.

"Yes," she replied. "Is all of Lynk like this?" She pointed to the mountain on her right.

"What do you mean?" the soldier behind her asked.

"Do steep mountain ranges cover most of your kingdom?"

"Yes. Why do you ask?"

"They're beautiful," she answered. Now she understood why Lynk needed food so desperately. It wasn't that the king focused all his resources on his military; it was that they had no land to farm.

The first soldier led them closer to the mountain range on the left. After a bit, they reached its base, and he took them to the entrance of a cave. He dismounted and ordered everyone else to do the same.

A soldier exited the cave, taking the reins of each horse. "If you need any of your personal belongings, be sure to take them," he instructed.

All of Sabine's things had been left with the carriage.

"Let's go," the man leading them stated as he entered the cave.

"What are we doing?" she asked, nearing the entrance.

"We're taking this tunnel to the palace."

"Tunnel?" she asked, her voice echoing as darkness closed in around her and panic set in.

Sabine blinked as her eyes adjusted to her darkened surroundings. The soldier ahead of them held a torch, lighting the way through the narrow tunnel, revealing slick black rock with water dripping from a few places.

"Is this a lava tube from a volcano?" Markis asked.

Sabine had never heard anything about there being a volcano on the continent.

"Yes," the soldier behind them answered. "Hundreds of years ago."

"What about our horses?" Sabine asked. The soldier who held the animals hadn't followed them into the tunnel.

"They'll be taken care of," the leader said.

The tunnel curved to the right, and it sounded like there was rushing water up ahead.

"Why are we taking the tunnel?" Sabine asked.

"It's faster than going around the mountain," the soldier answered.

They were going through the mountain. *Through.* The thought of being inside a mountain made Sabine's shoulders ache, as if a weight pressed down upon them. Having no idea how long this journey would take didn't help either. Even if going around the mountain added a week to their traveling time, she wouldn't have minded. At least then she could see the land. Here she saw nothing. Fear set in at the thought of a chunk of the mountain caving in and burying them alive.

The tunnel abruptly ended. The soldier leading the way held out his torch, revealing a waterfall to the left feeding into a river which went to the right. The soldier behind her moved to the side, pulling a small boat out from a cave.

"You've got to be kidding," Sabine said. "Do you expect me to get in there?"

"Not until it's in the water," he said, shoving it closer to the river.

"This will be much easier than walking," Markis assured her.

She glared at him.

He shrugged.

The two soldiers put some supplies in the boat before lowering it into the water and holding it in place.

"The princess goes in first," the one said.

Not wanting to overthink it and scare herself more, Sabine went over and stepped into the boat, sitting in the middle of it.

Markis joined her, sitting at her side. Then the soldiers got in, one in front, and one in the back.

"No oars?" Markis asked.

"Don't need them," the man in the back answered. "It's not that deep and the water will take us where we need to be."

Both men let go, and the boat floated away. The water rushed forward, taking them into another tunnel. Thankfully, they still had the torch so Sabine could see.

The farther they traveled, the deeper into the mountain they went. The air turned thick and heavy. The sounds of them breathing seemed loud above the water which was fairly quiet against the smooth sides of the tunnel.

They rode all day. Every few hours, the soldier at the front would grab a new torch, lighting it with the old one. Once the old torch burned out completely, he tossed it over the side and into the water. Sabine and Markis were offered something small to eat—a loaf of bread, some dried meat, or a piece of fruit.

Sabine didn't remember falling asleep, but she awoke and found herself on the floor of the boat, leaning against Markis's legs.

She stretched, realizing she needed to relieve herself. "Um," she mumbled, glancing about the small boat.

"If you need to go, there's a chamber pot in the back here. I'll switch places with you. No one will look. Then toss it over the side."

Horrified, Sabine realized what she was going to have to do.

"Being a man comes in handy sometimes," the soldier said as he switched spots with her.

Once she finished, she returned to the middle. "How long will we be traveling like this?"

"It's seventy-five miles long. About three days," the soldier answered.

Which meant she would not see or feel the sun on her face for three days. "We have enough food for that long?"

"We have what we need," he answered.

It was going to be a long three days since she had nothing to do to occupy her time but worry about what the future held.

Chapter Seven

T he next two days followed a similar pattern. They floated along the tunnel river, switching torches every few hours, eating small meals here and there, and sleeping on occasion. Just when Sabine thought she couldn't handle another minute in the mountain, she saw a faint light ahead. A minute later, the river exited the tunnel and entered a valley. The boat hit the bottom, and the soldiers jumped out, pulling it up onto solid ground.

Markis helped Sabine out of the boat. Her legs felt weak from being cramped in the small boat for the past couple of days. She reached up, stretching. The air felt wonderful and refreshing. Unfortunately, the sun had already set and dusk had descended over the land. At least tomorrow she would feel its warmth on her face.

"It's a good thing we exited in the evening," Markis said. "Otherwise, our eyes couldn't have handled the bright light."

Sabine hadn't considered that. She glanced around. "Do we walk from here?" She doubted their horses were on another boat following behind them.

"We have a place not far from here," the stockier soldier

said. "We will eat and sleep there for the night. There will also be horses there for us to use."

That sounded like a perfectly reasonable plan. As she started walking, she realized it felt as if the ground were moving up and down ever so slightly.

"It'll take a day or two to get your balance back," Markis said as he watched her.

She nodded and continued on, thankful to be on solid ground even if it didn't feel so solid right now. They traveled for another mile before coming to a small wooden house with a pen out back, filled with half a dozen horses. Inside the house, there were several bedrolls and a hearth piled with wood. That was about it. The four of them ate and then went to bed.

They set out on horseback early the next morning. Now that it was lighter out, she could focus on her surroundings. They were traveling in a valley between two steep mountain ranges, both of which appeared to have an abundance of black rocks and bright green moss covering them. There were a few trees scattered throughout—mostly pines. As they went, the vegetation became thicker and brighter in color.

That night, they stayed in another empty house. Sabine suspected these houses had been built specifically for soldiers to use when traveling through Lynk. She had yet to see a town or village.

The following day, as they rode their horses, Sabine noticed what appeared to be buildings carved into the side of the mountain. "What are those?" she asked, pointing toward the top of the mountain to their left.

"Homes."

She squinted, trying to get a better look. The structures

seemed to be part of the mountain, as if born from it. The only reason she even saw them was because whatever they'd been constructed with, the material stood in contrast to the green foliage and the black rocks.

"I can't imagine trying to build those." Markis whistled. "That's mighty impressive."

"People *live* there?" Sabine asked, needing clarification. All she could envision was a little girl leaning out of a window and plummeting to her death.

"Do people typically not live in houses in Bakley?" the soldier in the back asked.

"They do," she replied, irritated by his snide comment. "But our homes aren't hanging on the side of a mountain. They are on flat, solid ground."

He chuckled. "That sounds boring. And dangerous."

"How is having a house on the ground not safe?" she asked.

"If an enemy approaches, you're not at an advantage."

As they rode, she thought about that. This was a military kingdom. Everything, it seemed, reflected that. It made sense. Her own kingdom was the same. Since farming was Bakley's primary focus, the land, people, stores, and lack of a military reflected that.

A terrifying thought suddenly occurred to her. "Is the palace on a mountain like that?"

Both soldiers laughed, neither one answering her question.

The four of them traveled along the valley, between the mountain ranges, for several days. The farther north they went, the warmer it became. They finally left the valley, heading toward the mountain. When they reached it, they took a path carved into the side of it. The narrow trail wound back and forth as it gently ascended.

The sun started to set just as they reached the top of the mountain. Sabine didn't know what she expected to find, but this certainly wasn't it. An entire city stood before her. The homes looked like they hung over the edge of the mountain. Most of the structures were several stories tall, all constructed with stone. In Bakley, most of the homes were made from wood, and only the castle and the duke's homes were made from stone. Toward the center of the city, the buildings were even taller, maybe five or six stories.

"We'll walk from here," the soldier leading the way said as he dismounted.

Sabine slid off her horse, her legs shaking from the journey up the mountain.

Two young boys wearing loose pants and sleeveless shirts approached. They smiled and then took all four horses, leading them away.

"Follow me," the one soldier said as he assumed the lead. Sabine and Markis did as he asked while the other soldier walked behind them.

They took what must be the main street since it went straight through the city. Along the way, they passed several storefronts. Some had displays of fabric, others beads and jewelry. On top of the stores, lines strung from one window to another across the street, laundry hanging on them to dry. Sabine peered down one of the side streets. It, too, was lined with stores and homes. However, it only went fifty or so feet, right to the edge of the mountain.

The people all wore strange clothing. The men had on loose pants and thin shirts, many of the shirts unbuttoned. The women looked as if they'd taken a large swath of fabric and twisted it around their bodies, securing it with a belt. A lot of people didn't bother with shoes and simply went barefoot. Sabine didn't think it was a lack of money based upon the jewelry many of the people exhibited. It had to be a cultural thing. She couldn't help but chuckle at the thought of Alina seeing all of this for the first time. Her sister would have been horror-stricken to see so much skin exposed. However, based upon the warmth and humidity, Sabine guessed the people of Lynk dressed accordingly.

The buildings abruptly ended but the road kept on going for another thirty feet or so, appearing as if it led straight off the cliff. It was hard to tell because as the sun set, thick clouds rolled in, level with them at the top of the mountain. About five feet from the end of the road, two men clad all in black, including a black cloth that covered their heads leaving only a small cutout for their eyes, stood in the middle of the road.

"Halt," one of the men stated. "No one gets in or out. Direct orders from the king."

"I have a letter from the king's personal steward, Gunther," the soldier to Sabine's right said as he held out the letter Markis had handed over to them when they first reached Lynk.

The man on the right stepped forward, taking the letter. He quickly read through it. "We'll take it from here. You're both dismissed."

The two soldiers who'd accompanied Sabine and Markis bowed and then left without saying a word to them. Even though Sabine had never learned either of their names, she suddenly felt abandoned. Instead of showing any hint of unease, she kept her face blank and made sure to keep her head held high. She was going to be the queen of Lynk and needed to make sure she behaved as such.

One of the men knelt, opening a wooden door in the ground that Sabine hadn't noticed before. He pulled out a blue flag and stood, waving it in the air. After a few seconds, he returned the flag to its place. A loud groan resounded. Sabine could have sworn the ground beneath her feet shuddered.

"I'll be damned," Markis muttered.

Two large wooden planks began to lower, one from the mountainside where they stood, and the other from what appeared to be another mountain across the way. The other mountain ended up being more like an island, only surrounded by air instead of water. Perched precariously on that island mountain sat an elegant white palace. Sabine hadn't seen it at first because the clouds were so thick, concealing a portion of it, making the palace look as if it were floating.

Once the two bridges fully lowered, they connected, forming a long pathway from one mountain to the other. Two wooden doors opened on the other side and a dozen soldiers exited, coming straight toward them. These men, like the two with them, were dressed in solid black pants, tunics, and masks. Only seeing their eyes sent a chill down Sabine's spine. Each man also carried a spear and had a sword strapped to his waist.

They stopped just before the end of the bridge.

Sabine half wondered what would happen if the wind blew hard enough. She suspected the soldiers would be blown right off the bridge. The men kept their focus straight ahead, probably not wanting to look down. She wouldn't want to look down either.

One soldier stepped forward. "I am Captain Lithane, in charge of the palace guard." He held his hand out, and one of the other soldiers handed over the letter. He quickly read it. "It bears the king's steward's seal." He looked at Sabine and Markis.

"I am Lieutenant Markis Belle, tasked with delivering Princess Sabine Ludwig safely to the palace."

"We've been expecting you." He looked at Sabine again. "Though we didn't expect you to arrive like this." His eyes narrowed. "Lieutenant Markis, you may leave. I will escort Princess Sabine inside."

"I am not to leave her until she is delivered safely to the king." Markis's voice remained strong, not once wavering.

The sky began to darken and the air turned cold. "It is getting late," Sabine said, using her most sophisticated and haughty voice. "The journey here has been long and harrowing. I wish to go inside and retire for the night. Lieutenant Markis will remain at my side. That is not negotiable."

"The king will decide," Lithane replied. "If you wish to enter, you must be checked." He took a step toward Markis. "Spread your arms and legs."

Markis did as he said. "In addition to the sword at my waist, I have two knives."

Lithane quickly patted him down, retrieving the three weapons. "These will remain with me until you leave."

"I will discuss the matter with the king," Markis said.

Lithane ignored him and turned to face Sabine. "Now I will check the princess."

"You will maintain your place," Sabine said, her voice loud and firm. "And you will not lay a hand on me." She'd never been patted down by a soldier before and would not consent to being touched so brusquely now.

"I can't allow you inside the palace without making sure you are free from weapons."

She chuckled, like she'd seen her mother do when confronting a situation where she wished to have the upper hand. "Yet you all walk around with weapons. Weapons that anyone wishing the king harm could easily steal and use."

"No one gets past us."

"If no one could," Sabine said, folding her arms, "then

you're telling me my sister was assassinated by a Lynk soldier?"

She heard Markis's sharp intake of breath.

No one said a word for an uncomfortable minute.

"Are you accusing a Lynk soldier of killing your sister?" Lithane asked, his voice low.

"You will address me as a princess. And by your logic, you are admitting someone from your guard killed her since, as you stated, no one could get past you and your soldiers."

He opened his mouth to speak again but closed it, remaining quiet instead.

Sabine took the opportunity to maintain control of the situation. "As far as I'm concerned, I am entering the place where my sister was murdered. I will proceed with my dagger and my personal guard. You cannot—and will not—deny me these things. I am your future queen. Now take me to meet King Rainer."

Lithane stared at her for what felt like a full minute before answering. "I do not have the authority to admit you into the palace armed. Nor can I allow your…guard in. I will have to consult with my superior. Please wait here…Your Highness." He bowed and then returned to where his men stood waiting. They parted, and Lithane walked between them, back to the opened gate and into the palace.

Markis folded his arms and turned his back to the soldiers and the palace. "That was…a tad bit risky, don't you think?"

"No. It was necessary to establish my authority and make sure you remain at my side. I trust no one else with my protection."

He nodded. "Then let's hope this works. Otherwise, we're sleeping out here tonight."

The clouds continued to roll in, concealing the palace. Sabine shivered from the light wind and the moisture in the air.

"Who is he consulting?" she asked.

"I'm not sure how their chain of command works here. He said he was a captain, so I'm guessing he's pretty high up." He kicked the dirt with the toe of his boot. "Maybe we should have waited for the carriage to catch up."

"We've been over this. Stop second-guessing yourself." She needed food. And water. And a warm bed. Oh, and a bath sounded lovely. However, if she had to remain out here tonight to prove a point, she would.

About thirty minutes later, Lithane finally returned with a man at his side.

The man was dressed differently from the soldiers. He wore cream-colored pants and a matching tunic with the buttons open in the front, revealing his toned chest. Sabine had never seen a tunic like that before—worn like a jacket, only without a shirt beneath it. Beautiful gold stitching adorned the thick collar. As the man got closer, Sabine saw he had a thin crown atop his head though she didn't think he was the king.

He stopped in front of her. "I am Prince Axel Manfred." He bowed. When he straightened, his dark brown eyes scanned her from head to toe and the corners of his lips rose, as if fighting a smile.

She replied, "I am Princess Sabine Ludwig." From what she'd been told, the twins were twenty-two years old. He was certainly handsome in a generic sort of way. Square face, strong jawline, and dark hair.

"First, I would like to start by offering my condolences."

That surprised her. "Thank you."

"You have darker hair than your sister, but I see the resemblance. We did not expect you to arrive here at the palace so soon. We thought it would take at least another week for your carriage to arrive. Unfortunately, the king is not here to greet you." He clasped his hands behind his back.

Markis quickly introduced himself and explained why they were dressed the way they were and without a carriage and guard.

As Markis spoke, Sabine studied Axel, trying to determine if he knew about the attack on their carriage or not. Maybe he was behind her sister's death. No one could be ruled out.

"I'm sure you've had a long, tiring journey," Axel said. "Let's get you inside." He turned to face Lithane. "Princess Sabine and her guard are granted entrance. And the princess may keep any weapons she has in her possession."

"As you wish, Your Highness," Lithane replied.

Axel spoke quietly with Lithane for a moment, presumably giving the man instructions. When he finished, he turned to Sabine. "Princess, my men will show you to the room your sister was using, if that is okay with you? Her things are still there—we haven't packed anything up yet. It didn't feel right to touch her belongings. We thought it best for one of her family members to handle the matter. However, if you prefer, I can have another room prepared for you, in case her things hold too many memories."

Emotion overwhelmed her at the thought of being in the same room Alina had been in. "My sister's room is fine." Then she could wear her sister's clothing. The mere thought of touching Alina's things gave her a sense of comfort.

"Once you are washed and dressed appropriately, my siblings and I will join you for something to eat. I assume you are hungry from your journey?"

She was famished. "Yes, thank you."

He bowed his head, then left.

"Follow me," Lithane said. He led Sabine and Markis across the bridge.

The soldiers remained parted. Lithane, Sabine, and Markis walked in the center, past the soldiers. The bridge had more bounce than Sabine had anticipated, making her nervous to cross it, even if it was fifteen feet or so wide. She dared not look at what lay over the side—if she could even see down that far. Instead, she kept her focus straight ahead, on the two large wooden doors that seemed to be screaming her name, begging for her to reach them.

And then she was back on solid ground, entering through the doors. Once the soldiers were safely back in the palace, the bridge was lifted using cranks on the wall, and the doors were closed and locked.

"This way," Lithane said. He led Sabine, followed by Markis and half a dozen soldiers, under an archway and into a courtyard adorned with water fountains and roses. In the dim light of the early evening, it was hard to see much. The courtyard branched off into a dozen or so archways, some with doors and others leading to long corridors.

Lithane escorted them through one of the archways on the left and then down a hallway that seemed to extend along the side of the palace. To her right, there was a smooth white wall; to her left, there were several open archways—without windows—which appeared to have a complete vertical drop straight to the floor of the valley below. She couldn't bring herself to lean out and look to verify.

They turned and went along another hallway before Lithane opened a door and escorted them into a large room. They crossed it and went up four flights of stairs, down another hallway, and then stopped at a door.

"This is your room," Lithane said. "A servant has been called to attend to you. Your guard may remain on watch out here. Prince Axel is arranging for sentries to guard you as well. He should be along shortly and will show you to the dining hall once you are ready." He bowed his head and then left.

"Wait here," Markis said, opening the door. "I want to inspect the room first." He went inside.

Sabine remained at the threshold, the six Lynk soldiers spreading out in the hallway behind her. She peered into the room, observing her sister's trunks. Tears filled her eyes. A piece of her sister was in there. She forced herself to look away from Alina's things and examine the room. On the left side there were eight arched openings and a single doorway, without a door, revealing a sizable balcony. She suspected it jutted out over the side of the mountain. In the center of the room, there was a large bed with sheer fabric hanging around it. It wouldn't shut out the light, so she didn't understand why the fabric was there at all. The bed had several light blue blankets. To the right, it appeared there was a dressing closet and a bathing room.

"It's all clear," Markis said. "I'll let you get ready. Shall I send the servant in to assist you once she arrives?"

"Yes, thank you." She closed the door and took a deep breath. It was time to get to work. She swore to discover who killed her sister, and she planned to keep that promise.

Chapter Eight

To keep herself from being overwhelmed by grief, Sabine had to pretend her sister's belongings weren't in the bedchamber. All she wanted to do was run over to the trunks, throw them open, and hug Alina's things. However, she couldn't afford to be emotional. Not when Prince Axel would arrive soon to escort her to supper where she would meet his twin brother and their younger sister. When she had more time alone, she would look through her sister's trunks. Her priorities needed to be bathing and dressing so she looked the part.

Peering into the bathing room, she discovered the bathtub had been built in the ground and it was already filled with steaming water. Without questioning how such a feat was constructed, she peeled off her filthy clothes and climbed in. The warmth enveloped her, and she moaned. She could stay here forever. There was a block of soap next to the tub, so she grabbed it and began scrubbing her body and hair.

"Good evening, princess," a female voice said from nearby the doorway.

Sabine glanced over and saw a young woman, probably around her own age of eighteen, standing there.

"I'm Claire, and I'm here to help you dress for supper."

"Did you fill this bathtub for me?" Sabine asked.

"No, princess. There's a spring below the palace. Certain rooms always have warm water—this is one of them, which is why it's the queen's room."

That surprised Sabine—both the water part and the queen part. For some reason she'd assumed she'd be switching rooms once she married. "Does my room have an adjoining door to the king's room?" If the king could get in here, she needed to know.

"Yes. However, it is locked from both sides at the moment. Once the wedding takes place, the locks will be removed."

Relieved, Sabine went under the water one last time to ensure all the soap was rinsed from her body. When she resurfaced, Claire stood there holding a plush white towel.

"There are steps on the side," Claire said, nodding her head to the right.

Sabine used them to exit. She wrapped the towel around her body and headed out into the main portion of her bedchamber. The sky outside had turned dark. "Is it always this warm in Lynk? Even in the evening?"

"Yes, princess." Claire had followed Sabine into the bedchamber. "Shall I pick out something for you to wear?"

"No." She didn't want Claire touching her sister's things. "I'm not sure what will work. Alina was a little shorter and heavier than me. I'll need to look through her dresses to see." She eyed the trunks. "Have her things been packed? Or are her dresses still in the closet?"

"Princess Alina's possessions are packed. However, the king had the closet filled before your sister's arrival," Claire said. "Everything in the dressing closet is appropriate Lynk attire. I think you should choose one of the outfits in there as they are all the current fashion of our court. Your sister's clothing is a little different from what we wear here."

Sabine turned to study Claire. "Are you my lady's maid?"

"Yes." Claire's hair was pulled into a side ponytail. She had on a silky pale blue dress that only went on one shoulder and cinched around the waist.

"I wasn't sure by your attire." No proper woman in Bakley would wear a dress revealing a naked shoulder like that.

"All of the king's servants wear pale blue. It's the royal family's color."

Sabine went over to the door to the left of the bathing room and opened it, revealing an enormous closet filled with brightly colored clothes.

"I'm afraid everything was made for your sister," Claire said. "However, most of the outfits can easily be adjusted to fit your body."

Sabine walked into the closet, running her hands over the various items. The colors were bolder than what she was used to wearing, the fabric thinner and softer. "What do you recommend I wear?" She assumed she'd only be meeting the royal family minus the king. Regardless, she wanted to make a good first impression.

"I think you should go with something green," Claire said from the doorway. "With your gray eyes, you'll look stunning in that color." She pointed to a dress the color of grass after a dewfall.

"Are there any undergarments I can wear?"

Claire's brows drew together. "Undergarments?"

"A slip or a corset?"

"We don't wear anything like that here. With our heat and humidity, you'd melt."

Sabine nodded and put the dress on, feeling oddly naked since the dress hugged her breasts and curves, revealing far too much. "I'm not comfortable wearing this." A slit went up the front, showing the entire length of her leg.

"It looks perfect on you."

"I don't care." After removing the skintight dress, she went back into the bedchamber. She'd wear something of her sister's before prancing around the palace half naked. Going over to one of the trunks, she knelt and rummaged through it until she found a pale green dress with puffy sleeves and lace over the bodice. She slid it on over proper undergarments, pleased with how well it fit. Then the smell of her sister hit her. Instead of letting it overwhelm her, she breathed it in, taking strength from it. Alina's death would not be in vain.

She went over and sat at the chair to the vanity table situated in the corner of the room. Picking up a brush, she began untangling her hair. In the mirror, she noticed Claire with pursed lips. "Is something the matter?"

"That dress is very odd," Claire answered, standing behind Sabine.

"To you, perhaps, but to me it feels familiar. It is my first day here, I am far from home, and I need a little comfort." She smiled kindly at her lady's maid, wanting to forge a friendship with the woman. Her mother had told her that servants and her lady's maid would be an excellent source of information. If she hoped to navigate the complexities of this foreign court, she'd need all the help she could get.

"I can understand that," Claire said. "Would you like me to do your hair?"

Since Sabine wasn't sure what Claire would do with it, she pulled her hair over her shoulder and began braiding it. "I'll do it tonight. Next time, I'd love for you to help." She wrapped the braid around her head and pinned it in place. When she finished, she quickly applied a little dusting powder.

A soft knock sounded on the door.

Claire went over, opening it. Someone handed her a piece of paper and she read it before turning back to Sabine. "Prince Axel will meet you in the dining hall. Your guard will escort you there."

Standing, Sabine ran her hands over her dress to ensure she looked presentable. Satisfied, she exited the bedchamber.

In the hallway, she found six Lynk guards. Startled, she froze, wondering where Markis had gone.

"Princess," Markis said. One of the guards stepped forward.

Sabine recognized those eyes. "Markis?"

"I will be joining your guard," he said, stepping back in line with the rest of the men.

"Temporarily," one of the other men said. "This way, Your Highness." He gestured for her to follow him.

While she'd been getting ready, Markis must have changed. With the black uniform and the mask covering his face, it was hard to know which of the guards he was since they all looked identical. Maybe that was the point.

They traversed through several hallways, all of them white and bare and lit only by the occasional candle. Then they went down three flights of stairs and through an interior courtyard filled with water fountains and brightly colored flowers. She'd have to come back and examine it in greater detail when the sun was shining and she could see better. Back inside the palace, the guard led her to a room.

She stepped inside and found a large table taking up most of the space. One wall was completely open to a balcony overlooking the valley below. She suspected this wasn't the main dining hall due to its small size. However, this wasn't the royal family's personal one either since it wasn't attached to any of their private rooms.

"You're to wait here," the soldier said before bowing and taking up watch out in the hallway with her other guards.

Markis came inside the room and stood beside the door.

Sabine smiled at him to let him know how much she appreciated him being overly cautious. Since no one else had arrived yet and she didn't want to sit alone at the table, she ventured out onto the balcony. A low wall surrounded the perimeter. She was half tempted to peer over to see how far up she was. However, she decided not to. Maybe tomorrow when it was light out, she'd be brave enough to peek.

Tilting her head back, she gazed up at the stars. Now that the cloud cover had vanished, some of the stars seemed close enough to touch.

"Princess Sabine," a male voice said from behind her.

She turned and spotted Axel striding out onto the balcony along with a man who looked strikingly similar, but his brown hair was a little longer. That had to be Anton, Axel's twin brother. Anton was similarly dressed as Axel, though he wore red instead of cream. Sabine didn't understand why they wore tunics as jackets with the front open, exposing their chests. Even though she'd seen her brothers shirtless on occasion, she'd never observed a man outside of her family like that. At least they were both pleasant to look at—though she didn't want either of them to know she thought that.

Averting her eyes, she noticed a beautiful young woman behind them wearing a bright purple outfit that exposed her bare stomach. The skirt had two long slits, revealing her tanned legs. The woman's shoulders were bare, and her brown hair lay in soft waves down her back. Like her brothers, she had dark brown eyes and a squared face. She had to be their younger sister, Lottie.

Sabine blinked, feeling out of sorts. She'd never seen a woman dress like that before, revealing so much skin. Not knowing where to look, she tried to keep her focus on the three siblings' handsome faces.

Axel quickly made the introductions, confirming her assessment as to who each of these individuals were.

"It's late, and I'm sure you're hungry. Let's all take a seat at the table." Axel placed his hand on Sabine's lower back, ushering her inside. "It's a shame my brother isn't here to greet you."

"Where is the king?" Sabine asked, wondering why Axel felt the need to touch her. Even if it was a Lynk thing, it wasn't a Bakley custom and it made her feel even more out of sorts.

"He's investigating your sister's murder." Axel pulled out a chair for Sabine.

She slid onto it. "Didn't the murder happen here at the palace?"

A handful of servants entered, bringing trays upon trays of food, setting them all on the table before leaving.

"Yes," Axel finally answered. "However, he wanted to speak to a few people who have a special skill set and can possibly help in the matter." He waved his hand in the air as if that explained everything.

"How was your journey to the palace?" Lottie asked, tilting her head to the side as she spoke.

Sabine wanted to look at Lottie when she answered, but she found it hard to face the woman considering she barely had any clothes on. Focusing on Lottie's forehead, she replied, "Other than my carriage being attacked, it was uneventful."

"Either someone really hates your family," Anton said, "or someone desperately doesn't want Lynk and Bakley to form an alliance." He lifted his goblet and took a drink of his wine.

The siblings began helping themselves to the food, so Sabine did the same. The meat appeared to be some sort of fish. There were also small pieces of white stuff that was sticky and clumpy—she had no idea what it was—and cooked carrots.

"Luckily for us," Anton said, "we have our dear, older brother to investigate and figure it out all on his own. He doesn't need his family to do anything."

Sabine sensed the sarcasm in his voice and was immediately on edge. "Are there any suspects?"

"I am sure my brother has a list," Axel said with a wink. "You'll have to discuss the matter with him since he is handling it."

"Is that a traditional mourning gown worn in your kingdom?" Lottie asked, abruptly changing the subject.

"No," Sabine answered. "In Bakley, this is proper attire for supper." All her life, she thought her family prudes for being so modest and making sure to have their arms and necks always covered. She'd been the one to push the boundaries by exposing a little bit of her neckline or perhaps an inch from her gloves to her sleeves. Here, in Lynk, it seemed that modesty didn't exist and now Sabine was the prude. How the tables had turned. "I understand that this is not your fashion. However, is this not appropriate?"

Lottie raised her eyebrows and looked at Axel.

Sabine faced Axel, awaiting his answer.

"Well," he replied, "there's nothing wrong with what you're wearing but...well, what would your family say if Lottie showed up for supper dressed as she is?"

"They'd be horrified," Sabine admitted.

"Why?"

"Because it's not appropriate attire in Bakley."

"The answer is the same," he said.

So it was more than just not being in fashion, she realized. It had to do with offending the people here. Since she was in a foreign land, she needed to abide by their customs—no matter how crazy they may seem to be.

"I can help by showing you our proper attire," Lottie offered.

"I would like that," Sabine replied, touched by Lottie's kindness.

Anton drummed his fingers on the table. "I don't think we should announce the princess's presence until Rainer returns."

"I agree," Axel replied.

"We don't want gossip to start before our dear brother has a chance to present her to his court the way he wants to," Lottie said. "He'll need to figure out how to introduce this sister when he just introduced the other one not long ago."

"People are still jittery about the murder," Anton said.

Sabine realized that the palace was very different from her home in Bakley. At her castle, only the royal family resided there. "How many people live here at the palace?" she asked.

"Anyone of importance has rooms here," Lottie answered.

She had no idea how many people that would be. Lynk had dukes but she couldn't remember how many or if anyone else was considered important.

"At any given time, I'd say there are usually around twenty families here," Anton clarified. "And I'd say probably fifty servants and at least that many guards, though I've never counted before."

"I'm shocked you don't know the exact number," Axel mused, swirling the wine in his goblet before taking a sip.

This supper felt like being back home with her own family. The familiar banter carried on throughout their meal. While she didn't know these siblings well, it pleased her that they were comfortable enough to tease one another in front of her.

Once done eating, she excused herself. Her guards escorted her back to her bedchamber. When they reached it,

Markis went inside and checked the room, making sure it was safe.

"All clear," he said. "I'll be out here in the hallway if you need anything."

"At some point, I hope you sleep." He had to be exhausted and he couldn't watch over her all the time.

"Yes, Your Highness," he replied, bowing his head.

"Goodnight." She closed the door and locked it.

After putting on bedclothes, Sabine climbed into bed and fell fast asleep.

When Sabine awoke in the morning, a letter had been slid under her door. It instructed her to remain in her room until the king returned. She groaned. The last thing she wanted to do was waste time holed up in her bedchamber when she could be exploring her new home and trying to find information about her sister's assassin. She wouldn't be able to discover the killer unless she questioned the inhabitants of the palace.

Not wanting to upset the royal siblings, she did as they asked and remained in her room. She spent the day going through Alina's belongings and remembering some of the good times they shared growing up. A few bad memories managed to resurface. Like the one birthday when Sabine had asked for a white pony like Alina's. When she didn't get it, she was so mad she went out to the barn to take Alina's. Only, when she got close to the horse, it nipped at her, breaking the skin on her hand. Sabine had accused Alina of teaching the horse to do that. Alina cried and Sabine was punished for it. She was so furious she refused to come down for her own birthday celebration. Funny that she remembered that event now of all times.

After closing the last trunk, she stood and ventured out onto the balcony. The wind whipped around her, tossing her hair, and making it difficult to see. She pulled her hair back, knotting it at the base of her head. Breathing in, she reveled at the warmth of the air. It smelled lovely here. No horse or cow manure, only exotic fragrances from the plants. She made it half-way out onto the balcony before she froze in place. She could have sworn the balcony swayed ever so slightly. That was enough for her—she ran back inside.

It amazed her that someone had managed to construct a balcony sticking out over the edge of solid ground like that. Especially from so high up, over a hundred feet from the bottom of the valley floor. At least the palace itself was built on top of the mountain. Granted, it would be nice if there was some sort of perimeter around the palace instead of it going straight down.

Meandering through her room, she didn't know what else to do to occupy her time. She really wanted to start tracking down her sister's killer. With the murderer still loose, she couldn't feel at ease in the palace. Not only that, but her sister deserved justice. A thought occurred to her. Maybe the royal family had something to hide and that was why they insisted she remain in her room. It would give them time to get rid of the evidence. She glanced at the door. If she insisted on leaving her room, there wasn't much her guards could do to stop her. At least, she didn't think there was anything they could do.

Her sister would have followed the rules. Sabine was inclined not to. However, for now, she decided to stay put. She was used to doing things before thinking them through. This time, she needed to make sure she had a solid plan in place before she acted.

That night, Claire brought Sabine her supper. The three siblings seemed to be quite serious about not letting her step foot out of her bedchamber.

Frustrated, she took the tray and went over to her bed, setting it on there. "Do you know why the princes and princess wish for me to remain in here until the king returns?" Sabine asked before Claire could leave. She knew the siblings didn't want her to be introduced to the court before the king returned, which she accepted, but she didn't understand having to hide in her room.

"Oh, I, uh, assume they…"

"They what?" she prompted.

Claire's face turned red. "I think they're concerned about you looking queenly in case any of the Lynk people see you. They want to make sure everyone accepts you as their ruler."

Sabine sat on the bed, dumbfounded. She'd always taken pride in the dresses she wore and how she presented herself. "What does a Lynk queen look like?" It had been years since the late queen died. Regardless, people would compare Sabine to the royal siblings' mother.

"Beautiful and seductive. As a queen should be."

Sabine almost choked on her own spit. Not once had she ever thought a queen should be seductive. Elegant and refined, yes. Seductive? Absolutely not. Her sister must have been horrified when she came here.

"No offense, Your Highness, but right now you look like a foreigner."

Sabine ran a hand down her dress. "Did my sister wear Lynk clothing?" She couldn't imagine Alina putting on anything provocative since she'd always been overly modest.

"No, she did not."

"Was my sister introduced to your court?"

"Yes."

Sabine found this information fascinating. "How did the people here receive her?"

"Well, I don't think anyone really understood her. She looked and acted so different from us."

Which could be part of the reason they were afraid to introduce Sabine without Rainer's approval. "Thank you for bringing my food. You are dismissed."

Claire bowed before leaving the room.

While sitting on the bed eating her supper, Sabine considered all she'd learned. The royal family didn't want to introduce her to the court until the king returned because they wanted her to dress and look the part of a Lynk queen. Which meant this must have been an issue for her sister. If Alina looked like an outsider and made no effort to assimilate to the culture here, that could have been reason enough for someone to kill her. Which meant Sabine was going to have to do the opposite of what her sister did in the hopes of staying alive.

When she finished eating, the sun hadn't set yet. She wanted to snoop around the palace before the king returned —whenever that would be. She had no idea if it would be a day, a week, or a month. Regardless, the royal siblings couldn't order her around. They probably thought she was like Alina and would do what she was told. She snorted. They'd never suspect her to be wearing their clothing and walking around the palace in plain sight.

She went over to the closet, inspecting the outfits inside. The trouble would be finding something she felt comfortable wearing. There were many dresses to choose from. All brightly colored with hardly any fabric. She began searching for the most material she could find. When she came across a purple dress that covered one shoulder and didn't have any slits in it, she pulled it out, examining it. It seemed better than the other options.

Steeling her resolve, she put the dress on, finding it hugged her body a little more than she cared for. After locating some shoes that matched, she went back into the bedchamber, trying to decide what to do with her hair. Not knowing the Lynk fashion, she decided to leave her hair down as Lottie had worn hers to supper last night.

Satisfied with her appearance, she exited her bedchamber, holding her head high. There were only two guards on duty, and they both looked at her. Thankfully, one of them was Markis.

"I want to take a walk around the palace since my legs are stiff, but I don't want to attract any attention by having the two of you hovering."

"Yes, of course, Your Highness," Markis said, taking control of the situation. "Where would you like to go?"

"I don't know." She looked at the other guard. "Do you have any suggestions?"

"We can head to one of the courtyards," he said. "At this hour, there won't be many people around. I'll take the lead. You may walk a few feet behind me so no one will notice. Is that satisfactory to you?"

"Yes."

"And I'll walk behind you to make sure you're safe," Markis added.

The three of them set out. Even though she was dressed in Lynk clothing, Sabine still felt ill at ease moving through the palace. If one of the royal siblings found her, they'd be upset. However, she was on equal footing with them. Once she married the king, she'd be their queen and would outrank them. She never let one of her own siblings intimidate her, so she refused to let anyone here get the better of her either. She also assumed that the more she dressed in Lynk fashion, the more comfortable she'd get. Besides, she needed to keep her end goal in mind. She was doing this to start sniffing out the person who killed her sister. Sitting alone in her bedchamber all day would do her no good. And she'd always excelled at snooping.

The sun had just set, but the sky hadn't yet turned dark. When she reached the courtyard, someone was only just lighting the candles along the perimeter wall. She realized that was the first person she'd seen since leaving her room.

Markis and the other guard took up watch at one of the archways which allowed her to wander freely around the courtyard. She pretended to smell the flowers and observe the water fountain, all the while hoping to spot someone passing by so she could speak to him or her. However, if this was the royal wing, she doubted she'd run into anyone.

"I thought we asked you to remain in your room," Axel said, startling Sabine. He strode across the courtyard and joined her. "It's nice to see you're at least trying to assimilate." His eyes scanned her body. "You could use a little work, though." He winked.

"Your Highness," she said by way of greeting, hoping to remind him that he should address her with proper respect. She inwardly groaned, realizing she sounded like her mother.

He smiled. "We're not that formal when it's just the family. There's no need to be."

"We're not family. At least, not yet."

"What are you doing out here all alone in the courtyard?" he asked.

"I just needed to get out of my room for a bit."

"You could have asked one of us to visit you if you wanted company."

She was about to inquire what he was doing out at this hour when movement to the right caught her attention. In the nearby archway, a woman stood wearing a red outfit that covered her breasts, stomach, and then hung straight down to the floor. A slit ran up the front, exposing both of her long legs and thighs.

"Your eyes look as if they're going to fall out," Axel said with a chuckle. "Are you okay?"

She nodded, unable to believe women dressed like that in Lynk.

"I must go," Axel said. "You should remain in your room. When the king returns, he'll be furious if he finds you roaming the halls. Especially looking like that." He winked and then strode over to the woman, draping his arm around her shoulder. The two of them disappeared down the dark hallway.

The stars started to glimmer in the sky. Sabine sighed and headed back to her guards, upset that she'd discovered absolutely nothing of importance today. Tomorrow, she would try a different approach. One thing became clear—she couldn't remain in her bedchamber all day.

Chapter Nine

The next morning, when Claire arrived with breakfast, Sabine put her first plan into action. "Good morning," she practically sang. "Will you keep me company for a bit? I'm so lonely." She smiled sweetly at Claire, wanting to befriend the young woman. If Sabine was to have any hope of learning the secrets of the palace, she needed her lady's maid as a confidant.

"Of course. Shall we sit outside?"

"That is an excellent idea."

Situated on the balcony were a table and chairs on one side and and a sofa on the other side.

Claire set the tray on the table and took a seat.

Sabine sat across from her. "Why don't you tell me about yourself?" She pulled the tray closer, examining the bowl of oatmeal, the plate of cut apples, and the muffin. She didn't notice any yellow powder or anything odd smelling. Still, she hesitated, not knowing if it had been through a food taster.

"There's nothing to tell." Claire shrugged. "I'm the youngest of three girls. We all work here in the palace, including my mother and father. My mother works in the kitchen and my father is a guard."

Knowing her mother worked in the kitchen and the food had most likely gone from cook to Claire, Sabine relaxed and took a small bite of oatmeal. "I'm the youngest of six."

Claire smiled. "It's hard being the youngest sometimes."

"Yes, it is." She leaned back in her chair. "How long have you worked in the palace?"

"Since I was sixteen, so about three years now."

They were roughly the same age then. "What did you do before I arrived?"

"I was assigned to Princess Alina. Prior to that, I apprenticed for the resident seamstress."

Sabine found that interesting. She didn't know how one went from working with a seamstress to being the future queen's lady's maid. "Working with the seamstress sounds far more exciting than helping me." Not wanting to sound like she was fishing for information, she asked casually, "What about your sisters? What do they do?" She plucked an apple and put it in her mouth.

Claire's eyes widened. "Why do you ask?"

Obviously, Sabine had stumbled on something with regards to Claire's sisters. She needed to try and discover what it was.

Sabine shrugged, trying not to appear too interested. "I'm just curious. You told me what your parents do but not your sisters. Since you'll be attending to me, I thought we should get to know each other. I'm desperate for a kind friend here in this strange kingdom." Sabine forced a smile on her face, thrilled with the prospect of her first clue. Granted, it might not have anything to do with Alina, but there was something amiss and she was determined to discover what it was.

"The king tasked me as your lady's maid to ensure you dress and look the part. Given my background with the seamstress, I'm sure you can understand that I have a knack for fashion. That is the only reason I'm here." She abruptly stood.

"I'm sorry if I said something to offend you. Are we not permitted to be friends?"

"No. I mean, yes, we can be friends. But I need to go. I have some other tasks I must attend to."

Sabine wanted to ask what other jobs she had but refrained from doing so. Claire was far too skittish and untrusting now. Sabine would have to nudge her slowly.

That evening, Sabine sat at the desk composing a letter to her mother. For the first two paragraphs, she detailed her perilous journey to Lynk. Then in the next paragraph, she described the palace and the people she'd met. Her mother would be able to draw the same conclusions Sabine had with regards to possible suspects and motives.

Someone knocked on her door. "Come in," she called out.

Axel stepped into her room wearing loose black pants and a black tunic open in the front. It was stitched with intricate gold embroidery along the edges.

She stood, surprised to see him. "Is there something I can do for you?"

"I know it's late, but I'd like to escort you to the rooftop to show you the nearby town. It's exquisite at night."

She narrowed her eyes. "Why?" She doubted he wanted to be nice or get to know her. He had to have an ulterior motive.

He slid his hands into his pockets and watched her a moment before responding. "I thought you might like to get out of your room," he admitted. "The roof is secluded, so we don't have to worry about anyone seeing you. And...I thought we could talk."

Curiosity got the better of her and she wondered if he had anything to say regarding her sister. "I would like that." Not that she cared to go to a secluded place with this man, but for her sister and the possibility for information, she would.

Axel held the door open for her, and she exited the room.

"You're all to remain here," he said to her guards as he headed to the right.

She hadn't been down the corridor this way yet. "Markis will come with me," she said loud enough for Markis to hear.

"You don't need him. You have me to protect you." Axel winked. "Besides, it'll give us more privacy to talk."

Having seen him with that lady last night, she figured he had a way with women and enjoyed flirting. Or at least using his charm to his advantage. Too bad it wouldn't work on her. Having grown up with four older brothers, she knew most of their tricks. The key to dealing with Axel would be to treat him as she would one of her own brothers. "Markis will remain with me." She noticed Markis kept a careful three-foot distance behind her.

"Don't you trust me?" Axel asked, his hand to his chest as if wounded.

She tilted her head and looked up at him. "Do you trust me?" she countered.

He considered her for a moment. "I hadn't really thought about it." He led her to a flight of stairs.

"You never considered the possibility that I might have a weapon on me and try to assassinate you as revenge for the death of my sister?"

His face paled.

She laughed. "I'm only toying with you." She winked. "Maybe."

At that he chuckled. "You're nothing like Alina."

"No, I'm not." She stopped halfway up the stairs and turned to face him. "What do you consider me?" she asked. "Am I your future sister? A pawn? A toy?"

He chuckled, the sound low and sultry, and then gestured for her to continue up the steps. At the top, he placed his hand on her lower back and whispered in her ear, "You're all of those things and more."

She suspected he wanted something from her, and she'd need to keep her guard up around him.

The roof turned out to be a twenty-foot wide flat space on top of one of the palace turrets. There were other decks with slanted rooflines that she could see from where she stood.

Axel dropped his hand from her back and then meandered over to the edge of the rooftop, leaning on the railing. "Care to join me?"

Sabine stood in the middle, taking it all in. The view of the town and nearby mountains was breathtaking under the moonlight. Since she could see it all from where she stood, she decided not to go any closer to the edge, especially with Axel there.

"Why did you really bring me here?" she asked.

He leaned back against the railing, facing her. "You're much more direct than your sister."

"I'm a very different person than my sister." She folded her arms. "I thought we'd already established that."

Axel turned and faced away from her, resting his forearms on the railing. "Anton and I are opposites as well, even though we're twins. However, I assumed since you're so young…" He didn't finish his sentence.

Sabine could fill in the blanks. He'd assumed she was innocent, inexperienced, and naive. Especially after meeting Alina. "You thought wrong. Since I am the youngest of six…" She purposely didn't finish her sentence, allowing him to draw his own conclusions. Whatever came out of this, he needed to know he couldn't push her around.

"I'm sorry about your sister."

It was the second time he'd said something along those lines. "Why are you sorry? Did you have something to do with her death?" She hadn't meant to be so blunt, but she needed answers.

He glanced over his shoulder at her. "I'm going to pretend you didn't just ask that."

While he seemed genuinely offended, he'd failed to deny his involvement. However, she didn't say anything else. She simply stood there, waiting for him to get to the point of why he'd brought her here.

She glanced at Markis who'd remained in the stairwell, giving them the illusion of privacy. If she was aware of his presence, then Axel had to be as well. Markis nodded at her, as if giving her permission, so she moved closer to Axel, knowing Markis wouldn't take his eyes off her and he'd protect her at all cost.

If Axel simply wanted to get to know her better, he could have done so over supper, not an evening stroll on the rooftop. "Axel," she whispered, using his name, and foregoing his title, "what do you want?"

At first, she thought he hadn't heard her. She was about to repeat herself when he turned to face her.

"What do I want?" he mused, a small smile playing on his lips. "That is a good question. And one I'm used to only hearing in the bedroom." He smirked.

Sabine wanted to roll her eyes. He reminded her so much of Viktor. Instead of acknowledging his comment as she was certain he wanted her to do, she sighed, trying to look bored.

He rubbed his forehead and focused his attention back to the town in the distance again. "What do you know of Lynk's politics?"

Practically nothing. Instead of saying that, she answered, "Lynk is like any other kingdom. There is someone sitting on the throne, someone vying for the throne, someone who craves power, someone who doesn't want it…it's all the same. Different kingdoms, different players, same game."

"True." Axel chuckled. "You're more pessimistic than I expected."

"Why do you ask?" she said, trying to nudge him to get to the point.

A single shoulder rose and fell. "You're very different from Heather," Axel mumbled under his breath. "I wonder what he'll do about that."

She refused to take the bait and instead, filed the information away for later. She'd have to discover who Heather was and the man who Axel was referring to, though she suspected it was the king. She wished she knew more about the man she was supposed to marry. The man whom Alina had been writing to for weeks before they met in person.

"You're harder to read than your sister," Axel said. "I wonder how long you'll last."

A cold chill slid down Sabine's spine. Her initial reaction was to grab her dagger and ram it into Axel's back. However, she couldn't act so foolishly simply because he kept trying to bait her. "I think it's time I return to my room. My guard will escort me. Goodnight." She turned and left, not giving him a chance to respond.

At the stairwell, Markis took her arm and ushered her quickly down the steps. "I want you to stay away from that man," he whispered near her ear so Axel wouldn't overhear.

At the bottom of the staircase, he released her but kept a quick pace.

"Don't worry," she assured him. "I was just trying to

discover if he knew anything about Alina's death. I have no intention of forming any sort of friendship with that man."

"Sabine," Axel called after her, not even bothering to use her title. Footsteps pounded down the stairs not far behind them.

"Keep moving," Markis said. "I don't trust him."

The feeling was mutual.

"Sabine," Axel called out again. "Don't run away from me. Most women run *to* me, not *from* me. Running is only going to make me want you more."

"I'm going to kill him," she murmured.

"That makes two of us," Markis said. "Although I think he's just trying to get a rise out of you."

"Oh, I know he is, which is why I'm not stopping to engage with him." Anger, irritation, and fury rose within Sabine as she headed along the corridor back toward her bedchamber.

Markis steered her around the corner, and she slammed into something hard. Stumbling back, Markis grabbed her, keeping her upright.

"Watch where you're going," a man sneered.

"You watch where *you're* going," Sabine snapped, looking up and up until she found the face attached to the snide comment. A rather tall, devastatingly handsome gentleman stood before her, dressed similarly as Axel.

"Brother," Axel said as he came up behind her. "So lovely of you to join us. Princess Sabine and I are just returning from a romantic rooftop stroll. There are lots of stars out tonight. Beautiful, don't you think?"

Horror filled Sabine as she realized this man before her must be her future husband, Rainer, the king of Lynk. She didn't know if she should curtsy or apologize for barreling into him.

Rainer's eyes narrowed, focused solely on his brother, his

body blocking the entire hallway so Sabine couldn't move around him.

It dawned on her that Axel didn't seem at all surprised to see his brother. She'd been in enough dalliances to know a set up when she saw one. If she had to guess, she'd say Axel was next in line for the throne. Either he wanted to make his brother jealous by forming a relationship with her, or he wanted to prevent the wedding altogether so he could take the throne. If that were the case, it put him on the top of her list of suspects for her sister's murder. Not that she thought he'd dirty his hands by doing it himself. More likely, he'd hired someone to kill Alina for him.

"Axel," Rainer said, "it's late, and I am tired. We will talk tomorrow." His attention turned to Sabine.

She hadn't been prepared for the weight of his piercing gaze. As if he could see right inside of her with his mahogany-colored eyes. While he looked like his siblings, he had an older, more mature face adorned with dark hair that had a slight curl to it.

Axel winked as he walked by, leaving her alone with Rainer, Markis hovering behind her somewhere out of sight. The king towered over her by at least a foot, putting her eyes level with his muscular chest...which she did not need to be looking at or thinking about right now. She needed to stay focused.

"You're a little young," Rainer mused, his voice deep and appealing.

While there was a six-year age gap, she was old enough to marry and be queen of Lynk. Instead of responding to his jab, she forced herself to meet his intense eyes. "I'm tired and am going to bed. We can try this again tomorrow." She went to step around him.

He reached out, grabbing her arm and stopping her in place.

Markis made an odd sound, sort of like a hiss. Sabine tried not to laugh knowing Markis's hands were tied. While he may have wanted to protect her, he couldn't intervene with the king.

"Who are you?" Rainer demanded.

"Lieutenant Markis Belle, Your Majesty."

"You're not one of my guards." It was a statement, not a question.

The fact that Rainer knew Markis wasn't one of the guards since they all wore the same thing, including masks over their faces, said a lot. Sabine would have to remember that.

"No, Your Majesty. I am Princess Sabine's personal guard. I escorted her here and King Franz tasked me with her safety."

"The princess won't be requiring your services any longer. You're dismissed."

Sabine stiffened. If Markis left, she'd be all alone. She needed someone she trusted watching her back.

"With all due respect," Markis said, "given what happened with Princess Alina, I think it best I remain here."

Rainer's fingers tightened on her arm.

"You may release me," she said. "We can discuss this matter tomorrow when we aren't so tired."

"No one is allowed to cross the bridge and enter my palace unless I've vetted them." Rainer released Sabine and peered down at her. "I can't have another incident in my home."

"Incident?" She wanted to wrap her hands around his thick neck and squeeze. How dare he call her sister's murder an incident.

"However, if you can vouch for Lieutenant Markis, he can remain here until tomorrow."

"Tomorrow?"

"Tomorrow, when we discuss this matter." He articulated each word slowly, as if speaking to a child.

She needed to collect herself and get her emotions under control. "Of course, I personally vouch for Lieutenant Markis." She tried to make her voice sound as calm and haughty as possible so he wouldn't know how intimidated she was by his presence. Someone like Axel she could handle since she knew what to expect. But Rainer made her feel off kilter.

The king pinched the bridge of his nose, mumbling something under his breath. Sabine used the distraction to step around him. This time, he didn't try to stop her.

The next morning, Sabine awoke to a knock on her door. She went over and opened it and found Claire standing there. "Is something the matter?"

Claire folded her hands together. "The king wishes to have his breakfast with you this morning."

Sabine yawned and stretched. "Very well." She needed to speak with Rainer about her sister's murder and keeping Markis as her personal guard. "Please let him know I'll get dressed and be along shortly." She started to close the door.

Claire stuck her hand out, stopping it. "His Majesty sent me to help you get ready." She stepped into the room.

"Let me grab one of my sister's dresses." Sabine headed over to where she had the trunks organized.

"His Majesty gave me very specific instructions," Claire said. "I'm to make sure you're dressed *appropriately*."

Sabine glanced over at her lady's maid. "Which means I'm supposed to wear an outfit from the dressing closet?"

Claire bit her bottom lip.

"What?" Sabine asked.

"The king wishes for me to pick out your outfit and do your hair."

"I would love to have your help," she forced herself to say. Never in her life had a lady's maid picked out her clothing. However, she was in a foreign land and needed to assimilate. To get information on her sister's killer, she needed to play by their rules.

Claire's shoulders relaxed as she headed to Sabine's closet, exiting a few minutes later with three outfits. "I need to see these colors with your hair and skin tone." She held up each one to Sabine. "This is the one." She placed the pale yellow one on the bed and then returned to the closet.

Sabine removed her bedclothes and pulled on the outfit. "Are you sure about this?" she asked, looking down at herself. The fabric tied behind her neck, going straight down over her breasts, leaving her entire back exposed. It flowed to the floor and had two long slits in front of each leg, going up to her thighs. "I feel naked."

Claire stood back and examined her. "Hang on." She went to the closet and returned a moment later, tying a piece of braided fabric around Sabine's waist, letting the ends hang down off to the side. "You look perfect. This style is very fashionable right now."

At least the outfit was comfortable and light so she wouldn't sweat.

"Now for the shoes."

Sabine wouldn't call them shoes. They had a flat piece for the bottom and then leather straps that tied around her ankles. Regardless, she didn't say anything as she put them on, trying to be amiable.

"If you'll sit at the vanity table, I'll do the finishing touches."

Sabine felt like a doll as she sat, allowing Claire to make her presentable. Claire brushed out Sabine's hair, leaving it down which she appreciated since her back was exposed. Claire then applied some dusting powder to Sabine's face. Once finished, Claire handed her a handful of gold bracelets, matching earrings, and a simple necklace.

As Sabine put the jewelry on, a wave of sadness hit her. She used to do this sort of thing with her sister.

"Is something the matter?" Claire asked.

Taking a deep breath, Sabine realized she had an opportunity here that she couldn't pass up. She looked at her lady's maid in the mirror. "You remind me of my sister," she whispered. "She used to love helping me get ready for a party or a ball." She glanced away and twisted the bracelet around her wrist. "You mentioned you have sisters."

"Two," Claire answered. "Heather and Sarah."

Not wanting to push too hard and scare Claire off, Sabine stood. At least she had two names now. That was more than she had before. And she could start inquiring about Heather and Sarah who worked here in the palace.

She reached out and took hold of Claire's hand, squeezing it. "Thank you for your help. I appreciate your kindness. It means a lot to me." She released her. "You're certain I look okay?" The makeup seemed too dark and heavy. However, if this was the way people in Lynk wore it, then she would too.

"You look like our future queen—and that is the point."

The word *queen* gave her goosebumps. When she heard that word, she thought of her mother, not herself. This entire situation still felt surreal to her. And right now, she was about to face the king of Lynk. Hopefully, by looking the part as the future queen, King Rainer would be more amiable toward her. She needed to have a decent rapport with him to glean what information she could about her sister's murder.

"Where am I meeting the king for breakfast?" Her hands started to become sweaty, a nasty product of being nervous.

"I'll escort you there."

The two of them exited the bedchamber.

Out in the hallway, Markis's eyes widened at the sight of Sabine, and the tiny bit of skin visible around his eyes turned a deep shade of red. While she understood this was not an appropriate outfit in Bakley—if her brothers saw her like this, they'd cover her with their jackets and probably pull a sword on the person responsible for dressing her—it was the Lynk way. Rolling her shoulders back with false bravado, Sabine ignored Markis and followed Claire. They turned down the corridor to the left and went to the end, stopping before a door.

Claire knocked, and the king's personal steward—the one who'd delivered the news of Alina's death—opened the door.

"Your Highness," he said with a bow.

"Good morning, Gunther," she said, hoping she'd remembered his name correctly.

He smiled. "Please come in." She stepped inside, and Gunther closed the door, leaving her guards and Claire out in the hallway. "The king is expecting you."

The steward led her into the royal quarters. They passed by several sofas and chairs, all lightly colored. If this was considered the king's personal sitting area, it lacked a fireplace. Come to think of it, her room did as well. Perhaps it didn't get cold enough for one. She had a hard time imagining that.

Gunther stopped before a small, private dining room where the king sat at the head of a rectangular table with six chairs. Four archways adorned the wall to the left, sheer curtains hanging next to them, gently blowing in the breeze, revealing a narrow balcony, only three feet wide on the other side.

The king stood, commanding her attention. "Princess Sabine Ludwig. Welcome." He wore a sleeveless vest that exposed his tanned, muscular torso and arms. It looked as if he spent his days training with the army. Maybe he did. After all, Lynk was known for its military might.

"King Rainer Manfred," Sabine said as she stepped into the room.

Rainer motioned for her to take the seat to his right, so she did.

A servant rushed in, placing several trays laden with food on the table.

"Help yourself," the king said.

Sabine scooped some fruit on her plate and a piece of bread drizzled with honey. Examining the food, she didn't notice anything of concern. However, she kept her focus on her plate instead of the man sitting next to her. The king. Who made her slightly uncomfortable. While he was the same age as Alina, Sabine felt the gap in years acutely between them. Physically, he felt much older than her, older than Rolf and Karl even. Perhaps it was the wide set of his shoulders, his towering height, or the light dusting of hair on his chest.

"Thank you for meeting with me this morning," he said, his deep voice rumbly like horse hooves racing across the field. "I would like to first offer my condolences. Alina— Princess Alina—was a remarkable woman who didn't deserve to die as she did. I hold myself fully responsible and vow to find the murderer."

Stunned by his words, Sabine set her fork down, observing him. "Thank you." His eyes held hers, making her face feel warm. "I want nothing more than to discover the person who killed my sister." She hadn't expected him to care about Alina's death since he barely knew her. If they worked together, they could solve her murder.

"I hear you had a dangerous encounter on your trip here." He reached out as he spoke, placing his large, calloused hand on her forearm.

"I did." She blinked a few times, not knowing what to make of his touch. In Bakley, such an intimate gesture was something only two people who were familiar with one another did. But they were to marry soon, and such things were common among couples. It was just that his warm hand felt like boiling water, searing her with a burning warmth she didn't understand. Over the years, she'd danced, walked, and even conversed in dark corners with men. Well, technically boys her own age. This, whatever this was that she felt toward King Rainer, seemed different. Somehow more potent and it scared her.

"When my men and I met up with your carriage and soldiers, I was stunned to learn what had transpired and that you had gone on ahead with a single soldier for protection." He removed his hand from her arm and leaned back in his chair, watching her with his dark eyes.

Axel had told her Rainer was out investigating Alina's death. If that were the case, he had no business being anywhere near her carriage. She couldn't help but wonder if he had something to do with the attack. She licked her lips, trying to find a way to ask him what he'd been doing there in the first place. "Is my carriage here at the palace?" she asked, pulling off a piece of her bread and eating it.

"No. It'll be here in a day or two. After I spoke with your soldiers, I returned home, hoping to arrive before you did. I'm sorry I was not here to greet you."

"Why did you meet up with my carriage?" she asked, needing to hear his explanation. Her hands began to shake, so she set them on her lap where he couldn't see them. Maybe him touching her and looking at her as if she were important was his way of trying to throw her off. She'd done the same by flirting with men to learn a bit of gossip or to get something she wanted. Right now, it seemed like Rainer was trying to get her to trust him, which meant she needed to keep her guard up. While she wanted to believe he was sincere, they'd only just met, and she was no fool.

Rainer took a drink from his goblet before answering. "I had to travel to Carlon to meet with the League. When your father wrote to me, telling me you'd take your sister's place, he changed a few minor details of the contract. I had to give the League the new contract for approval."

His answer only caused Sabine to question even more. However, she didn't want to appear like a simpleton, so she refrained from speaking.

"On my way back to Lynk, I came across your carriage as there are only two main roads leading to my kingdom."

She was certain Axel told her that Rainer was out investigating Alina's murder. Which meant that either Axel had lied, or Rainer was lying right now.

He was staring at her, as if waiting for her to say something.

"My father didn't mention that he'd altered the contract at all." She would have to write to him to ask if he had and if so, why.

"Minor details. Regardless, I am required to follow protocol."

She nodded as if she knew this already.

"I'll be honest," he said as he propped his elbow on the back of the chair, pulling his vest wider and exposing his entire muscled stomach to her. "I was disappointed when I learned you weren't with your carriage."

"Why?" The question slipped out before she could stop herself.

He stared at her for an uncomfortable minute before replying. "I wanted to meet you to make sure we are aligned in our goals."

The hair on the back of her neck stood on end, and Sabine felt danger rising like a lake during a downpour.

"Please explain." It sounded an awful lot like he could be her sister's killer. As if he would have done the same to Sabine if he found them not aligned. Maybe he'd kill her now if he discovered that to be the case. She needed to tread carefully.

"Alina and I exchanged letters before we agreed to marry one another. I am intimately aware of your kingdom's troubles, just as Alina knew about mine. We...agreed on several issues."

Markis had mentioned something about Alina and Rainer's letters. He wanted to find them so her brother Rolf could read them to see if there was anything important in them.

"It is my understanding that you sent a contract, asking for my sister's hand in marriage, and she agreed. Is that when you started writing to one another?"

"No," he revealed. "If I'd simply wanted a wife, I could have chosen anyone. I chose Alina after we wrote to one another on two separate occasions and decided on some issues."

Sabine knew her sister, but her sister had never told her any of this.

"After the contract was signed, we wrote to one another more intimately." The way he said that sentence, softer, almost like a secret, made Sabine's toes curl.

With raised eyebrows, she considered this man before her. He was the most sensual man she'd ever met—and she was going to marry him. However, he'd chosen Alina, not her. "Are you suggesting you don't wish to proceed with the wedding?" Bakley needed his soldiers. If Lynk backed out, her father would accuse her of ruining the alliance, and her mother would be devastated Alina hadn't received the justice she deserved.

"No," he answered. "I signed the new contract your father

sent to me. I've agreed to its terms. He told me a little about you, though I'd like to get to know you for myself."

"What would you like to know?" She couldn't think of a single question she wanted to ask him about himself at the moment. Everything she thought of related to his kingdom, the palace, or her sister. But not him personally.

He leaned forward, resting his arms on the edge of the table as he neared her and said, "Everything I need to know I've learned watching you eat your breakfast."

She leaned back in her chair, wanting to put some space between them, realizing she was in over her head.

"Do you have any questions for me?"

Knowing he expected her to ask something about himself, she decided not to. "When will our wedding take place?" In other words, how long did she have to get her bearings around this palace before she became queen.

"Everything is ready. Once we have permission, we'll wed."

"Permission?"

"From the League."

She needed to figure out what this League was. As soon as she had the chance, she'd write to Rolf and ask him. He had to tell her, especially now that she was going to be Lynk's queen. She had a right and deserved to know.

"Before you go," Rainer said, "we have one last matter to discuss. You understand that I must maintain a secure palace. I have a duty to protect my people and ensure no one else is killed here in my home."

"Of course."

"Then you understand why your guard, Markis, must return to Bakley."

Terror gripped her. If Markis left, she'd be completely alone in a foreign kingdom with no one to protect her. Right now, she didn't trust a single person here besides him. "And you must understand that this is where my beloved sister was assassinated. I won't feel safe unless I have someone loyal guarding me."

"I will ensure your safety," Rainer insisted.

She shook her head. "Until the assassin is caught, Markis will be my personal guard."

"I can vouch for each of my men," he said. "Your safety is my top concern."

"I'm sure you told Alina that same thing." And look how that had turned out.

He stiffened. "Your sister had her Bakley guards with her. They failed to protect her." His voice held a hint of suppressed fury. "I will not allow you to be guarded by subpar sentries. My men will protect you."

"And your men can protect me so long as Markis is one of them." She stood, wanting to end this argument.

"I'll make you a deal," he said, standing as well. "I will personally assess Markis and decide if he is worthy to be in my guard. If I deem him capable, he can remain under my employment so long as he swears fealty to me."

"Markis has a family to return to. All I'm requesting is that he remain with me until I'm settled. I'm not asking that he remain here permanently."

The corners of Rainer's lips pulled down ever so slightly, the only indication that what she'd said surprised him.

He folded his hands behind his back and walked out of the dining room. "Very well. If I deem Markis capable, he can remain here for the time being. However, no one else from Bakley will be allowed to stay. When your carriage arrives, your things will be unloaded and then your soldiers dismissed." He stopped by the door and turned to face her.

"Very well." She could live with that. She hoped.

Chapter Ten

B ack in her own bedchamber, Sabine stood there, staring at the door leading to what Claire had said was the king's room. Claire said it was locked from both sides. While Sabine could visibly see the latch was secure from her side, she couldn't be sure about the other. She assumed it led not to the king's personal room but into what would be their shared bedchamber. The king probably had his own room, like hers, on the other side of that one. What bothered her was the separate entrance she had leading out into the palace. If she had one, then the king likely did as well.

A lot of royal couples took lovers, so the thought of her future husband taking one shouldn't upset her so much. She'd assumed, with time, they'd have a loving relationship like her parents had. Just because Rainer had a private bedchamber with a separate entrance didn't mean he'd have concubines. But a small part of her understood that she didn't know this king and she didn't know Lynk's customs. It could be normal for royalty here to have affairs.

Sometimes, when snooping, the best explanation for

being found doing something she shouldn't or being somewhere she shouldn't be was to play dumb. With a shaking hand, she reached forward and unlocked the adjoining door. When nothing happened, she placed her fingers on the knob and twisted it. The door swung open, revealing a narrow hallway leading to the sitting room she'd passed by when meeting the king for breakfast.

Gunther, Rainer's personal steward, was walking by when he noticed her and stumbled to a halt. "Is there something I can help you with, Your Highness?"

Her brows pulled together in confusion. "I didn't know this door in my personal bedchamber led to here," she said.

Gunther approached her. "Allow me to explain. King Rainer's personal bedchamber is right next to yours." He gestured to her left, indicating the door a few feet away. "After the wedding, the room the two of you will share is there." He gestured to the door on her right.

She found it strange that the three bedchambers didn't connect. Servants, such as Gunther, would know if, when, and how often the two of them shared a bed. "And these rooms here," she indicated the sitting and dining rooms before them, "comprise the royal suite?"

"Yes, Your Highness."

"Earlier, when I came around and used the main entrance, why was that? Wouldn't it have been easier and faster for me just to come through this door?"

Gunther glanced over his shoulder. "May I be frank?" he asked, his voice suddenly softer and lower than before.

"Please."

"I'm not sure King Rainer is ready to share the royal suite with a stranger."

"I understand." She wasn't ready to share anything with the king either. "I'm just trying to learn how things are done here in Lynk. Everything is so different from Bakley."

She smiled, hoping to gain another resource here in the palace.

"Just know you're not the only one learning to adjust. King Rainer moved into the royal suite a few months ago. It's hard for him being in his parents' old rooms now that they're both deceased. He wouldn't even let Lady Heath—I mean, he is still getting used to being in here himself." Gunther studiously focused on his feet, not meeting her gaze.

Sabine nodded, as if she understood what he'd said. "Thank you." She shut and locked the door.

Sabine finished writing a letter to Rolf. She was as cryptic as possible, asking about the League without specifically asking about it. Hopefully he'd understand what she was getting at. After sealing the envelope, she gave it to Markis in the hallway. He'd make sure it went through the proper channels and made it to Bakley. She started to write another letter to her mother. However, the sun shone so brightly outside that she went to her balcony and laid down on the sofa out there.

She must have fallen asleep because the next thing she knew, the sun had shifted to the other side of the sky, indicating it was past noon. How strange for her to have fallen asleep like that. Sitting up, her tongue had an odd tang to it. She wanted to go to the kitchen to get something to drink.

Not knowing if she was still confined to her bedchamber since the king had returned, she went over to the door leading to the royal suite and knocked, hoping to discuss the matter with Rainer. It immediately swung open.

"Your Highness," a guard said, bowing his head. "I've been stationed here for your protection. Is there something you need?"

A soft laugh, half snort escaped her mouth. More likely, the guard had been stationed there for the king's protection, not hers. Rainer couldn't have her sneaking into the royal suite without him knowing—which verified her suspicion that the door only locked from her side.

"I'm tired of being in my room and wish to see the palace. Would King Rainer like to escort me on a tour?" Hopefully he'd show her where the kitchen was so she could get something to drink since her mouth was so parched.

"Please wait here while I go see if the king is available." He bowed before heading down the corridor, away from her.

Sabine leaned against the doorway, examining the sitting room in greater detail. Two sofas were situated in the middle, facing each other, and the wall to the right was lined floor to ceiling with shelves. Her feet moved of their own accord, taking her into the room so she could examine the contents of the shelves. There were dozens and dozens of sculptures carved from wood. Some were animals, others were people. She picked one up in the shape of a flower, running her finger over a petal, unable to believe how real it looked. The person who'd carved it had even managed to replicate the veins in its leaves.

"Your Highness," the guard said from behind her.

She put the flower back in its spot. "Yes?" She turned to face him.

"The king said he will introduce you to his court this evening at supper. After that, you will be able to visit the gardens in the courtyards at your leisure."

Dumbfounded, she stood there staring at him. Not only was the king not going to escort her around the palace, even after being introduced to the court, she still wouldn't be able to wander through the halls of her own free will. Maybe things would change once they married. "Thank you for your help," she said before returning to her bedchamber.

After closing and locking the door, she went over to her desk to finish writing the letter she'd started to pen to her mother. She was about to sit down when she paused. Something looked different. Since she wrote with her right hand, the paper should be tilted to the left slightly, but the paper was tilted to the right. Perhaps she'd unknowingly bumped it when she'd stood. As she examined everything else on the desk, an odd feeling came over her. She pulled open the top drawer. The papers inside weren't stacked as she'd left them. Someone had been in here going through her things.

Her skin turned clammy. She glanced around her bedchamber, making sure no one else was in the room. Not seeing anyone, she tried to calm down. Instead, the panic only intensified. Going over to her door, she threw it open, making sure her guards were out in the hallway in case she needed them.

Markis immediately stepped forward. "What's wrong?" he demanded.

"Someone has been in my room." She opened the door wider, granting him entrance. She wanted him to check everywhere to make sure an assassin wasn't hiding somewhere. Like in her dressing closet behind an outfit.

"Are you certain?" Markis asked, stepping into her room flanked by two additional guards. The remaining guards stayed in the hallway.

She nodded. "Has Claire been here?" she asked. Maybe her lady's maid had been tidying up.

"No, Your Highness," one of the guards answered.

The only other feasible option was the man who'd murdered Alina had returned to kill Sabine.

The three guards began searching through her room, looking under the bed and in her closet to be certain no one was hiding in there.

"A few of the items on my desk are moved," she explained. Turning in a slow circle, she examined her room, not seeing anything else out of place. Then she remembered falling asleep out on the sofa on the balcony and the funny taste in her mouth. "I think someone slipped something in my food," she whispered.

Markis rushed over, examining her eyes, skin color, and hands. "Do you feel okay?"

"I do now." She hadn't before. Looking directly into Markis's eyes she said, "I took my breakfast with the king." If someone had slipped something into her food, it had to have been then. "Do you think the king did this?"

"Why would he do such a thing?" Markis whispered so the other guards wouldn't overhear their conversation.

"Maybe so he could look through my things?"

"It's a possibility. Especially since we didn't see anyone enter your room."

Fury built. How dare the king drug her and go through her possessions, especially since Alina had been poisoned. This didn't bode well for Rainer as it only made him look guilty. She went over to the door leading to the royal suite and pounded on it. When no one immediately answered, she threw it open and stormed inside, stepping past the guard on duty.

"Can I help you, Your Highness?" the guard asked as he hurried after her.

Sabine ignored him. "King Rainer," she shouted, peering into the dining room, and not seeing him. She called his name again.

A door opened and Rainer strolled out of his bedchamber, wearing nothing but loose pants, his chest and face covered with sweat. "Is there a problem?"

Sabine blinked, startled to have found the king half naked.

"I just finished working with my soldiers and am about to take a bath. Do you need something?"

Regaining her wits about her, she said, "Someone has been in my room."

"That's because I had your room searched."

"Why would you do that?"

He smiled and made a placating gesture with his hands. "I wanted them to check your room to ensure it was secure. When they deemed it was, I ordered two men to remain at the exterior door and one to always remain here at this door, even when you leave your room. That way, when you return, it will not have to be searched every time. It will afford you more privacy as well."

"And when they checked my room, did you tell them to read my personal letters? To go through my desk and look at my papers?" Knowing someone had touched her possessions made her feel violated.

His eyes narrowed ever so slightly. "Not in those exact words, but yes, I did." He ran his arm over his forehead, wiping the sweat away.

"How could you?" Shock and anger boiled inside of her. She took a step forward, wanting to wrap her hands around his thick neck and squeeze that smug look off his face. How dare he order his servants to touch her personal belongings. Her hands balled into fists.

He took a step closer to her as well. They now stood less than a foot apart. "I don't know you," he said, his voice low and lethal, like steel cutting through stalks of wheat. "Captain Lithane informed me that you entered my home with a weapon. I ordered my guards to go through your things to see what else you might be hiding." His eyes raked over her body, as if looking for where she'd concealed the dagger. "I have a duty to protect my people."

"You can't possibly think I'm a threat."

Rainer cocked his head to the side. "How do I know you're really Princess Sabine and not an assassin sent to kill me?"

She scoffed at the suggestion.

"How do I know you didn't kill the real Sabine and take her place? After all, you didn't stay with the Bakley royal carriage after it was attacked. Instead, you showed up here, not dressed like a princess, with only one man as a guard. I have to consider the possibility that you're not who you say you are."

She folded her arms. "Is that why you haven't introduced me to your court? Why you're making me stay in my room?"

"I'm introducing you to my court tonight," he said, his voice rising a bit as anger seeped through.

"Why bother if you're not sure who I am?"

"With the help of my men, your carriage will arrive here today before sunset. I plan to have the Bakley soldiers verify your identity. If you're Princess Sabine, I'll introduce you to my court. If you're not, you'll be executed."

She shook her head. Unbelievable. And she was expected to rule along with this overbearing, insufferable man.

"Did you need anything else?" Rainer asked, his voice calm.

"I only came here because I thought the person who'd murdered my sister had snuck into my room. I was frightened." She turned and headed toward her door. She paused, remembering the other reason she'd stormed into his room. "Did you drug me as well?"

"Excuse me?" It was the first time his voice held a hint of confusion.

"Did you put something in my food to make me fall asleep?" She kept her back to him as she spoke.

"No. I would never do that."

She peered over her shoulder at him. "I have no way of

knowing that or if you're even telling me the truth." She entered her bedchamber.

"Princess Sabine," Rainer called after her.

She ignored him and closed the door, being sure to lock it from her side.

Someone knocked on Sabine's door, so she went over and answered it. Captain Lithane and Claire stood there.

"Your Highness," Lithane said. "I'm to escort you to the southern balcony overlooking the front of the palace."

"Whatever for?" She was glad about the opportunity to leave her room but had no idea what to wear for the occasion. She looked at Claire who had to be there to help her dress.

"Your carriage has arrived along with your soldiers," Lithane answered.

"And when you return," Claire said, "I am to help you get ready for your presentation to the court this evening."

Sabine couldn't help but laugh. "The king honestly wants my own soldiers to verify I'm me." It wasn't a question.

"Yes, Your Highness."

Instead of rolling her eyes or protesting at the ridiculousness of it, she went into her dressing closet and grabbed a cape she'd noticed earlier.

"You won't be needing that," Claire said.

Sabine ignored her lady's maid and followed Lithane out into the hallway where her guards were dutifully waiting for her. She wrapped the cape around her body knowing she didn't need it in this heat. However, if the Bakley soldiers saw her dressed as she was, they might not recognize her. The cape would help her look more like herself.

Walking through the palace hallways, she scanned her

guards, searching for Markis and not finding him. Perhaps he was with the carriage and Bakley soldiers.

After a few minutes, they reached the southern balcony. Sabine strolled out onto it, going right to the railing overlooking the bridge leading to the town. The balcony was only two levels above the bridge, affording her the ability to see her men.

She smiled. "Greetings Bakley soldiers," she said, using the term she'd so often heard Rolf say when addressing his men.

All five Bakley soldiers knelt on one knee, bowing their heads, clearly acknowledging her as their princess.

"Rise," she commanded them. "Thank you for bringing my carriage and belongings to Lynk." She spotted Markis who was easy to identify dressed as a Lynk soldier. "I assume Lieutenant Markis Belle has briefed you on the state of things."

The men nodded their heads.

"That's all you're needed for," Lithane said. "Let's go."

Sabine looked at her men one last time. "Thank you." She waved to them and then left the balcony, following Lithane once again through the palace.

"Was that sufficient, Lieutenant Lithane?" she asked, knowing she'd used the wrong title. However, he didn't seem keen on addressing her appropriately, so she was hoping to make a point.

"Captain."

"No, I'm Princess Sabine. Not Captain."

One of the guards chuckled.

"Yes," Lithane said, irritation seeping through his voice. "That was good enough for me."

When they reached the corridor leading to her room, she stepped around him and hurried ahead, entering her room and shutting the door before he could protest.

"I'm not going to be executed," Sabine announced as she went over to her dressing closet where she found Claire.

"Why would you be executed?"

Sabine shook her head. "Never mind."

"The king is going to wear a midnight blue jacket lined with silver," Claire said, holding up an outfit. "This will match him perfectly."

Sabine removed her cape. "Are those diamonds on the dress?"

"Yes. The king wants you to look like a queen tonight." Claire exited the dressing closet and went over to the bed, laying the dress across it.

As Sabine removed her clothing, she asked, "When my sister was here," she had to keep her voice steady so it wouldn't wobble from the grief she felt whenever she mentioned Alina, "who did she spend time with?"

"The princess wasn't here very long before…" Claire's voice trailed off. "Your sister was friendly and kind to everyone here at court. However, I don't recall her doing anything with anyone in particular. She wasn't here long enough to form any friendships."

Sabine pulled the midnight blue dress on. Going over to the mirror, she examined herself in the reflection. The sheer material loosely covered her arms, tapering around her wrists. On her shoulders, instead of the fabric going up and over them, it cut across at an angle and wrapped around her neck. Then another section of the sheer fabric attached near her underarms and covered her breasts, leaving a lot of the skin on her torso exposed. The material tightened around her waist and then flowed to the floor. Two large slits had been cut up the front, showcasing her legs. Though the material was see-through, it darkened around her breasts and other intimate areas so no one would be able to see anything uncouth. When she moved, the hundreds of diamonds sewn all over it caught the light and shimmered.

"What do you think?" Claire asked.

Instead of answering, because Sabine truly did not know how she felt about it, she countered, "What should I do with my hair and makeup?"

"Sit," Claire said, her voice sounding far too excited.

Curious, Sabine did as she instructed.

Claire applied dusting powder to Sabine's face. After she finished, she combed Sabine's hair back, leaving it unbound. "Now for the finishing touch." She pulled out a silver crown adorned with diamonds and sapphires, setting it atop Sabine's head. "Take a look."

Her makeup had been applied darker than she normally wore it, accentuating her eyes and her cheeks in an odd way. However, that, coupled with her hair and the crown, completed the ensemble.

"I think you look stunning," Claire said, standing back to examine her work. "Exactly as you should. Beautiful and desirable."

"I am doing my best to understand and embrace your customs. Thank you for helping me." She was getting the feeling that Rainer wanted a pretty wife to look at and not one to help him rule his kingdom. Hopefully in time, she could change that. For now, she'd go along with things and not cause problems.

"That's what I'm here for," Claire replied. "I'm happy to help. We need to get going. The sun is about to set."

"Is there anything I should know for tonight?" No one had mentioned what would take place, so she had no idea if she'd be speaking to the people or if there were any customs she needed to be aware of.

"I don't think so."

"If anything comes up, please be sure to help me. I look to you for guidance."

Claire shifted from foot to foot. "I won't be there this evening."

"But you're my lady's maid." Back home, her mother's lady's maid always attended royal functions in case the queen needed anything.

"That's not how it works in Lynk."

Sabine shook her head, realizing she had a lot to learn. Thankfully, she'd been to enough royal functions to have a general idea of what to expect tonight. Those with money or vying for power would immediately introduce themselves, trying to get on her good side. Those threatened by her would approach her later in the evening. She would need to make sure to keep her face devoid from all feeling and emotion. She couldn't let anyone know if they got to her. And during all of this, she needed to ask questions about Alina and discover if anyone knew anything about her death. In other words, she needed to snoop without appearing to snoop.

Out in the hallway, two soldiers stood guard on either side of her door while the rest followed close behind her. She didn't see Markis among them. He was probably still with the Bakley soldiers. However, she felt ill at ease not having him with her.

Claire led the way down to the first level of the palace and then to a balcony on the west side. "This is where I'm to leave you," Claire said. "I'll meet you back at your room afterward to help you prepare for bed." She bowed then left.

Sabine stood alone on the large balcony, her guards hovering near one of the entrances. Growing up with five siblings meant she never had to attend a royal function by herself. She always had one of her brothers or her sister by her side. Especially since she was the youngest. Never in her wildest dreams did she think she'd be in a foreign kingdom, let alone the queen of one, having to do something like this on her own.

Gunther exited through one of the archways and smiled at her. "Princess Sabine."

"I didn't realize you'd be here tonight." Since Claire wasn't going to be in attendance, she assumed Gunther wouldn't be either.

"I'm not. King Rainer just wanted me to inform you that your belongings from the carriage are being brought up to your room. I am personally overseeing it, so you have nothing to worry about."

"Thank you."

"And the Bakley soldiers are all being fed and will rest here for the night. They will return home tomorrow."

It surprised her that Rainer was feeding them and allowing them to spend the night. He'd seemed so against anything like that earlier today. "I appreciate your help," she replied, forcing a sweet smile on her face. The more friends she had here, the better.

As Gunther exited, Anton and Lottie walked out on the balcony and approached Sabine.

"I can't believe Rainer threw this party together so quickly," Anton mumbled. "I was supposed to head down to the docks tonight for the seasons celebration."

Sabine hadn't realized it was already changing from summer to fall. Back home, the leaves would start shifting colors. Here, she hadn't noticed anything of the sort.

"I'm sure you can still make it," Lottie said. "This isn't going to take all night. But you do need to stop complaining about it. We should to be happy for Rainer. This is his engagement party, and Sabine will be our sister-in-law soon." She smiled sweetly at Sabine.

"Well, well, well," Axel said as he casually strolled out

onto the balcony. "What have we here?" He stopped before Sabine, his eyes roaming up and down as he slowly took her in. "You almost look like you belong in Lynk." He smirked.

Lottie rolled her eyes. "Yes, it's amazing what a bit of cloth will do."

Instead of responding to Axel, Sabine focused beyond him, trying to see inside the palace. Soft music floated out onto the balcony along with the voices of people talking and laughing mixed in with music. However, she couldn't see the room or what she'd be walking into in a few minutes.

Lottie and Anton were talking with one another, ignoring Sabine.

Axel faced away from his siblings and then leaned toward her. "Be on guard tonight," he whispered.

"From you or from the people inside?" She honestly couldn't tell if he was flirting or warning her.

He chuckled. "Both."

The music stopped.

"It's time for us to go in," Lottie said. "Except for you, Sabine. You are to wait until my brother announces you. Just make sure you don't stand in front of the entrance. Wait over there, off to the side, so no one sees you until it's time."

It irked Sabine that these siblings were always rather informal with her, not bothering to use her proper title. Alina would have insisted they were doing it because they were trying to welcome her into the family. But Sabine didn't think that was the case. She got the feeling they didn't want to acknowledge her title or the fact that she would soon outrank them.

The twins and Lottie entered the room, leaving Sabine alone on the balcony. She meandered over to the side, close enough to hear Rainer's voice as he spoke, but not too close where those inside could see her. The sun was setting in the distance, casting the sky in a brilliant orange.

A moment later, a soldier came through one of the entrances and waved her forward.

Holding her head high, she glided toward him and stepped through the archway. Rainer stood a few feet away, his hand outstretched to her. She hesitated a moment, almost unable to move at the sight before her.

The king looked stunning dressed in midnight blue pants that went straight down, quite different from the tailored ones people in Bakley wore. His tunic matched the color of his pants, and tonight, was buttoned closed concealing his muscled torso beneath. The crown atop his head complemented her crown, although it was larger to indicate his station. And his chiseled face held a pleasant smile, his eyes almost sparkling. He was the most handsome man she'd ever seen.

"Princess Sabine?" he mumbled, low and sultry, stirring something deep inside of her.

Forcing a smile on her face, she placed her hand on his. He guided her forward to the edge of a platform, stopping at the top of the steps that led down to a large room packed with people. As the two of them stood there, the sun setting in the distance behind them, Sabine couldn't help but be stunned by the sheer number of people in attendance.

Standing before her soon-to-be subjects, she watched as the hundred or so people bowed their heads in veneration.

"My wedding to Princess Sabine, followed by her coronation, will take place in a fortnight," Rainer bellowed. "Join me in welcoming my future wife to the great kingdom of Lynk."

Everyone straightened and clapped.

Rainer led Sabine down the steps to where his three siblings stood in front of everyone present. One by one, each sibling welcomed Sabine to Lynk. Rainer then escorted her over to an elderly couple and introduced them as the Earl and

Countess of Geslock. From there, he continued to introduce her to different people, so many that she had trouble keeping track of them all.

Rainer released her hand but remained at her side as he made more introductions. Every so often, he'd place his hand on her side or back, making her shiver from the intimate touch. However, she noticed most of the men behaved similarly. It had to be a Lynk thing.

A squire announced that dinner was served. Everyone moved to the other side of the room where tables had been set up for the occasion.

Rainer once again took her hand, leading the way.

"Now the real fun begins," Axel whispered from behind her, a low chuckle to his voice.

Chapter Eleven

The king pulled out a chair at the rectangular head table, indicating for Sabine to sit. She slid on the chair while he took a seat next to her. The three royal siblings also took their places at the head table; everyone else sat at the round tables situated before them. Plates loaded with fruit, bread, and pork were placed on the tables, and people began helping themselves. Bottles of wine were on each table as well. A group of musicians continued playing soft music. On the other side of the room, directly across from where Sabine sat, the entire wall contained a dozen archways leading to the large balcony she'd been on earlier.

"Eat," Rainer said. "Then we'll dance. After that, many of the people here will wish to take a turn with you. When asked questions, be vague with your answers."

"I may be young, but I am a princess." Sabine scooped a little bit of everything for her plate. "I know how to handle social climbers and busybodies." At least the food was tasty and the wine decent.

Ignoring her, Rainer continued, "Later tonight, you will repeat your conversations to me. Are we clear?"

Setting her fork down, she looked at him, irritated that he was treating her like a child.

He sighed. "The simplest thing said can mean nothing to you, but it can reveal an important detail to me. Until I discover who killed your sister and why, everyone is a suspect. Since you don't know these people, you will report all conversations to me."

Since she happened to agree with him, she nodded. Picking up her fork she asked, "You suspect one of the people living in the palace?"

"We'll discuss this later, in private."

Axel chuckled, though he wasn't looking their way.

Sabine resumed eating. She noticed many of the people glancing at her while involved in conversations. As if they were all talking about her. If a foreigner came to Bakley to marry one of her brothers, she supposed everyone would behave similarly. And she had no idea what—if anything— Rainer had told them about her. These people may be unaware that her kingdom would be sending food. Granted, it was in exchange for soldiers. However, it seemed as if both kingdoms were benefiting greatly from this match.

"Is something the matter?" Rainer asked, startling Sabine.

She hadn't realized he'd leaned in and was only inches from her. "Everything is fine," she replied with a forced smile.

He raised a single eyebrow, the gesture indicating he didn't believe her. "Then perhaps you shouldn't stare at your food as if it's a puzzle to figure out. Even now, you're looking at me like I just asked you to eat a spoonful of dirt. Why don't you try and at least relax your face. I don't want people here to think I'm forcing you into anything."

She hadn't realized her face gave so much away. "Better?" It felt as if she now had a pleasant look on her face.

Rainer leaned in even closer, his hand gliding up her arm, sending a chill through her. "One of the issues I discussed with your sister ahead of time was the need to put on a united front," he murmured, speaking to her as if whispering a secret shared between lovers. "We're going to dance now. You need to look besotted. Are we clear?"

"Yes." It was becoming very clear that he wanted a wife who was beautiful, alluring, and fawned all over him. Not a partner. Not a queen. But someone who followed his directions and did as he wanted. She now understood why he'd chosen Alina. A pang of jealousy swept through Sabine because she was none of those things.

"Ready?" Rainer asked as he stood and held out his hand to her.

She took it, allowing him to lead her to the dance floor. The last time she'd danced was with her sister. Vivid memories filled her, bringing tears to her eyes. She looked down, averting her gaze so Rainer wouldn't see her grief.

"Do you know the Carilke dance?" he asked as he stopped and pulled her into an embrace.

She forced everything she was thinking and feeling away. Rainer made it clear what he wanted, and she would give it to him. For now. She'd play along and do as he asked in order to find her sister's killer. He didn't need to know what she was really thinking or feeling because he clearly didn't care. She suspected he was putting on a show for his subjects, and she would do the same.

"I do not," she said, placing her other hand on his shoulder and looking into his eyes.

"Just follow my lead. It's a slower song." Rainer held her gaze, his eyebrows raising ever so slightly, as if trying to figure her out.

She forced a half smile on her face, the one she used when flirting with a man. Confidence was something she'd never lacked. And it was time Rainer understood she was nothing like Alina. While she may be playing along and doing as he wished, she expected to get something in return. It was time he started to realize she could be a valuable ally, but one who wouldn't roll over like a dog.

The music began. Something in the air shifted as Rainer took a step closer and slid his other hand on the small of her bare back, sending a jolt of warmth through her. They began moving to the music. However, this dance was very different from anything she'd experienced in Bakley. Usually, when dancing with a partner, they moved away from one another and then returned. The music was oftentimes upbeat. But this...this was slow and intimate. They swayed to the music together, not breaking contact.

Sabine held his eyes, following his lead. For the first time, she didn't feel like she had the upper hand. Normally, men were putty in her hands, and she could do as she pleased. But she hadn't been with many older men. Her brothers wouldn't allow it.

"I'm assuming you danced this very dance with my sister when you introduced her to your court?" Sabine said, wanting to talk to tame the odd feelings rising within her.

"Actually, we did not. She was introduced to my court, but very briefly." His eyes glanced down, as if taking Sabine in.

Something occurred to her. "My sister wouldn't wear the clothes you wanted or play along, would she?" Sabine knew her sister would never wear a dress like this. And Alina would never dance this way. Both went against all her years of being trained by their mother in proper Bakley protocol. It would have made Lynk hard for Alina to assimilate to.

"Play along?" he asked, his voice deep and rumbling.

She smiled and leaned in closer. "You and Alina may have

agreed on a great many things before she arrived, but she wasn't what you expected, was she?" The thought of someone—even the king—killing Alina because she didn't fit in here was starting to seem like a plausible motive. Fury began to simmer.

"That's where you're wrong," Rainer replied, turning them in a slow circle. "I need a well-bred woman who can have my child. Whether it's her or you, it makes no difference to me. A woman is a woman."

A soft laugh escaped her lips. She had to be throwing him off, and his comment was meant to rile her up, put her in her place, and gain the upper hand.

"I can see you want to argue with me," he said, smiling, as if enjoying this.

"Perhaps." She moved her hand from his shoulder to the back of his neck, her fingers playing with his longer hair.

His smile deepened, and she realized she'd just issued him a challenge without meaning to.

He pressed his body against hers, his hand holding her in place. Lowering his lips to her ear, he whispered, "It appears we have some things we need to discuss."

"Yes. I agree."

He moved his head back, only slightly, so his lips now hovered mere inches from hers. The simmering she'd felt before began to grow, and it seemed as if a fire had started in her stomach. Usually, she was the one pushing the boundaries, teasing the men she danced with. Now she felt as if this man was toying with her. Only, her body seemed to be reacting to his in a way she didn't want. She'd used that tactic one too many times and would be damned if she let a man use it on her. While her brain understood that, her body did not.

"Tomorrow, come to my office. We'll talk privately there." His warm breath caressed her cheek.

She pulled back to look him in the eyes. "I want to know everything you do about what happened to my sister." Since they were the only two people dancing, they could have this conversation without anyone eavesdropping.

"That seems only fair as you are behaving exactly the way I want."

His eyes cleared for a second, showing a seriousness Sabine hadn't seen before. It also made his expectations abundantly clear. A small part of it irritated her. It made her feel like an animal being trained. Do this and receive a treat. However, she wasn't the only one performing right now—he was, too. And that—and only that—made this tolerable. Somehow, they were in this together. It was the first time since arriving that she felt a sense of hope.

As they turned, she caught sight of Markis standing alongside another guard at one of the entrances. Since she hadn't seen him earlier, he must have just started his shift. His eyes were solely focused on her—the only part of him visible with the mask on. Thankfully she knew him just by the shape of his body and eyes. A sense of calm filled her. With Markis here, she was safe.

Rainer's eyes flickered in Markis's direction and then back to Sabine. His mouth opened, as if to say something, when the song ended, and an older gentleman approached them. Rainer took a step back, away from her. "Thank you for the dance." He turned his attention to the man. "Duke Vadil, my beautiful fiancée is all yours." He strode away, heading toward an older woman who was probably the duke's wife.

Sabine faced the duke, and they began dancing. After a minute, the duke asked her some generic questions about her journey to Lynk and what she thought of the kingdom so far. As Rainer had instructed, she answered vaguely. When the music ended, another man asked her to dance.

After half a dozen dances in which two of the men

bombarded her with suggestions about how she could help improve the living conditions and military might of Lynk, Anton approached her. While she was glad to see a familiar face, she was instantly on guard. She didn't know if he had a purpose for seeking her out this evening. He wasn't any less threatening than the men she'd danced with. Everyone here had an ulterior motive; she couldn't forget that.

The music began, and Anton took the lead. His movements were slightly jilted, lacking the elegance of his brother.

"I'm surprised you have nothing to say to me," Sabine said, hoping to have some sort of conversation with Anton so she could get to know him better.

"What is there to say?" he mumbled. "I'm surprised my brother bothered having this party at all considering the circumstances."

She didn't think he was talking about the festival he'd mentioned earlier. "Are you referring to my sister's death?" Her heartbeat sped up, wondering if he knew something.

He shook his head. "The problem with your marriage contract."

"What problem?" This wasn't the first time it had been mentioned.

"The change your father made. The League isn't happy about it."

"I don't understand. Didn't my father just swap Alina's name for my name?"

Someone chuckled behind her. She turned to find Axel standing there.

"Anton can be a little blunt sometimes," Axel said. "Can't you, brother? You've never been one with words. Especially where the ladies are concerned."

"If anyone's blunt, it's you," Anton muttered before shaking his head and stalking away.

Axel slid up closer to Sabine, taking her hand and placing his other against her bare back. His hand felt cold, unlike the sensation of fire that she'd had earlier with Rainer. They began dancing even though the song was almost over.

"I think Anton had a thing for your sister," Axel revealed. "He likes his women docile." He winked. "I don't."

She couldn't tell if he was joking or not. "It's inappropriate for either of you to have feelings of any sort for your future queen." She knew she sounded like her mother right now. She tried not to cringe at the mere thought.

Axel smiled as he pulled her closer, their chests touching. His chin rested next to her head, so she couldn't see his face.

"What do you want?" she asked.

"Who says I want something?"

"Everyone wants something." She glanced over to make sure Markis was still watching her. He hadn't moved. When Axel didn't respond, she decided to change course. "Are there usually this many people staying in the palace?"

"No. Most people only stay for a season and then return home. Since the king is to marry, everyone is here for the ceremony. Afterward, a lot will leave." As he spoke, his breath ruffled the hair next to her ear. "Keep your guard up around Cutler. He's going to want to speak with you."

She didn't recall meeting anyone with that name yet.

"He's a captain in the army. His father, Felix, is the commander. Felix is a good man, but Cutler has jealousy issues." The song ended and Axel took a step back. "Watch yourself." He winked before striding away.

Needing a drink, Sabine declined the next man who asked for her hand. She headed over to the beverage table and was about to pour herself a glass of wine when she thought better of it. Anyone could have slipped poison into the jug. Looking up, she saw Markis still watching her. She used her hands to pretend to drink. He nodded and then spoke to the guard next to him before ducking out of the room. She knew he'd understood and would be back with something for her to drink in a few minutes.

Scanning the dancers, she spotted Rainer with a woman she'd neither met nor recognized.

"She's stunning, isn't she?" a man said from beside her, gesturing to the woman the king was with.

"Yes," Sabine admitted. Out of all the women here, the one currently dancing with Rainer was easily the most beautiful. The blue dress she wore revealed supple breasts and long, toned legs. Her brown hair hung down her bare back in soft waves. The word *desirable* came to mind. Sabine tilted her head to the side, watching the woman. Her outfit coordinated with the king's. An odd feeling took root, almost as if Sabine had entered a room turned sideways. She tried to shake off the feeling.

"She's my fiancée," the man said as he stood tall, almost puffing out his chest.

"Is that so?" Sabine wished she had a drink, so she had something to do with her hands. She awkwardly stood there knowing this man beside her had sought her out for a reason. One she probably wasn't going to like.

"Yes," he cooed.

Taking a deep breath and letting it out slowly, Sabine decided she might as well get this conversation over with. "I'm sorry, have we met?" she asked, looking at the man's face for the first time. He was good looking with short hair and wide shoulders, reminding her a bit of her brother, Rolf.

"Not officially. I'm Captain Cutler." He bowed his head.

This was the man Axel had warned her about.

"And do you know who I am?" She wanted to be clear that she outranked him and was not one who could be pushed around.

"Yes, Princess Sabine. Everyone knows who you are."

She turned back to watch Rainer with this man's beautiful fiancée. She suspected Axel's warning about Cutler may have had to do with his jealousy that Cutler was engaged to such an alluring woman. Axel probably had a thing for her. But many matches were made based on family alliances rather than love or attraction.

"It's a beautiful night," Cutler said. "Let's take a stroll on the balcony." He held out his arm for her to take.

She stared at him, trying to decide how best to handle this situation.

"We need to talk," he said, his voice a whisper.

He must have something to discuss with her in private, away from prying eyes. Given that her fiancé was dancing with his, she figured it was important. Glancing through the nearest archway where two guards stood watch, she saw there were only a few couples on the balcony thus affording them the space they needed.

Sabine slid her hand onto his arm, letting him lead her outside. Even though the sun had set, the air was warm and still. When they reached the railing, she removed her hand from Cutler's arm and stared into the distance, marveling at the beautiful night sky. "I've never seen stars so large," she said. "They seem closer here than they did back in Bakley."

Cutler rested his arms on the railing beside her. "Lynk is a unique place."

Peering over her shoulder, she noticed Markis standing inside near one of the archways, watching, with a cup in one hand. She shook her head ever so slightly indicating she didn't want it right now. He nodded.

"Next week, Heather and I are to marry."

She'd heard that name before but couldn't remember where. "Will the two of you be taking a honeymoon right after?"

"I wish we could, but we can't, considering the circumstances."

Somehow, she knew he'd brought her out here to tell her exactly what circumstances they were dealing with. Unfortunately, she suspected it had to do with Rainer and Heather. Sabine was a fool for coming to Lynk and thinking she could take Alina's place. Everything was so much more complicated than she'd thought it would be.

"It seems the king is in love with my fiancée," Cutler said.

"It seems your fiancé is in love with the king," she replied, not knowing if that was true or not. However, she didn't want Cutler thinking she was some heartbroken young woman who would fall to pieces. She had no illusions as to what her marriage to the king really was. She was here for a political alliance, not love. If Cutler understood that, she could be his ally. It was up to him how things would proceed from here; she'd merely opened the door for the possibility.

"I love her," he revealed. "I've loved her since the day I saw her almost ten years ago."

She had so many questions and had to force herself to refrain from asking any of them. She needed to let Cutler lead this conversation.

"She never looks at me the way she looks at him. I can't compete with that. He's a king."

Sabine wondered if Heather was in love with Rainer or his title.

"I'd hoped once the king married, he'd lose interest in Heather," Cutler said. "Not because you're not beautiful," he hurried to add.

Sabine chuckled since that's what his comment had implied. A part of her was vain enough to have been stung by his words.

"They've been seeing one another intimately for years," he revealed.

Then the two of them were in love. Sadness filled her. Rainer reminded her of Alina. Both were in love with someone they weren't to marry. "Why bring me out here and tell me all of this?"

"I want you to know that the king will never love you."

She understood that. The part she didn't get was why bother telling her. She couldn't figure out his motive and whether he'd be an ally or a foe.

"He will *use* you." Cutler straightened and turned to face her. "He will sleep with you because he needs a child of royal blood to hold onto his throne. But you'll be like a whore to him. There to fulfill a basic need. Once he's done with you, he will cast you aside. Just like his father did to his mother."

Sabine straightened and faced him, reeling from all he'd said. "I'll ask you this one last time. Why are you telling me this?" What did he hope to gain?

"I just want you to know that your soon-to-be husband is in love with another woman."

She didn't know how to respond to that. Did he expect her to thank him?

"He'll never love you."

"Step away from the princess," Markis demanded, his voice harsh.

Cutler jerked, as if he didn't realize Markis had moved from the archway to Sabine's side, standing only a foot away.

"We're having a private conversation," Cutler said. "Leave us be."

Markis stepped even closer, rage simmering in his eyes. "Step away from the princess," he repeated.

Cutler's brows drew together. "Do you not recognize me?"

"You're too close to the princess, and she seems distressed. You will put space between the two of you."

"I'm your captain."

"You're not my captain," Markis said. "I only take orders from Princess Sabine."

"What's going on?" Rainer asked as he and Heather rushed out onto the balcony, side by side.

It was time for Sabine to step in. "Nothing. Captain Cutler and I were simply having a discussion."

"Then why is your guard involved?" Rainer asked.

"In Bakley it is not appropriate for a man to confront someone in the royal family in such a manner."

"Explain." Rainer turned to Markis, expecting him to answer.

"Your Majesty," Markis said. "Captain Cutler moved in close proximity to the princess, less than a foot away. She stiffened, appearing distressed. I intervened as I've been trained to do."

Rainer looked at Sabine, his eyes scanning her from head to toe. "Are you okay?"

"Yes." She forced herself to keep her focus on Rainer and not to look at or acknowledge Heather. As a princess, she bowed to no one except the king. Once she became his queen, she'd be his equal. Everyone here needed to see and understand that. She would not have the king's mistress thinking she had any power here.

"Captain Cutler, it's getting late. Why don't you take Heather home." It wasn't a request.

Sabine found it interesting that Rainer didn't introduce Heather or use a title when mentioning her. He'd used Cutler's title and if Heather had one, it should have been given. Perhaps she was a commoner. Sabine would have to find out.

Rainer moved to stand beside Sabine, sliding his arm around her waist in a protective gesture.

"Yes, Your Majesty," Cutler said. He looked at Heather who rushed to his side. The two of them retreated from the balcony.

"Lieutenant Markis, thank you for protecting the princess," Rainer said.

"I apologize for causing a scene," Markis said. "But given what happened with Princess Alina, I decided to err on the side of caution."

"Understood. However, in Lynk, we tend to be a bit friendlier."

Sabine had noticed that. Men and women tended to touch one another more freely without it meaning anything.

"Noted." Markis nodded and then went back to his post near the archway.

"Let's stay out here for a bit." Rainer motioned toward the railing. "I want you to repeat your entire conversation with Cutler before you forget anything."

Sabine did as he requested, hoping that Rainer would volunteer some information about Heather.

He didn't.

When she finished recalling everything, Rainer rubbed his chin. "What, exactly, is your relationship with Lieutenant Markis?"

She bit her lip until she got her temper under control. She wanted nothing more than to answer his question with a counter question about Heather. "He is my guard."

"Why do you want him to stay?"

She thought they'd already been over this. Instead of answering, she simply looked at Rainer, waiting for him to get to the point.

"Please don't take this the wrong way," he said, "but are you not capable of defending yourself?"

"I have some basic training," she admitted.

"But not enough to keep your personal guard from interceding just because a man steps too close to you?"

Sabine had no idea how to respond to that.

Rainer studied her. "Let's revisit this conversation tomorrow when we talk."

She nodded.

"Come. We need to return to our guests." He took her hand, escorting her back inside.

Chapter Twelve

The next morning, Sabine sat on the balcony, examining the breakfast tray Claire had left for her. She had her usual plate of fruit, some biscuits, and a box. Reaching forward, she opened the box, curious to see what it contained. Instead of a special pastry as she'd expected, she found a stack of letters tied together with a note.

> *Princess Sabine,*
> *These are the letters your sister wrote to me along with the notes I sent her. I want you to have them.*
> *Rainer*

Shock rolled through her. Not only had he signed the paper informally using his first name—no title—but he'd give her *his* letters. Returning her sister's made sense. However, giving her *his* showed a major gesture on his part. Curious as to what insight they could possibly reveal, she untied the ribbon and began reading them.

The first thing she noticed were the dates. Alina and Rainer had begun writing to one another before the marriage contract had been signed. And Sabine hadn't known about it. A pang of hurt filled her. She wished her sister had confided in her. Then the engagement wouldn't have been such a shock.

Each of Alina's letters were open, honest, and touching. Alina shared that she was in love with a man she hoped to marry. She told Rainer she didn't think she could ever love anyone else. However, Alina expressed concern over her kingdom's troubles. In her latter letters, she shared her desire to have children and her willingness to be a queen.

Surprisingly, Rainer's letters were much the same. He spoke about a great love of his life whom he couldn't marry because of her station. He didn't want to try to find someone to replace her; however, he needed to marry and have an heir as soon as possible to keep his crown. He asked if Alina would consider marrying and being friends but nothing more. He didn't want anything from her other than being a queen for Lynk and giving him a child.

Leaning back in her chair, she tried to digest all she'd learned. Rainer had shown Sabine these letters for a reason. Maybe he wanted her to know he had no interest in having a relationship with her—which was fine. They could be married and nothing more. Truth be told, she didn't even care if they were friends. All she wanted was to bring her sister's killer to justice and make sure the king sent soldiers to help Bakley so they could secure their border.

She found it hard to reconcile the Rainer she'd met with the one in the letters.

Markis had told her he was supposed to find these letters and send them to Rolf in case they offered any insight into who was responsible for Alina's murder. After reading them, she knew they didn't reveal anything of that nature. Instead, they showed a private side of both Alina and Rainer that Sabine didn't feel anyone else had the right to see.

After carefully stacking the letters together, she tied the ribbon back around them. This was a part of Alina that she'd chosen not to share with Sabine. She would respect her sister and return them to their rightful owner.

She went inside and over to the door leading to the royal suite, knocking softly on it.

A guard answered. "Is there something I can do for you, Your Highness?"

"I want to speak with King Rainer." She had no idea what she'd say to him, but she'd start by returning the letters and thanking him for his kindness.

"He's at the training grounds." The guard started to close the door.

"Can I tour the facilities?" she asked, curious as to not only where they were located but wanting to see Rainer with his men. Her brother, Rolf, often trained alongside his soldiers, running through drills with them. However, her father rarely stepped foot in the training yard.

"You'd like for me to escort you to the training grounds?" the guard asked.

"Yes." She held her head high, as if making it a command and not a request. She had no idea what orders Rainer had given to his men regarding her, but she was going to be their queen and they'd have to obey her eventually. She might as well start acting like it now.

"I'm not able to leave my post, Your Highness."

"Very well. I will have one of my other guards escort me." She shut the door before he could respond.

After placing the letters in the top drawer of her desk for safekeeping, she exited her room, scanning her guards' faces for Markis and not finding him. She quickly spoke, taking control of the situation. "I want to be escorted to the training facility."

"Of course, Your Highness," one of the guards said. "This way, please." Two men remained at her door while the other four loosely surrounded her.

They traversed along hallways and stairwells until they reached the front of the palace where her guards spoke with the sentries on duty. Having their faces all covered with masks made it hard to tell what these men were thinking and if they'd permit her to leave the palace. She made sure to keep her head held high with the expectation that her orders would be obeyed.

After a moment, a groan resounded and the bridges on both sides of the mountains began to lower. Once they connected, Sabine and her guards were granted passage. The wind wasn't nearly as strong as before, and she crossed easily without an ounce of panic.

Back on solid ground, her guards led her to the left instead of along the main street as she'd suspected they would. It felt strange being out of the palace since she'd been holed up in there for so many days.

There were several plain buildings along the side of the street. They stopped before the last one, right next to the edge of the cliff, no windows visible in the two-story structure.

One of her guards knocked and an elderly woman opened the door, granting them entrance. Sabine stepped inside. A single torch lit a square room. Once the door closed and locked, the woman knelt and opened a door built into the floor, revealing a steep staircase. Two of her guards began the descent.

Sabine hesitated.

"You going to the training grounds or not?" the elderly woman asked, a slight accent to her words.

"That's Your Highness to you," the guard beside her said.

The woman's eyes widened. "Forgive me, Your Highness."

"Of course," Sabine said, peering down the steps. There was no end in sight since she didn't see another level. "Does this go down *into* the mountain?"

"Aye," the woman answered.

The first two guards stopped, waiting for her.

"We'll be right behind you," the guard to her right assured her.

Sabine nodded. She couldn't show any fear. Gripping the railing, she began the climb down. The first thing she noticed was the slight chill in the air. The deeper she descended, the colder it got. An odd smell filled the air though she couldn't pinpoint what it was. After twenty feet, the staircase abruptly turned to the right. It continued in this pattern, and she realized she was descending in a square-shaped vertical tunnel of sorts. The stairs eventually stopped at a door.

One of her guards knocked, paused, knocked three times, and then kicked the bottom with his boot.

The door opened, revealing an enormous cavern. Based upon the sheer size of it, it had to be under the town. She stepped out onto a ledge that wrapped around the upper portion of the cavern where a few people stood watching the activity twenty feet below. She went to the right, out of the way, before stopping next to the railing.

Ten groups of men, all dressed in black, were spread throughout the area. One group had swords and seemed to be doing some basic katas. The group next to them was busy sparring. Some used weapons, others worked on hand-to-hand combat techniques. Each seemed to be doing something different.

"Are these all soldiers in the army?" Sabine asked no one in particular.

"Soldiers and people from the town who serve when called upon," the guard to her left answered.

She stood there watching, amazed by the talent of some of these men. Cheering erupted from the sparring group toward the middle. One man flew onto his back, blood pouring from his nose, his arm at an odd angle. The victor reached down, helping the defeated man to his feet. They went to the edge of the circle and two different men entered the ring.

A hush descended over the cavern, and everyone turned to watch the fight about to take place.

The two men stood across from one another, each taking up a fighting stance. She instantly recognized the one on the right—it was Markis. She had no idea what he was doing here training with these Lynk men. Markis's opponent took the first swing. He was a few inches taller than Markis but other than that, they appeared to be about the same weight. The two men circled one another. As the man's face came into view, shock rolled through Sabine. It was the king.

Markis swung, and Rainer jumped back.

"What are you doing here?" Lottie asked as she came to stand beside Sabine.

"I wanted to speak to Rainer," she said lamely, pointing at him.

"He won't talk to you here." Lottie leaned against the railing, watching the two men circle one another. "When he trains, he is very focused. You'd swear he was a soldier and not a king. Then when he's in the palace it flips. All king, no soldier."

"What are you doing here?" Sabine asked.

"I heard Rainer was going to fight, so I came to watch. I'm sure Axel and Anton are here as well."

Rainer threw another punch. This time he managed to hit Markis in the stomach. Markis hunched forward but quickly straightened, once again bouncing on his feet. The two men eyed one another, two animals each seeking blood.

"I love when Rainer challenges someone," Lottie said. "Since being crowned king, he's rarely had the chance to fight."

"You enjoy watching this?" Sabine always hated it when one of her brothers fought.

"Yes." Lottie smiled and glanced at her. "Rainer has a natural talent for fighting. It really is amazing to see."

Markis swung but Rainer turned, so he missed. Rainer countered with a strike to Markis's head.

"They're holding back, right?" Sabine whispered. "So no one will get hurt?"

Lottie laughed. "I doubt it. Don't you have brothers?"

Sabine nodded. "I have four."

"Then you know when they fight, they don't hold back."

"What if they get hurt?" In the last fight, it looked like the one had a broken arm and nose.

"Other than a few bruises and some scratches, my brother has managed to come out mostly unscathed. He's also never lost a fight. My dad trained his sons to be warriors. That's what Rainer is." She peered at Sabine. "Does this side of him scare you?"

"No." And that was the truth. She found his ability to fight so well fascinating. Karl had trained his entire life to be king, so his fighting skills were lacking. But Rainer...the way his body moved, the muscles along his torso, and the speed with which he fought could only be accomplished from years and years of training.

"Then what made you upset?"

"He's fighting Markis, and I fear he'll be injured. As his

sister, I'm surprised you allow him to do this now that he's king."

Lottie laughed. "No one *allows* Rainer to do anything. He does as he pleases."

Markis managed to hit Rainer's shoulder, and the king stumbled backward a few steps.

"When do they stop?" Sabine asked.

"When one is too injured to continue."

Sabine didn't think she could stand there and watch this any longer.

"Do you know why the guards wear masks?" Lottie asked.

She'd considered it many times. So far, she'd only managed to come up with one possibility. "So no one knows who they are so they can't be bribed?"

"That, and so no one sees their bruised faces."

Rainer swiped Markis's legs out from under him. Markis landed on his back, rolled out of the way, and jumped to his feet.

"I've never seen a fight take this long," Lottie said. "Rainer is going to be thrilled."

"Why is that?" She would have expected him to be upset.

"Markis has a different way of fighting. It's challenging Rainer. My brother will want to learn Markis's ways and teach it to his soldiers."

Markis spun and then punched Rainer's stomach. Rainer wrapped his arm around Markis's neck, flipping him to the ground. The two men continued in this manner for the next several minutes. Finally, another soldier called the fight, raising both of their arms in a tie.

Relief filled Sabine.

"Interesting," Lottie said. "I've never seen a tie called before either."

Rainer and Markis went over to the side, talking together while another pair entered the ring and began sparring.

"I think I've seen enough for one day," Sabine mumbled.

"If you're leaving, I'm going to head down."

"Down?"

"To practice with the soldiers."

"Women are permitted to openly train?"

Lottie nodded. "My brother encourages it."

The sound of dogs barking echoed in the cavern. "What's that?"

"We have a training facility down here for dogs as well. My brother likes to use them for hunting, sniffing out poisons, and sometimes he'll use them in battle depending on the situation."

"Dogs?"

"They're intelligent and easily trainable."

There was so much Sabine didn't know.

Lottie reached out, taking hold of Sabine's hand, and squeezing it. "I'm here if there's anything you need. I can show you around the palace, teach you some of our Lynk history, anything you want. All you have to do is ask."

"Thank you."

Lottie smiled. "Us women have to stick together." She released Sabine's hand.

"Yes, we do." While no one could possibly replace Alina, Lottie could be a much-needed friend in what was turning out to be a very lonely place.

Sabine made her way through the palace, heading back toward her bedchamber. There was so much about Rainer that she didn't understand—starting with why he'd been sparring with Markis in the first place. If it were to test his skills, they could have taken precautions so neither would be injured. However, they'd been fighting as if it were a real fight. Her stomach still didn't feel well after witnessing such unrestrained violence.

Turning the corner, she caught sight of Axel standing with a woman in the doorway down the hall. The two were locked in an embrace, the woman's lips on Axel's neck as he twirled a strand of her hair, a lazy smile on his face.

Sabine moved around her guards and headed directly toward him, stopping a few feet away and tapping her foot with impatience.

When Axel noticed her, surprise filled his face. He quickly hid it and asked, "What can I do for you?"

"Ditch the woman."

He extricated himself from her, then whispered something in her ear. The woman glared at Sabine before sauntering away. Once she turned the corner, Axel shoved his hands in his pockets and came closer to Sabine, his eyes gleaming in delight. "Well, well, well. What has you in this delightfully feisty mood?"

"I want to know why you told me to watch out for Cutler."

He shrugged. "Don't like the guy."

"Are you sure that's all?" she said, folding her arms.

"What other reason could I possibly have?"

She nodded. "That's all I needed to know." She turned and started to walk away.

After she'd gone about ten feet, Axel said, "Wait."

She stopped but didn't face him.

"I figured he'd want to talk to you. Tell you some things you might not be ready to hear."

At that, she turned toward him. "He did. Our conversation became quite animated. Markis had to intervene."

He tipped his head back and laughed, the sound echoing

down the hallway. "Oh that's rich. That explains why Rainer is with him."

"I saw the two of them fighting. It wasn't pretty."

The smile disappeared from Axel's face. "Here is not the place to be having this conversation." He tilted his head to the side, an invitation for Sabine to follow him.

She wasn't a jealous woman, and she didn't care what Rainer did. However, she wanted to know about Heather, and she didn't want to ask Rainer about her. If the king had a relationship with another woman, that needed to be considered with regards to Alina. This woman—Heather—could have had Alina killed. At this point, all options had to be considered.

Axel led the way along the hallway, stopping before a large door. He opened it, ushering her inside.

Sabine stepped into a luxurious sitting room filled with plush sofas and large pillows.

"Wait out there," Axel instructed her guards. They remained in the hallway. "You, out." The guard stationed inside bowed and then left the room. Axel closed the door. "Now that we're alone, we can speak freely."

"Where are we?" she asked, wondering if this was a royal wing shared by Axel, Anton, and Lottie.

"We're in my private rooms." He went over and plopped on one of the two cream sofas, stretching his arms across the back of it. To the right, archways led to a balcony lined with tall bushes which blocked the view.

"We shouldn't be in here alone." They were both unmarried. There needed to be at least one guard present.

"I forgot how uptight people from Bakley are," he said with a moan. "No one is around—which is the point—so you can ask me whatever it is you want to know."

Not wanting to waste the opportunity, she said, "Why is King Rainer fighting with my guard, Markis?" She sat on the sofa across from Axel. The slit up the front of her tan dress parted, sliding over her legs, and exposing them from ankle to thigh. She had the urge to pull the material together to cover them. However, she left it, wanting to show she was acclimating to the culture here.

Axel's eyes focused on her legs. "Your skin is pale. I can tell you're used to being covered up." He winked. "Glad that's changing."

"Please answer my question." She needed to show him he couldn't rattle her.

After watching her for a minute, Axel shrugged. "Who knows. My brother has always done what he wants. Rainer doesn't care if his actions hurt or affect others."

A loaded answer she'd have to think about in more detail later. "King Rainer seems to be a good ruler." Not that she knew much about the sort of king he was, especially since he hadn't been sitting on the throne that long.

"Everyone is entitled to his or her opinion."

"You don't think he is?" she asked, wondering if Axel should be on her list of suspects.

He glanced at the ceiling before responding, "Don't ever tell him I said this." He looked her in the eyes. "But yes, he's a good ruler. Just a little soft sometimes. Like the whole mess with…"

"Heather?" she whispered.

He nodded. "Cutler told you?"

"Cutler told me he is engaged to Heather."

"Of course he did." Axel shook his head. "The bloke's been in love with her for as long as I've known him. Obviously. No man in their right mind would marry a woman carrying another man's child."

It felt as if Sabine had been punched in the stomach. Heather was pregnant with Rainer's child. "Did my sister know any of this?" While the letters had revealed that the king was in love with another woman, they said nothing about it being Heather or that she was pregnant. Sabine didn't know why this piece of information was important, but it was. She needed to know.

"Not sure. Your sister didn't confide in me."

She rubbed her forehead. This had to be why Rainer shared the letters with her—he wanted her to know, as her sister had, what she was getting herself into. Then she'd have no reason to ever be resentful or jealous. She couldn't believe Alina had agreed to any of this. The thought sickened her.

"Why do you care who my brother loves?" Axel asked, his voice holding a hint of genuine curiosity.

"I don't." Her priority was finding her sister's killer, not worrying about love or who was sleeping with whom.

"Then why do you look upset?"

"All of this makes Heather a suspect in the death of my sister." And if Heather were responsible for Alina's death, she doubted Rainer would do anything about it. Most likely, he'd hide all evidence on Heather's behalf.

"I doubt Heather is capable of murder."

"You'd be surprised what a woman would do in the name of love."

"Oh, I have no doubt. I've seen some crazy things over the years." Axel crossed his legs and folded his hands in his lap. "Are you aware that my brother is required to have an heir to maintain the throne?"

"Yes." She just didn't want to think about having sex with her soon-to-be husband right now. Even if he was handsome. Even if she could imagine him sliding his hands over her body, his lips trailing kissing along her neck, his tongue...

"Then consider this. Heather's child is a backup in case you can't have a kid."

His comment snapped some sense back into her. "I am not a horse to be bred."

He chuckled; the sound dark. "I'm afraid you are. And Rainer needs a child to keep his throne. Power, and the need to maintain it, makes people do crazy things."

She abruptly stood and went over to the archway, looking out at the balcony. "Do you know who killed my sister?"

"No." He sighed. "But I wish I did. Princess Alina didn't deserve to die."

"I need to find out who killed her," she whispered.

"Honestly, there are too many possibilities both here in the palace and in other kingdoms."

A rustling sound came from behind her, but she didn't turn around.

"My brother is looking into it," Axel said from what sounded like a few feet away.

"That's not good enough." It had already been weeks. "I have to find the person responsible."

"So you can get revenge?" His voice sounded even closer.

"Yes." The air seemed to crackle around her. She knew Axel was mere inches behind her, but she refused to face him.

"If you want to find your sister's killer, I suggest you start playing nice with everyone here at the palace."

"How so?" Now they were getting somewhere.

"If I were you, I'd host a private, exclusive tea party to welcome a few select people into your personal inner circle. They'll start talking to gain your favor. It might give you some direction."

That was an excellent idea, and one she should have thought of. "Thank you." She could almost feel Axel behind her. She half expected him to touch her shoulder or back, but he refrained from doing so. After a moment of silence, she turned around and looked up into his eyes. "Why was Rainer fighting Markis?" she asked again.

"My guess would be to see if he's worthy to be your protector."

"And Rainer couldn't watch Markis fight one of his soldiers?"

Axel smiled. "That's not how my brother operates." He suddenly looked away, shaking his head.

"Axel," she whispered. "What do you mean by that?" She had a feeling he wanted to say more.

His brow furrowed, and he looked at her as if he were seeing her for the first time. "You're everything my brother wanted with Alina but didn't get."

Silence hung between them. She wanted to ask more but knew when to keep her mouth shut. She'd already gotten more out of Axel than he'd intended to give. "Thank you for your advice." She stepped around him and went to the door.

"Be careful out there," Axel said. "You're an outsider, and a lot of people don't want the king of Lynk to marry someone from Bakley."

She glanced over her shoulder at him. "Like some of the people in your court?"

"And ruling families from other kingdoms. They're afraid of the power the two kingdoms will gain by forming an alliance."

"I understand." She left the room, more confused than ever.

Chapter Thirteen

S abine stood in the archway leading from her bedchamber to the outside balcony, gazing at the beautiful view before her.

"I have everything written down," Claire said as she stood from the table. "Is there anything else you'll be requiring?"

"No, that will be all." Sabine couldn't believe she'd asked Claire to help her plan a small tea party. Back home, the last thing she ever wanted to do was sit in a room having tea all afternoon while making idle chatter with other women. However, after her conversation with Axel, she knew she needed to start forming connections with the wives of the powerful men in Lynk.

"I'll get the invitations out later today and have all of the food and drinks arranged to your specifications." Claire gathered her papers and writing utensils. "I would like to apologize."

"For what?" Sabine asked.

"I should have mentioned sooner that my sister is Heather. She told me she met you last night."

"Your sister is a beautiful woman," Sabine replied, trying

to keep her face neutral and devoid of any emotion revealing that she knew Heather was Rainer's lover. "There is no need to apologize so long as you don't keep information from me in the future."

Claire smiled. "I won't. And thank you. I'll get started on this right away." She left the room.

Letting out a sigh, Sabine turned her attention back to the landscape before her as unwanted thoughts wormed their way in. She had no idea where Claire's loyalties lie. Claire could have been given this job as a favor to Heather since being a lady's maid was far more prestigious than a seamstress's assistant. However, she could also have this job to keep tabs on Sabine. She could be reporting everything Sabine did back to Heather. Or even Rainer. For some reason, this felt like a small betrayal. It only solidified the fact that Sabine couldn't trust anyone.

Someone knocked on her door. She called out for the person to enter.

"Princess Sabine," a warm, masculine voice said from behind her.

She forced a pleasant smile on her face and headed inside where she found Rainer standing in the middle of her bedchamber. "Yes, Your Majesty?"

"We need to talk," he said by way of greeting.

"Yes, we do." She folded her arms as she examined the man before her. The last time she saw him, he'd been fighting with Markis. Now, his hair appeared damp, he smelled of soap, and he wore a tan tunic and matching loose pants.

"Let's go to my private office." He headed to the door that led to the royal suite.

Sabine went to her desk, opening the top drawer and gathering the letters he'd given her, wanting to return them. She followed him past the sitting room, past the dining room, and to a closed door. He opened it, ushering her inside.

Back home, her father's office had dark wood walls, a desk that always seemed to be littered with piles of papers, and several shelves full to the brim with books stacked in no particular order. This space was the opposite. A small desk sat in the middle of the room, there were no books, and three of the walls were bare. Where the fourth wall should have been, it was entirely open to the outside. The space felt rather impersonal.

"Go ahead and make yourself comfortable," Rainer said as he moved around her and took a seat at his desk.

"There's no wall," she said, as if he didn't know that. Since the palace was built atop a mountain, if she went too close to the opening, she feared she'd topple right down the side of the cliff and die. Maybe that was the point. If someone upset him, he could just shove the person right off the mountainside.

"There's a large pool below," he said, tracking her movements—or lack thereof. "Worst thing that can happen, you'll fall one level into the water."

"How is there a pool?"

"This room stops well before the edge of the palace and mountain."

She inched forward, trying to see without getting too close. Sure enough, she spotted a body of water fifteen feet below. It looked as if it went under where she currently stood making it an indoor and outdoor pool. She'd never seen anything so amazing in all her life.

"When it rains, the water cascades off the roof above here and into the pool."

"I would love to see that," she said, taking a seat across from him. "Everything here is so different from Bakley." She set the letters he'd given her on the desk. "I want to return these to you."

He picked them up and slid them in a drawer, not even questioning her about them.

"Could someone down there hear us?" She pointed to the open wall.

"No. Below this room is my own personal training room next to the pool. Even if someone was down there, they'd never hear us unless we spoke very loudly and much closer to the edge of the room."

She wanted to see the training room. However, now was not the time. He'd brought her into his personal office for a private conversation. If she wanted to know about her sister, now was the time. "Do you have any leads on who killed Alina?" She spoke with an air of confidence, expecting an answer.

He leaned back in his chair. "I have it narrowed down to a few suspects."

"Are they citizens of Lynk?"

"No," he said, not breaking eye contact with her. "They're from other kingdoms, though we believe one could be in Lynk at the moment. We're trying to locate him."

Thrilled he was sharing this information with her, she asked, "Who are they?"

"The first is a group of soldiers from Carlon who have been very vocal about not wanting your sister and I to marry. They don't want Lynk and Bakley forming any sort of an alliance. Another suspect is one of Carlon's well-known assassins. He was seen spending an obscene amount of money at a brothel a week ago. We haven't been able to link him to anyone though, so we have no idea who hired him."

"Any others?"

"A powerful noblewoman from Nisk has also expressed her displeasure with Lynk uniting with Bakley. She threatened to stop the wedding but gave no specifics beyond that. However, she is quite wealthy and has extensive resources."

"Who do you believe is in Lynk?"

"The assassin from Carlon has a brother who hasn't been seen since the assassination. The two men usually work together. I believe he may have stayed behind to ensure the job was complete, or he may be here now for you. I don't have proof—it's just a feeling. There have been a few odd things that have happened which is why I've kept the palace closed to outsiders, why I sent your men home, and why I have six guards assigned to you."

At least he seemed to be taking her safety seriously. "Once you discover who killed my sister, what do you plan to do with him?"

"I'll discuss the matter with your father and then decide how to proceed with his recommendations."

Tears filled her eyes. When her sister had first left Bakley to marry Rainer, Sabine hadn't once considered other kingdoms would be opposed to the union and her sister would end up dead. Even when she offered to take her sister's place, her only thought had been seeking the killer and getting revenge.

"Do you have any other questions?"

"You've ruled out everyone here in Lynk?" she asked. There had to be at least one person from this kingdom who opposed the marriage and had the means to pull off an assassination.

"While I am sure there are some who'd love to see this union fail, I do not believe any of them would have killed your sister."

"Why is that?"

"Because if one of my own people killed her, the

punishment would be the death of the killer's entire bloodline."

Silence hung in the room. An extreme punishment for the family, especially if they weren't corrupt like the killer.

"Thank you," she said. "For telling me all of this." She needed to write to her mother, letting her know all she'd learned.

Rainer stood and walked around the desk, perching on the edge of it near Sabine. "Can I ask you something?"

"Of course." She sat back, trying to figure out why he'd moved so close to her.

"Will you promise to answer honestly?" he asked, his voice low and rumbling like water over stones.

"Yes," Sabine replied, her own voice coming out breathy, "as long as I can ask something in return." She had no idea why this man had this effect on her. Whenever he looked at her, his eyes seemed to be undressing her, making her body ache in a way no one else ever had. Even though she had a desire to touch him, to run a finger along his arm, she refrained from doing so and instead, tried her hardest to pretend she wasn't attracted to him.

"That's only fair." He clasped his hands together and asked, "What is your relationship with Markis?"

"My guard, Markis?" She'd never considered defining her friendship with a soldier in her father's army.

"Yes."

And then it dawned on her what he was insinuating. Her face heated with the implication. She decided to play dumb. "What do you mean by our relationship? He's my guard."

"Forgive me, but he seems like more." He reached out, placing his warm hand on her knee, practically making her jump from the contact.

She crossed her legs, forcing him to remove his hand. "I hadn't met Markis until the day I left my home to journey here to Lynk. After my carriage was attacked, the two of us traveled together. I trust him to keep me safe."

Rainer rubbed the back of his neck. "You don't fancy him as something more?"

She raised her eyebrows at that. "No. The thought never crossed my mind. Why are you asking me these questions?"

"The two of you seem close." He stood and went over to the open wall, gazing outside. "He cares for you."

It irked her that Rainer was inquiring after Markis while he was intimately involved with another woman. She didn't think he was jealous but more along the lines of not wanting to look the fool. It was her job then to ease his mind. Men could be so fickle. "Of course Markis cares for me—my father tasked him with my safety. I am his princess, and he has sworn fealty to me." She stood and took a couple of steps closer to Rainer, facing his back. "You of all people must understand that my kingdom needs your soldiers. Our marriage is imperative. Markis knows children that have been kidnapped. He wants Bakley and Lynk to unite. He is here to help us."

"That's exactly what he said."

"Then why are you questioning me?"

He peered over his shoulder at her. "To see if your stories align."

"Will he be allowed to stay?" She wanted to ask why they'd been fighting this morning in the first place.

"Yes. I've tested him, and he's proved himself capable."

Relief filled her. But now it was her turn to ask him something. "After we marry, what will your association with Heather be?"

He turned his attention back outside. "I was wondering why you agreed to answer my question so readily." He shook his head. "Heather and I have a long and complicated relationship."

She waited for him to explain because she would not leave this room without some sort of understanding. She couldn't be the queen of this kingdom without having a level of respect from the king. She moved to stand alongside Rainer, her focus also outside on the stunning scenery before them.

"Heather was my first love," he said, his voice almost wistful. "When my father discovered I fancied her, he made it clear I was free to dabble on occasion but that I could never marry or have a relationship with Heather. Naturally, I rebelled. I saw her more frequently and made promises to her that I couldn't keep. I thought I could have a life with Heather before my father died. I assumed I had twenty or so years until I needed to worry about taking up the crown. When my father passed at such an early age, I was stunned. No one expected it. I told Heather I had to marry someone else, and for the most part, we ended things. We see each other on occasion, but that is all. She is marrying Cutler. We will each go our separate ways."

"If that's the case, then why did Cutler tell me about the two of you?" It had been bothering her all day. The only reason she could come up with was that Rainer and Heather would continue their affair even after both married someone else.

"Cutler is hotheaded." He turned to face her. "Why are you asking me about Heather?"

She wanted to say *for the same reason you're asking me about Markis;* however, she refrained from doing so. The two of them needed to form some sort of friendship and a level of trust. "I wasn't sure of the customs in your kingdom and if you'd take a consort or not."

He chuckled and rubbed his chin. "It is within my right to do anything I wish, including taking a lover. However, I have no desire to bother with love because it clouds a person's judgment. Now that I am the king of Lynk, I need to see things clearly and rationally." He placed his hands on her bare shoulders, sending a jolt of warmth through her. "Your purpose here is to bring strength to my kingdom. I help you; you help me. This is a business deal." His right finger slid from her arm to her collar bone and then up to her chin, forcing her to look directly into his eyes. "I need an heir within the year; otherwise, I lose my throne. Until your end of the deal is met, your activities will be restricted to ensure your wellbeing and safety. Your sister understood and accepted all of this." He leaned in, as if to kiss her, his warm breath caressing her face. "You will behave in such a way that it is clear you are my wife, that we are married, and I am the only one in your bed."

She nodded, unable to form a sentence.

Rainer's finger slid up her cheek and then across her lips. She held completely still, not sure what his intentions were. If he leaned forward and kissed her, she was pretty sure she'd kiss him back. Not because she felt anything for him as a person, but because he made her body react to his in strange, alluring ways. She wondered what it would feel like to have his large hands remove her dress, caress her skin, hold her in bed.

"You are not to be alone in a room with anyone—including my brother. There can never be a question as to whose child you bear. Understood?"

"Yes," she whispered, blinking. She needed to pull it together. It was just that she'd never had the tables turned on her like this. Usually, she was the one leaning in, saying something semi-scandalous, getting young men to do as she wanted.

"Good." He removed his hands and took a step back.

Without him physically touching her, it became easier to

think clearly. Wanting to change the subject, she said, "Lottie mentioned she trains with your soldiers."

He nodded. "It's important she knows how to defend herself since she refuses to have any guards in the palace."

She twisted her fingers together, trying to figure out how to ask him. Finally, she just came out and said, "Can I train with them?"

He shook his head. "I will not have the future queen training with my soldiers."

"I understand." She started to head toward the door.

"However," he said.

She froze, her back to him.

"I'd be willing to train you."

The two of them, alone together, training. "Okay."

"Oh, and there's one other matter to discuss before you leave."

She turned to face him. "Yes?"

"The only kingdom that hasn't specifically expressed concern over our union is Avoni."

"You didn't mention any suspects from that kingdom either."

"Exactly. Which naturally makes me suspicious, so I sent the king a letter inviting him to our wedding."

"Did he reply?"

"He wrote back thanking me for the invitation. He politely declined but said he is sending a small delegation in his place to witness the joyous occasion. His words, not mine."

"Are you going to let them in the palace?" Rainer must not have expected that response.

"I have no choice but to welcome them here," he said. "They will arrive shortly. Once they do, our wedding will take place." He turned his back to her, facing out toward the mountains in the distance once again.

Sabine didn't bother to say anything else as she left the room, wondering about Avoni. If the assassin was from that kingdom, he could come with the delegation and be granted entrance into the palace. If so, he could try to kill her to stop the union.

Chapter Fourteen

S abine entered the courtyard, inspecting it. Her tea party was due to start in fifteen minutes, and she hoped there wouldn't be any problems. A large round table had been set up near the center of the area, next to the water fountain. A white cloth covered it along with several plates and teacups.

Claire approached with a large smile on her face. "What do you think?" she asked. "Is it to your liking?" She swept her hand out toward the table. In the middle, a vase with bright pink flowers stood.

"It's beautiful." The sun was out, the air was the perfect temperature, and the flowers smelled divine.

"A few minutes after everyone arrives, a servant will bring the refreshments along with some treats. The guards have been instructed to remain at the perimeter of the courtyard." Claire folded her hands behind her back, giving the area a once over. "Anything else?"

"And you're sure it's acceptable for me to be serving mead with fruit instead of traditional tea?"

Claire laughed. "Yes. Besides putting everyone more at ease, I'm sure it'll get the ladies talking more freely."

"Which is what I want if I'm to make any real friends here."

Claire placed her hand on Sabine's shoulder. "I'm glad you listened to me and wore the red outfit. It looks stunning with your eyes. Now if you'll excuse me, I'm going to make sure everything is ready in the kitchen."

This centrally located courtyard was the perfect location. People at the palace would see her talking and laughing with the few carefully chosen high ranking ladies that would be in attendance. By making the small gathering exclusive, she hoped others would want to befriend her and be included in future events. To find the killer, she needed all the gossip she could get. And what better way than through those married to the most powerful men in Lynk. Since Rainer only seemed to be focused on suspects from other kingdoms, Sabine wanted to be sure there wasn't someone right in his own palace that he'd missed. Or at the very least, see if anyone saw or heard anything that could help find the killer.

A woman in her early fifties strode through one of the archways. With her head held high, she glided over to Sabine and bowed. "I'm surprised you invited me given how my son spoke to you the other night." She straightened.

This had to be Cutler's mother, Lady Regina. Given that her husband was the commander of the army and Cutler a captain, Sabine needed to tread carefully. "Welcome." She forced a pleasant smile on her face. She didn't recall meeting this woman the night she'd been introduced to the court. "I believe your son was just making sure I knew he was going to marry Heather."

Regina raised a single eyebrow. "I believe he wants to make sure everyone in the kingdom is aware of that fact."

Lottie entered the courtyard, her arm clasped with

another young woman's who looked vaguely familiar. "Greetings," Lottie said. "I ran into Duchess Marin on the way here."

Sabine silently thanked Lottie for reminding her who the woman was. Duchess Marin had just married a man who owned the smallest and weakest duchy of the kingdom. However, a duchess was a duchess, nonetheless. While Sabine remembered meeting the woman, she didn't remember having a conversation with her.

Movement through the archway to the right caught Sabine's attention, and she looked to see Duchess Cassandra and Lady Karmen enter the courtyard. "The last of our party has arrived." She'd invited Cassandra because she was the duchess of the wealthiest duchy in the kingdom. Karmen, on the other hand, had been invited because she seemed to know a little something about everything.

Once the women had all assembled around Sabine, she said, "Ladies, I hope we can all forgo our titles for this afternoon. I don't feel the need to be called princess every time someone wishes to speak to me, and I invited you all here so that I can get to know some people here in Lynk. I could use a friend or two." She smiled sweetly at all of them, wanting to come across as non-threatening but needing to show she could be a powerful ally as well. Besides, since people from Bakley seemed to have a reputation for being stiff and overly formal, this was Sabine's chance to show them she could be one of them—that she was more Lynk than Bakley.

"I believe every one of us could use a friend," Lottie said. She headed to the table.

Everyone else agreed and followed suit.

After they were all seated, Cassandra said, "I was surprised to receive your invitation to this gathering, but when I saw it was a tea party, it made sense." She was a large woman in her late forties with beautiful chestnut hair that was starting to turn gray.

"And why is that?" Sabine asked, amusement dancing in her voice.

The servants entered, setting several trays on the table, and then leaving.

"Everyone knows how much people from Bakley like their tea."

"That we do," Sabine said, gesturing to the table. "Why don't you all help yourself to some *tea*."

The guests began reaching for the tea pots and pouring the liquid into their cups.

Karmen took a sip and then began laughing. "This isn't tea." Her eyes sparkled with amusement. "I like you. I think we are going to be great friends." She saluted her teacup in Sabine's direction.

The other women looked confused.

"No, it's not tea," Sabine explained. "Oftentimes things aren't what they appear." She reached forward, taking her own cup in hand.

The women all took small sips, then smiled in understanding.

"Forgive me," Cassandra said, "but you're nothing like your sister."

"Do you have siblings?" Sabine asked.

"I do."

"And you are the same as your siblings?"

"Well, no. We are each vastly different. I see your point."

Sabine pretended to take a sip from her own cup. The last thing she wanted was for her own lips to be loose, so she couldn't drink the strong mead. Hopefully, everyone else would open up once they started drinking.

"I think court is going to be much more interesting with

you around," Karmen said. "You've already livened things up."

Within a few minutes, the women began to gossip. Apparently, two different women had been seen kissing the very handsome and available Duke Trenton. Then the conversation steered to what fashions seemed to be up and coming for the season, who Lottie should consider marrying, and so on. No one said anything about Alina and her murder. Sabine would have to find a way to steer the conversation in that direction if the opportunity afforded itself.

"My servants are all gossiping about a new handsome guard here in the palace," Marin said. "I think he's one of your soldiers." She nodded her chin toward Sabine.

"Markis?" Sabine said, startled by the change in topics. "My guard from Bakley?"

"Oh yes," Karmen said. "He's all anyone is talking about."

"He is easy on the eyes," Lottie added, smirking. "I'm sure that's why Sabine keeps him around."

"How do any of you know what he looks like since he's always wearing a mask?" Sabine asked.

"When he fought the king, he didn't have a mask," Marin said. "All of my servants were there watching."

"More like drooling," Lottie mumbled with a chuckle.

"And it's his eyes," Karmen said with a sigh. "There's something so powerful and sexy about them."

Glancing at the perimeter of the courtyard where her guards stood watch, Sabine hoped they couldn't overhear them—especially Markis. Wanting to redirect this conversation, Sabine leaned forward. "I'll let you all in on a little secret." All the women leaned forward as well; their eyes gleaming with excitement. Sabine took another pretend sip of her drink, as if she might be slightly tipsy, which was why she was so readily divulging this information. "Markis is here to help me find my sister's killer." She put her finger at her lips, as if this were a secret.

The information seemed to surprise them all.

"And once you find the killer," Cassandra asked, "then what?"

"I need to make sure I stay far away from him," Sabine said, trying to keep the tone light, so the women would continue to talk.

"Let's face it," Regina said as she poured herself another cup of mead, "it's a trained assassin. No regular person could have slipped the princess poison like that."

"Cutler told me the poison made it past the royal food taster. That's why the person was executed."

"If it was a trained assassin from another kingdom, he is probably long gone," Cassandra said. "Surely he went back to wherever he's from, don't you think?"

"Possibly," Sabine mused. "Or..." She set her cup on the table for dramatic effect. "He is hiding somewhere in the palace. He could be among us now. Waiting to strike again."

No one spoke and all eyes focused on Sabine.

"If he's still here in the palace," Lottie whispered, breaking the silence, "then why hasn't he killed you yet? What do you think he's waiting for?"

A very good question. "Perhaps he just hasn't had a chance."

Lottie glanced at the mezzanine above, as if searching for an assassin lurking in the shadows.

"Maybe you should go inside," Marin suggested. "That way you aren't so exposed."

Sabine loved that these women seemed to care for her wellbeing. "I'm tired of hiding inside. I just want to find this killer."

"Don't worry," Lottie said. "I'm sure my brother will find him. He was furious the murder happened in his own home and wants to prove he is in control. When he sets his mind to something, he always follows through."

Lottie made a valid point. Rainer was a new king. If someone here at court wanted to prove the king incompetent, a murder such as Alina's would certainly accomplish that. Especially if there were no suspects. Sabine would have to start learning who here at court didn't want Rainer to succeed as the next king.

"How would one even go about hiring an assassin?" Karmen asked. "I'm assuming we have them here in Lynk, but who are they and how do you contact them?"

"There are a few men in the army tasked with such things," Regina said. "I'm sure they do side jobs. I imagine the pay would be astronomical."

The conversation turned away from Alina and moved to other topics. The more the women drank, the louder they became. By the end of the afternoon, Sabine found herself laughing right along with them even though she hadn't finished a single cup of mead.

Sabine sprawled out on her bed, thankful for the soft breeze coming into her room. Exhaustion consumed her from her tea party, and her eyes became heavy.

A soft knock sounded on the door.

"Your Highness," Claire said as she stepped into the room. "The king wishes for you to take your supper with him and his family this evening."

Sabine groaned. "Any idea why?" She'd been planning on skipping supper and staying in bed.

"I am simply the messenger."

With a dramatic sigh, she sat up. "The tea party was a hit," she said as she slid off the bed and stretched.

"So I hear. Gossip is already spreading through the palace as to who you invited."

Pleased with that bit of information, Sabine ran her hands through her hair. "Should I change for dinner?" She still had on the red outfit from earlier.

"What you have on is appropriate. Besides, King Rainer wants you to come now."

Sabine glanced outside at the sun still shining brightly. "Isn't it a little early for supper?"

Claire shrugged.

"Very well." She gestured for Claire to lead the way. The sooner she got supper over with, the sooner she could climb back into bed to sleep.

Out in the hallway, the guards fell into place behind Sabine. Peering over her shoulder, she spotted Markis on her left. She had no idea how to do this stealthily, so she just decided to be blunt about it. "I need a word with my guard." She pointed to Markis.

Claire's brows bent together and she opened her mouth to say something, but Sabine turned her back to Claire and faced Markis.

"Is everything all right, Your Highness?" Markis asked in a soft voice so the others wouldn't overhear.

"I want you to do something for me," Sabine whispered. She glanced at the other guards, making sure they kept their distance.

"What do you need?"

"Find out who the designated assassins in the army are. See if any were recently hired for a private job or if any are missing."

"I understand."

Knowing she could trust him to handle the matter, she resumed her trek to the dining room, her guards once again falling into place behind her.

"Is everything all right?" Claire asked.

"Yes." As the future queen, she didn't have to justify her actions. However, she wanted to make sure Claire trusted her, so she smiled and said, "I simply told him since he will be staying here for a while, he is permitted to write home to his family. I'm not sure he wants anyone here to know about his private life."

Her explanation seemed to appease Claire since she didn't press the matter any further.

When they reached the dining room, Sabine entered alone. It felt like the last time she was here had been a lifetime ago. A moan came from the right. She swung toward the sound and found Lottie sitting at the table, her head resting on her arms. "Are you all right?" Sabine inquired.

"I'm sleeping," Lottie mumbled.

"Did you have too much to drink this afternoon?" She tried to sound shocked and not as if that had been her plan all along.

Lottie tilted her head, opening an eyelid. "Your *tea* is quite potent." She closed her eye again. "I'm assuming that's a reflection on you."

Sabine patted Lottie's back before heading out onto the balcony. She slid her hands over the railing and sucked in a deep breath. A hawk flew a few feet below.

"It's going to rain," Anton said as he came to stand beside her. "I can feel it."

She eyed him. "You feel rain coming?" There wasn't a cloud in the sky.

"My knee hurts—and it's never wrong."

"From an old injury?"

He nodded. "Axel dared me to jump from one rooftop to another. I missed."

That sounded painful. "I assume you were much younger when this happened?"

"Sort of." He laughed. "Axel and I have a long history of getting into trouble. If it's not me, it's him to be sure. We used to drive my father crazy." His voice sounded wistful.

He reminded her of her brothers, making her miss home even more today. "You're twenty-two but not engaged?" she asked. That seemed a little old, at least by Bakley standards, to not be betrothed.

He raised his eyebrows and looked at her. "No. Why?"

"Just curious." It was odd that not one of the four siblings was married.

"I'm not sure how it is in Bakley, but for us here in Lynk, the king will decide who Axel, Lottie, and I marry. I can't believe my brother is going to choose my bride."

"Do you fancy someone?" She bumped her shoulder against his. "Maybe I can put in a good word for you," she teased. This was what she missed about her home. The banter with her siblings.

"I wish it were that simple. Unfortunately, the three of us must marry to strengthen our kingdom. I'm sure you understand that seeing as how it's why you're here."

"Yes." Her finger trailed along the edge of the railing. Duty. What an ugly little word that could be quite inconvenient. However, she supposed everyone had it in some form or other. Her duty was to her family and kingdom. Someone like a servant had a duty to provide for their family as well, just on a different scale. It seemed everyone had a rope tethering them to something.

"What are you two discussing out here?" Axel asked as he joined them on the balcony.

"Nothing of importance," Sabine said, turning back to look at the sun setting over the mountain in the distance.

Axel shoved his hands into his pockets. "Can I ask why Lottie is passed out on the dining table?"

"She drank too much tea," Sabine said, trying not to smile.

Axel chuckled, the sound deep and throaty. "That so?"

"Rainer is here," Anton said, nodding inside.

The three of them made their way into the dining room.

"Did you see what Sabine did to Lottie?" Axel said to Rainer as he sat down.

Rainer's eyes narrowed. "Is she drunk?" he asked with disbelief.

"I'm fine," Lottie moaned. "I just went to Sabine's *tea* party."

"At any minute she is going to start snoring," Anton mumbled.

"Tea must mean something different in Bakley," Axel said, a grin on his face. "And here I thought all those tea parties your kingdom had were a total bore."

Sabine ignored them and took her seat, wondering why Rainer had insisted they all have supper together.

The servants brought in a dozen or so trays of food and then left.

"Eat something," Rainer commanded Lottie. "I need you alert for this conversation."

Lottie rolled her eyes and sat up, grabbing a tray of food and pulling it closer so she could load her plate with chicken and rice. When she finished, Sabine did the same.

"What's going on?" Axel asked.

"What I say right now remains in this room with the five of us. Understood?" Rainer looked at everyone, waiting for each to acknowledge and agree. "A delegation from Avoni is on their way here."

He'd mentioned that to Sabine before, so she didn't think too much about it as she shoved a spoonful of rice in her mouth.

"Whatever for?" Lottie asked. "People from Avoni are so weird."

Sabine didn't know much about Avoni, so she had no opinion whether they acted or behaved strangely or not. According to Lottie, people from Bakley were probably odd, too.

"A member of the League will be traveling with them," Rainer said. "This person will be the deciding vote as to whether my marriage to Sabine can take place or not."

Sabine almost choked on her mouthful of food. *Deciding vote?*

"The tiebreaker vote?" Axel said.

"Yes." Rainer leaned back on his chair.

"Besides swapping out princesses, what else changed?" Axel inquired.

Sabine nodded, wanting to know as well.

"King Franz asked for an additional five hundred soldiers. I agreed."

If her father had asked for more soldiers, it was for good reason. They needed to get their border secure. When her mouth was empty, she said, "I don't understand why anyone else has a say in what we do."

The siblings all looked at her as if she were daft. Now was probably not a good time to admit she didn't even know what the League was.

"Father did warn you the other kingdoms would be testing you once he died," Axel said, his voice soft. "Maybe this is their way of doing it by seeing how you handle the situation."

"Why would anyone test King Rainer?" Sabine asked. "Everyone knows Lynk has a huge army." To go up against them would be suicide. And just because he was the youngest ruling king on the continent didn't mean he wasn't qualified for the job.

"That could be why someone assassinated Princess Alina," Anton said. "It's a way to test our king without using an army. One simple assassin. What will the king of Lynk do?"

This entire time, Sabine had assumed her sister's assassination had to do with preventing a wedding, not testing a king.

"It's a possibility," Rainer said. "Since I'm young, people are probably wondering if I can maintain control over my army or not. I'm sure the neighboring kingdoms fear that someone from within could assassinate me. Then who would be in control, and would they follow the League's treaty? Plus, Princess Alina was killed under my roof—that shows I'm weak. Vulnerable. If I don't find the assassin and bring him to justice, I'll constantly be challenged from both home and abroad." He took hold of the stem of his goblet, twisting it.

"I have my men investigating," Anton assured him. "We'll find the assassin."

"Your men?" Sabine asked.

"I oversee intelligence."

She had no idea Anton handled the spies for the kingdom.

"Lottie, make sure you keep up with your training," Rainer said.

Lottie shoved some bread in her mouth. "No need to worry. I have great motivation to stay alive. I won't miss a session. What about Sabine?"

"Tomorrow before breakfast, Sabine and I will train together."

"When is Avoni due to arrive?" Axel asked.

"My guess is within the next fortnight. I'm hoping once they're here, we can gain their approval and move forward with the wedding as planned."

"No offense," Axel said, "but are we sure we want this wedding to happen?"

Sabine eyed him, wondering what he was getting at.

"Our people need Bakley's food," Rainer said. "I won't sacrifice my own people just to appease some League."

"Are you saying if they don't approve, you'll go against the League?" Anton asked. "As Lynk's representative, I need to know."

"I'll make that decision when the time comes," Rainer responded. "For now, we need to put all our focus on getting them to agree."

"Rainer," Anton said, his voice low. "You can't consider going to war."

"Every treaty eventually comes to an end. Now, I'd prefer to maintain peace. But I won't sacrifice my people to do it."

Anton nodded. "Duly noted."

"All of this talk about politics is giving me a headache," Lottie said.

"I think that's Sabine's special tea and not our stimulating conversation," Axel said. He lifted his goblet and saluted Sabine.

"Are we free to go?" Lottie asked.

"Yes," Rainer replied.

Lottie shoved her chair back and stood. "Now that my head has cleared, I'd like for Sabine to accompany me."

"Where to?" Axel asked.

"None of your business." Lottie headed toward the door. "Are you coming?" She glanced over her shoulder at Sabine.

Nodding, Sabine got up and hurried after her, assuming Lottie wanted to have some girl time. While Lottie could never take Alina's place, Sabine welcomed the friendship. Craved it even.

Out in the hallway, Lottie looped her arm through Sabine's, a wicked smile on her face. "Now it's time to make sure you actually drink and enjoy yourself. I watched you this afternoon. You didn't touch your tea."

The keen observation startled her. She hadn't thought anyone noticed. "Sure I did," Sabine lied as Lottie dragged her along the corridor.

"You may have touched it, but you didn't drink it." She eyed her sidelong. "Well played, by the way. I'm impressed."

The two of them traveled down several stairwells, the temperature dropping.

"Are we still in the palace?" Sabine asked. She thought there were only five levels, but they'd gone down more than that.

"Technically."

They descended another narrow stairwell and came to a door. Lottie knocked.

The top portion of the door slid open, and a man eyed them. "Just the two of you?"

"Now, Tim," Lottie said, her voice practically singing, "you know our future queen can't come in without a guard."

He grunted. "Fine. She can have one."

Lottie smiled and looked at Sabine. "Now it's time to have some real fun."

Chapter Fifteen

The man swung the door open, revealing a tavern. A group of three musicians played instruments off to the side while a dozen or so people danced. The fast, upbeat, lively music was unlike anything Sabine had heard before. On the other side, thirty or so tables filled the space, most occupied with patrons. Along the entire back wall, a bar spanned from one end to the other, every stool filled. The stone walls appeared to have been chiseled right out of the mountain.

"Are we below the palace?" Sabine asked as Lottie pulled her into the tavern.

"If you're asking if this is in the mountain, it is." Lottie patted Sabine's arm. "Don't tell me you've never been to a tavern before." She led the way to one of the open tables.

Sabine had been to a tavern or two, but always with her brothers, and only to the more reputable ones in which people of similar station frequented. Her father never would have permitted her to go to the local tavern where the townsfolk went. "Are we allowed to be here?" As she scanned the people's faces, noting most wore plain clothing, she figured these people were probably workers in the palace, not its noble inhabitants. She had no idea where the guard who'd followed her inside had gone.

Lottie rolled her eyes. "Why wouldn't we be allowed?"

"Do people from the royal family frequently consort with commoners?" she asked as the two of them each took a seat.

"Ah." Lottie folded her hands on the table and leaned forward toward Sabine. "Here, there are no titles. Everyone is equal. No questions asked."

Sabine had never heard of such a thing. However, she found the notion intriguing. Looking at those around them, no one seemed to be paying them any attention, as if the people didn't know that their princess and future queen were sitting amongst them.

Lottie waved a server over. "Two cups of your house ale."

The server nodded and left.

"I don't see any other noble people here," Sabine commented. Unless they were dressed as commoners, but she didn't think so. She and Lottie definitely stood out based on the coloring of their clothing.

"Their loss." Lottie shrugged.

"Do you come here often?"

"I do since I can't very well leave the palace grounds and go to a tavern in town."

"I'm surprised your brother allows this."

Lottie suddenly became very interested in a scratch on the table. "Well," she said, "when he ascended to the throne, he asked that I not come here any longer and I promised him I wouldn't."

Sabine scoffed at her. "Then why do you?"

"Because it's fun. Besides, nothing is going to happen." She leaned back in her chair. "Rainer used to come here all the time before my father died."

Sabine understood why the royal siblings would want to come here—the need to escape for a few hours.

"Oh look," Lottie said, gesturing across the room, "Markis is here." She smiled and waved at him.

Sabine peered across the room and saw Markis dressed in an outfit similar to everyone else in the tavern. It was nice to see him without his mask on. And now his eyes were glaring at her. Of course he'd be upset she was here.

The server returned, setting two mugs of ale on the table. Sabine knew better than to drink it without it having gone through a taster first. Lottie, however, took a long sip from hers, not seeming at all concerned about it being laced with poison.

Markis made his way over to Sabine. "What are you doing here?"

"I brought her," Lottie answered. "We're here to have some fun. You can join us."

Markis didn't look Lottie's way—he kept his focus on Sabine. "Do you have guards with you?"

She nodded. "Sit so you don't attract attention."

He plopped on the chair, running a hand over his face, revealing dark circles beneath his eyes.

A guy who looked about twenty-five came over and asked Lottie to dance. She joyfully agreed and jumped up to join him.

"I actually need to talk to you," he said, his voice low so no one nearby would overhear.

Sabine leaned toward him.

"I've been asking around," Markis mumbled.

"And?"

"All evidence points to a professional assassin from Carlon."

She nodded, trying to process the information.

"I also think someone in the palace hired him."

Shock filled Sabine, and her pulse quickened. "Why do you think that?" If it were someone in the palace, then Sabine was definitely in danger.

"A lot of people don't want a union between Bakley and Lynk."

"Including the people in Lynk?" She assumed everyone would welcome the union since it meant bringing large amounts of food to the people here in this kingdom. And then it dawned on her. "It has to be someone wealthy or powerful."

"Exactly. Someone who doesn't want the king to succeed. At least, that's what I think based upon my limited investigation."

It was more than Sabine had managed to come up with. "Which means I probably met the person the night I was introduced to the court." A shudder rippled through her at the thought of having danced with the man responsible for her sister's death.

"My guess is the assassin didn't even know who he was working for. He was paid handsomely and disappeared after. It was a job for him and nothing more."

"We have to find out who hired him." Which would be infinitely more difficult.

"Yes," Markis replied, looking at her with his brows raised. "And the person who hired the assassin is probably upset you took your sister's place."

"Do you think the person will hire the assassin again?"

Markis shrugged. "Who knows?" He leaned on his elbows, rubbing his forehead. "You will need to continue to be extra cautious."

Glancing around, Sabine said, "I should leave." There were so many people in the tavern that any one of them could easily pull out a knife and stab her.

"You're probably safer here with the servants than you are walking the halls in the palace with the nobles around."

She grabbed her drink but then set it down, remembering it hadn't been through a food taster. "Why are you here?" she asked, wanting him to distract her before she panicked.

"I'm here for the gossip. Servants see and hear things others do not. Then when they have a little alcohol in their system, they tend to talk. If I can piece together enough conversations, enough clues from the servants, I can come up with a list of possible suspects. At least, that's what I'm hoping for." Markis yawned.

"When's the last time you slept?"

He shrugged. "There's work to be done."

"You need to take care of yourself, so you don't get yourself killed trying to protect me."

"Yes, Mother."

She wanted to slap him for the jab. "Are your knuckles scabbed from fighting Rainer?" She hoped nothing else had happened that she didn't know about. Either way, she wanted to hear what he had to say about it.

"They are. He insisted on testing my fighting abilities. If I didn't pass his test, I would've had to return to Bakley."

"It's a good thing you passed."

The corner of his mouth turned up in a half smile. "Was there any doubt I wouldn't't?" He stood and tapped the table. "I'm not going to learn anything from sitting here."

"Go," she said, shooing him away.

The music reverberated through the room, the sound loud and pulsing through Sabine's body. She really wanted to dance—it looked like so much fun. Couples spun about, stomped their feet, and clapped to the music. People were laughing and cheering. Lottie was out there in the middle of it all, looking like she belonged. As if she'd done this a hundred times before. Maybe she had.

"How come you're not out there dancing?" an older man at the table to Sabine's left asked.

"I don't want to dance," she lied. As the future queen of these people, dancing with other men while engaged to the king didn't feel right to her. It might be what people here in Lynk did, but it wasn't something done where she came from. She couldn't forego her morals just because the people here had different ones. And yes, she sounded so much like her mother it made her inwardly cringe.

"I'm not much of a dancer myself," the man said.

The last time Sabine danced with such joy it had been with her sister. Tears filled her eyes at the memory. Overwhelmed with emotion, she needed to leave before she broke down crying. She glanced around, looking for her guard who stood near the door, still wearing his mask, watching her. She waved him over. "I want to go."

He escorted her from the tavern. The rest of her guards stood waiting for her on the steps. She hoped Lottie wouldn't be upset she'd left her behind. She exited the stairwell and bumped into Axel.

"What are you doing here?" they each said at the exact same time.

Sabine took a step back, away from him.

"I came here in search of my sister," he said. "Did she drag you down there with her?" He pointed at the stairwell she'd just exited through.

"She did."

"I'm surprised you're leaving already. I thought that would have been something you enjoyed." He tilted his head to the side, eyeing her.

"How do you know it wasn't?"

"Because you seem...upset."

He didn't know her well enough to determine such things, and she didn't feel like standing in the corridor having a heartfelt conversation with him. It was late, she was tired, and something about tonight felt off. "I'm exhausted from the day." She bid him goodnight and hurried to her room.

After changing into her nightclothes, she heard the distinct patter of raindrops. She went over to the archway leading to her balcony. In the darkness, she could barely see the rain, but she could hear and smell it. It reminded her of home. A pain gripped her chest, and her eyes filled with tears. She missed her sister so much.

"I'm so sorry," she said out loud to the sky, as if Alina could hear her. Tears started to fall. She'd been so wrapped up in wanting to find the murderer and dealing with being in a foreign kingdom that she'd shoved all her emotions aside. Not facing the pain had been easier than dealing with it. Now, everything came flooding in and grief overwhelmed her.

Stepping out onto the balcony, she tipped her head back and let the rain bathe her face. She gripped the fabric near her chest, as if that would help stifle the hurt. Her sister should have married, had children, and lived a full life. Sabine shouldn't even be in Lynk. Everything was a disaster.

She stood there until there were no tears left to cry.

The next morning, Sabine awoke feeling exhausted instead of refreshed. Her sleep had been a mixture of nightmares about someone chasing after her, trying to kill her, intermixed with sweet memories of her and Alina playing together as children.

The sky remained gray, and soft rain continued to fall outside. It was the first gloomy day since she'd arrived, and she welcomed it. It matched her mood.

Someone knocked on her door, and she called for the person to come in.

Claire entered. "You're supposed to train with the king before breakfast," she said, cringing when she saw the state of Sabine. "He sent me to find out what is keeping you."

"It won't take me long to get ready." Sabine climbed out of bed, stripped her clothes off, and went to take a hot bath. The warm water enveloped her, waking her up, washing away the tears from last night. This was just what she needed before starting her day.

When Sabine got out, a simple shirt and pants had been laid out for her to put on. Claire was nowhere to be seen. After dressing, Sabine went over to the adjoining door and knocked.

A guard opened it, letting her in. "His Majesty is downstairs in the training room." He pointed to the open door next to the king's office.

Sabine headed that way and went down the stairwell. At the bottom, she found a large, empty room. One wall was open, showcasing a pool that extended from inside to outside. Where the wall should have been, water cascaded down into the pool. She remembered Rainer saying something about when it rained, the roof was slanted in such a way to allow the rain to slide down, forming a waterfall into the pool. Which meant the king's office was directly above this room.

"Oh good," Rainer said as he came out of a doorway in the wall to the right, "you're here. We can begin." He was dressed similarly as her with loose pants and a shirt.

At least he wasn't half naked like he'd been when fighting Markis. If he'd shown up without a shirt, she wouldn't have been able to be alone in the room with him. At least not until they were married. His presence was so overpowering.

"Do you have any formal training?" he asked, standing a few feet away from her.

"No. But my brothers have shown me a few things." Better to be as vague as possible.

"Do you know how to get out of a chokehold?" He stepped forward and gently took hold of her neck with his large, calloused hands.

For some reason, she hadn't expected him to jump right in. Taking a deep breath, she forced herself to focus and remember what Rolf had taught her. She slid her arms up, her hands going between his arms, and then pulled her arms outward, breaking his hold on her.

"Excellent. Then knee your attacker in the groin and run."
She nodded.

His eyes remained locked on hers, not once looking elsewhere. It was unnerving. He placed his hands on her shoulders, turning her body so her back was to him.

"If someone comes up behind you," he mumbled, close to her ear, sending a shiver down her spine, "what do you do?" He splayed his hand against her stomach, the heat of it penetrating through her shirt.

He was trying to rile her up, she was sure of it. Two could play that game. Gathering her courage, she leaned back into him and said, "Lean back and kiss him?" She lifted her chin, her lips hovering near his neck.

He sucked in his breath, clearly not expecting that to be her answer.

While he was distracted, she grabbed one of his fingers, pulling it back while simultaneously slamming her foot down on his. She easily moved away from him. Turning to face him, she patiently waited for his next challenge.

"Who taught you to fight?" he asked, folding his arms across his chest and studying her as if she were a puzzle he couldn't quite figure out how to put together.

The way in which he looked at her made her toes curl, and something deep inside of her yearned for more. She shoved her attraction toward this man aside, so she could keep her wits about her and not get lost in his eyes. "My brothers."

"What about weapons?"

"I know the basics of a dagger. That is all."

With his arms still folded, he lifted his right hand and rubbed his chin. "You definitely have some work to do. For now, I think it best if we focus on what to do during a physical attack. For example, if someone blocks the corridor or comes running at you with a sword."

Sabine thought that wise and welcomed the chance to physically train in how to defend herself since Rolf had only taught her the basics. A small part of her acknowledged that if someone poisoned her, there was little she could do. At least her mother had shown her the most commonly used poisons and how to recognize them. For now, she would learn everything she could about how to keep herself safe— even if that meant working with this devilishly handsome man before her.

The two of them spent the next hour going over various scenarios and how to quickly escape each one. Rainer kept things professional and didn't once try to be anything other than a teacher. He must have realized that she wasn't one to be trifled with.

When her stomach growled loud enough for him to hear, he chuckled. "Let's go eat. I'm starving."

Sabine followed Rainer out of the training room, up the staircase, and to the dining room where food had been spread out for them. She sat and began eating.

"I have two things for you," Rainer said around a bite of food.

She peered up at him, wondering what he could possibly

be referring to.

"First, a letter arrived from your father." He withdrew an envelope from under the platter on his left. He slid it across the table to her.

Sabine picked it up, examining it. Her father's seal was still attached, which meant Rainer hadn't read its contents. "Thank you." She set it aside, wanting to read it when she was alone so she could savor every moment.

"The, uh, second thing is a little unconventional." He pushed his chair back slightly and twisted toward her. "I thought it might be a good idea. I figured you could use the companionship since you're alone in a foreign kingdom, and it'll be good for security reasons."

"What are you talking about?" she asked.

He whistled, and a dog ran into the dining room, sitting beside Rainer. "This is for you. Her name is Harta, which means protector and defender."

The dog looked expectantly at Sabine.

She'd never had her very own dog before. In Bakley, dogs were used out in the fields for herding and things of that nature. They were rarely indoor companions. She eyed the adorable creature, trying not to fall in love. "May I?"

"Of course."

She slid off her chair and squatted before Harta. "Hello there."

Rainer said, "Release."

The dog immediately stood and began licking Sabine's face. She laughed, running her hands over the dog's short, brown hair.

"We train dogs to use for battle," he said. "I have a facility over in the training grounds."

Sabine remembered hearing the dogs and Lottie mentioning something about them.

"This one here has been trained to smell certain poisons.

She's also been taught a few other things I'll need to go over with you. For example, if you want her to chase someone, there's a command for that. If someone makes you uncomfortable, you give a command and she'll move in front of you and protect you. You can also have her bark on command to get a guard's attention."

Sabine kissed the dog's head then stood. "It seems you've thought of everything."

"Do you like it?"

"I love it."

The corners of his lips rose. "Good."

Chapter Sixteen

The dog, it seemed, did not care for Markis. As Sabine walked across the courtyard with Lady Karmen, Harta trotted along behind them, occasionally growling at Markis if he got too close. Every time it happened, Markis mumbled under his breath and backed up a few steps. Sabine tried not to chuckle. Unfortunately, it seemed Harta didn't care for paper either. Sabine still couldn't believe the dog had grabbed her father's letter from her hand and ate it. She'd have to write to her father later today, letting him know what happened. She hoped there wasn't anything important in the letter.

"I'm glad you seem to have settled in at the palace," Karmen said.

Sabine had been around long enough to know when something was worded one way but meant something else. Karmen wouldn't have used the word *seem* otherwise. "While it is quite different here in Lynk, I am finding the change refreshing." She forced a smile on her face, waiting for Karmen's response. After all, she'd invited the woman to walk with her for a reason.

"I've been worried with so many of the women being upset with your arrival." Karmen patted Sabine's arm.

While she assumed there would be those vying for power upset by the union, they should have gotten over it already. Especially since Sabine was the second one betrothed to Rainer. Regardless, she played along. "What women are upset?" This was the information she wanted anyway—to see if there were any suspects that hadn't been considered.

"The usual ones," Karmen said, waving her hand. "Those who want power, money, or feel they're entitled to sit on a throne. I'm sure you have the same in Bakley."

Sabine nodded. "We do. And I feel bad that King Rainer is marrying a foreigner. I am sure many here in Lynk would prefer him to marry one of their own. However, this marriage is mutually beneficial for both kingdoms." She needed that message spread through court. "My kingdom will be sending a substantial amount of grain to Lynk. That will feed hundreds, if not thousands, of people." She realized she had no idea how much her father had agreed to send.

"I understand," Karmen replied. "But I think the concern is that you won't produce a child soon enough. Many believe the king shouldn't have wasted so much time finding a woman to marry. If he doesn't have an heir by the time he turns twenty-five, he forfeits the throne. Naturally, people are worried."

In other words, they were questioning the king's judgment. Sabine glanced back, making sure Harta still followed close behind. She was such a good doggie.

Karmen waved to someone walking on the second level's outdoor hallway to the right. "Being seen with you is going to get everyone talking," she purred. "I love it."

Sabine chuckled. "I can understand why a lot of people are worried since the king and I don't have a lot of room for error." Alina's death had set the king's timetable back quite a bit. "And I'm sure many wouldn't be happy with Axel as the king." She laughed at the mere idea.

"Oh no, he wouldn't be king."

"Anton then?" Sabine assumed the twin born first would be next in line for the throne. However, she couldn't imagine Anton leading a kingdom either. Rainer was the best choice out of the three brothers.

"You don't know?" Karmen asked, pulling Sabine to a stop, and glancing around.

"Know what?"

Karmen leaned in closer and whispered, "The twins can't take the throne. They're not the previous king's legitimate heirs."

The news surprised Sabine. "I hadn't realized the king had two children out of wedlock."

"He didn't." Karmen's eyes widened, as if willing Sabine to understand what she wasn't saying.

It dawned on her. "The *queen* cheated on the king?" She didn't think the previous king—or any king for that matter—would have allowed something like that to stand. "And he raised the twins as his own? I don't understand." She'd never heard of something so preposterous.

"Rumor is that the king was gone when the queen became pregnant. Some say it was a palace sentry. When the king returned and found out, he had all her guards killed."

Sabine recalled Rainer's unwarranted reaction to Markis and her soldiers from back home. Given what his father had gone through, she understood him better now.

"The king loved his wife, so he let her live. After she gave birth, he claimed the twins as his own. However, he made it clear they would never sit on the throne. Which means Lottie is the next in line."

No wonder Rainer had insisted Sabine never be alone in a room with a man—even his own brothers. Sabine resumed walking. "Is this common knowledge here at court?"

"Yes, though no one talks about it publicly."

That had to be why Axel didn't take things seriously. He had nothing to lose from his questionable behavior. "There is still so much I need to learn about Lynk."

"You have plenty of time." Karmen patted Sabine's arm. "And there are several of us here rooting for you. We'll help you in any way we can."

Sabine had to force the smile on her face to appear genuine and not triumphant. "Thank you," she said as demurely as possible.

Since the king declared his marriage to Sabine would take place shortly after the Avoni delegation arrived—which would be any day now—Sabine made her way to the seamstress's room for a fitting. She couldn't help but inwardly cringe at what she expected the wedding dress to look like. It wouldn't be the beautiful style she'd envisioned growing up, but rather, something in the Lynk fashion.

When she arrived, her guards waited outside while she went in, Harta at her side.

"Good morning, Princess Sabine," the seamstress, Lillian, cooed. "I can't wait to see how the dress fits you." The seamstress was an elderly woman, maybe around sixty, with a short stature and a slightly plump shape, her dark hair piled on top of her head in a messy bun.

"Where is it?" she asked, not seeing anything resembling a wedding dress amidst the yards of fabrics and cutting tables spread throughout the room.

"It's hidden from prying eyes." She wiggled her eyebrows. "Now go in there," she pointed to a door on the right.

"Remove your clothes. I'll get your dress and help you put it on. Leave the door open so I know when you're ready." She eyed the dog. "Is that creature going in there with you?"

"She goes everywhere I do." Sabine rubbed Harta's head.

"Just make sure it doesn't rub against my fabrics. I don't need dog hair everywhere." She shooed Sabine toward the dressing room.

Once inside, Sabine sat on one of the small stools and removed her shoes. Harta diligently sat at the threshold, guarding her. As she slid her shirt up over her head, she thought she heard a whistle but couldn't be certain. When she tossed the shirt onto the stool, she noticed her dog wasn't sitting in the doorway any longer.

"Harta?" she called out. The dog didn't appear.

Ever since she'd received the dog, it hadn't left her side. It slept at the foot of her bed, sat next to the bath, and even laid next to her chair while she ate. Afraid something had happened to Harta, Sabine tiptoed over to the doorway, peering out into the main portion of the seamstress's room. Neither the dog nor Lillian were anywhere to be seen.

"Lillian?" Sabine called out. The woman didn't reply.

She turned back into the dressing room to get her shirt so she could find out what was going on. Something hit Sabine from behind. She screamed as she fell forward, landing with her chin, hands, and knees smacking the floor. She felt a large man on top of her, so she twisted, trying to get away from him. A loud sound reverberated through the room, as if a door had burst open. Growling and barking filled the space. Relief filled Sabine since Harta was here. She screamed again, trying to alert her guards out in the hallway.

Footsteps pounded and shouts rang out.

The person on top of her cursed, kicking at her dog.

The thought of him hurting Harta infuriated her, so she reached for the nearby stool. Her fingers wrapped around one of the legs and she swung it, hitting the man's head with a satisfying crack. His dagger fell from his hand, clinking to the floor.

Without thinking, Sabine reached for the weapon. She grabbed it, holding it the way Rolf had shown her, and she rammed it down into the man, stabbing his leg. Sabine kept her fingers gripped on the hilt, not wanting her attacker to get ahold of it. He grunted and rolled off her.

She scooted as far away from the man as she could. He reached down, holding his thigh as blood soaked through his pants and dripped onto the floor.

Shouts rang from somewhere in the palace. The man cursed and got to his feet, limping as he ran from the dressing room holding his thigh. Harta barked as she chased after him, snapping at his leg.

Sabine grabbed her shirt and put it on. She sat in the corner of the room, blood on her hands. Her entire body shook, and her heart thudded in her chest as she tried to process all that had just happened.

Soldiers rushed into the dressing area, surrounding her.

More shouting came from outside the room.

One of her guards squatted before her. "Princess Sabine, are you injured?"

"I don't think so." Other than being sore, she didn't notice anything broken or bleeding.

He helped her stand and then escorted her from the seamstress's room.

Out in the hallway, her guards formed a tight, protective circle around her as they made their way through the palace. Sabine wondered what had taken them so long to enter and help her. How had the attacker gotten in there in the first place? He could have come in through a window. But when he left, he used the door. She knew that because Harta had followed him. Presumably, the attacker would have run right into them on his way out, which meant they had to have him in custody. That had to be why it took them so long to get to her.

Panic seized her as she looked around. "Where's Harta?" she demanded.

"Once you're in a secure location, I will personally find Harta for you," the guard to her right said. "I'm sure she's around here looking for you."

"She didn't get injured when she went after my attacker, did she?"

"I can't be sure, princess," he answered.

Her stomach rolled with nausea. She prayed nothing had happened to her dog. Even though her bedchamber always had guards, those accompanying her insisted on searching it before allowing her to enter. Once it was deemed safe, she went in and headed to her bathing room, scrubbing the blood from her hands. Once clean, she wandered back into the main portion of her room, not knowing what to do.

She'd been attacked. Someone had tried to kill her. Her head started to pound.

"Where is she?" Rainer said as he burst into the room, his eyes wild.

"Your Majesty, she is all right," one of the guards answered.

Rainer ran to Sabine, taking her face in his hands. "Are you okay?"

She nodded, unable to speak, still too shocked at the events that had just transpired.

He turned and spoke with her guards, demanding to know the details of the attack.

"We have men in pursuit of him now. As soon as we have him in custody, we'll let you know."

Shock filled her that her attacker hadn't been caught yet. She didn't know how he could have escaped when her guards were right outside in the hallway. It didn't make any sense. Especially since the man was injured.

"Good. Double the number of guards on the princess."

"Where's Harta?" she asked, realizing her dog hadn't returned. Maybe she was still pursuing the assassin.

"And someone find out where Harta is," Rainer snapped. He came over and took Sabine's hand, leading her to the bed where they both sat. "Are you sure you're not injured?"

"I'm fine. Everything just happened so quickly." She didn't understand how her attacker had gotten into the room in the first place. It seemed strange that her guards had been right out in the hallway but didn't enter the room until a minute or two into the attack. Even her dog had disappeared right before it took place. She rubbed her forehead, not liking the implications and fearful voicing them would make them real. Regardless, the king needed to know.

She reached out, taking his hand. "You've asked your soldiers what happened, but you haven't asked me for my account."

"You're correct. Forgive me."

She quickly told him all that had happened, not leaving out a single detail.

A soldier entered the room, breathing heavily. "The suspect got away, but I managed to retrieve this." He motioned behind him.

Harta trotted into the room, her tail wagging. She jumped onto the bed, licking Sabine.

Rainer stood. "Got away? How is that possible?" His low voice sent shards of ice through Sabine. It was the voice of a man she never wanted to cross.

The soldier seemed to shrink into himself. "He just... disappeared. He didn't use any of the palace exits."

"Perhaps he scaled the exterior palace walls. Did you look

out of the windows to see?" Rainer asked, folding his arms and standing a solid foot above the man.

"No. He went around a corner, out of sight. When those following rounded the corner, he was nowhere to be seen. The corridor had no windows. We're doing a palace-wide sweep right now. We're checking all the rooms."

Rainer took a deep breath, his shoulders rising and falling. "Fine. Get back to searching. I want everyone on duty looking for the assassin."

The word *assassin* sent a shiver through her. She'd just survived an assassination attempt. That could have been the man who killed Alina.

Rainer ordered all the soldiers out of the room, so it was just the two of them. He went over to the door leading to his rooms, opened it, and called for his steward. They spoke so quietly Sabine couldn't hear a word they said.

When Gunther closed the door, Rainer turned to her. "I'm getting you out of here."

"Where are we going?"

He came over and placed his lips next to her ear and whispered, "My private vacation home. Pack a few things. We're leaving in fifteen minutes. I don't want anyone to know what we're doing or where we're going."

"Excellent idea."

After gathering a few necessities and shoving everything into a leather bag, Sabine went to the royal suite to find Rainer, Harta trotting alongside her. She found Rainer exiting his bedchamber, a small sword strapped to his waist. The weapon made his alluring demeanor look intimidating.

"You're not taking a bag?" she asked.

"I keep the home supplied with everything I need. That

way I don't have to worry about taking things back and forth." He held his hand out to her. "Let's be on our way."

She hesitated a moment. He was taking her to his private residence. Alone. She clasped onto his warm hand. He led the way down the stairwell to the training room. He put his finger to his lips, and she nodded. On the far wall, there were two doors. He took the one on the right. They traveled along a plain corridor. At the end, they came to a large bathing room, the floor made from squared tiles. Rainer released her hand and knelt in the corner, lifting four of the tiles and setting them aside. He waved her over.

Peering down, she saw a narrow stairwell leading into what had to be the mountain.

Rainer motioned for the dog to go first. Harta carefully descended the steps. Sabine went next, holding onto the railing as she went down. Rainer gathered the tiles and then entered the stairwell, putting the tiles back in place above him, sending them into complete darkness.

Without talking, Sabine continued descending what felt like hundreds of steps. Finally, her feet came across a flat surface. Harta brushed up beside her. A moment later, a light blossomed.

Rainer stood beside her with a torch in hand. "There are a series of stairwells we must navigate," he whispered. "The lower we go, the more they tend to get wet and slippery, so be careful."

She nodded, thankful for the light.

"I'll lead the way." He turned and descended another flight of stairs.

Sabine went next, the dog close behind her. At least this time she could see the steps. The lower they went, the eerier it became. The silence turned so deafening that she could almost feel the stone walls around her whispering as a dull sound rang in her ears.

Her legs began to burn, so she stopped to rest for a few minutes. She hadn't thought going down stairs would be so difficult. Rainer glanced back and saw her standing there. Wordlessly, he stopped and waited, holding the torch, and rubbing the dog's head. When Sabine's legs recovered, they continued their descent. Clinging to the railing, she felt steadier on her feet.

Just when she thought things were getting better, her hand slid over something wet. She shivered, assuming it was water from the walls, and wiped her hand on her pants. The steps got slicker, water now visible in a few places. The echo of a dripping sound pinged every few seconds.

After what felt like forever—it had to be a solid hour—the floor leveled out. Sabine's legs shook. She feared she wouldn't be able to walk tomorrow. Rainer led the way down a tunnel that reminded her of the lava tube she'd traveled through when she first came to Lynk.

"We're almost out," Rainer said. A minute later, he stopped before a warped wooden door. "Strange," he mumbled. "The lock isn't on. I can't even remember the last time I came through here." He opened the door and bright light inundated them.

Squinting, Sabine stepped outside into a jungle, breathing in the fresh air. Bright green trees with vines hanging from them and exotic shrubs with leaves larger than her head clung to the land in every direction.

Rainer secured the door. "Follow me." He led the way, though no trail was visible.

They traveled for about a mile. The farther they went, the thinner the vegetation became until they exited the jungle and came to a steep cliff, the ocean below a brilliant blue that smashed against the rocky shoreline.

"Now what?" she asked, her legs shaking. She wiped the sweat from her forehead.

"One last descent."

"I'm not climbing down that." And there was no way the dog could make her way down either.

He chuckled. "Not that way." He nodded his head away from the cliff. "Over here." He led her twenty feet to a group of black rocks. He moved one of them aside, revealing a hole in the ground. "It's sloped," he assured her.

At this point, as long as she didn't encounter any more steps, she could handle it. She climbed inside and made her way down the muddy path to a cave filled with water. A boat was tied to a wooden post.

Rainer stepped around her, getting into the boat.

"Where are we taking that?" Because if he intended on rowing that small thing out into the ocean, there's no way they'd survive. Not with the cliff and rocks right there. The waves and current would be too ferocious.

"Have a little faith," he chided her. "The cave won't dump us in a dangerous part. I promise." He whistled, and Harta jumped into the boat.

Sabine remembered hearing a whistle right before being attacked. That's when Harta had left her. She'd mentioned it to Rainer, but he hadn't said anything. There had to be a way to find out who knew the dog's commands. She shivered, realizing it had to be someone inside the palace.

"Give me your hand," Rainer said, extending his arm to help her.

Reaching out, she noticed her palm had smeared blood on it.

"Did you hurt yourself during the altercation?" Rainer asked, noticing the blood.

"Not that I'm aware of." She glanced down at her pants and saw blood there as well. "When we came down the steps, I felt something on the railing. I remember thinking it was just water, so I rubbed my palm on my pants."

His eyes widened. "Get in," he said, a hint of urgency to his voice.

She did as he said, fearful the assassin would jump out at them at any moment.

He quickly untied the boat and grabbed hold of the oars, allowing the boat to drift deeper into the dark cave. The only way Rainer could steer the boat was by allowing the current to push them along. He had to use the oars to make sure they didn't hit the sides of the cave. After about five minutes, the air around them started to lighten.

"There's an alcove ahead," Rainer explained. "It's protected so the boat can easily exit there." He started rowing. Bright light inundated them as they left the cave and went into the open water.

"Are we going there?" She pointed to the island not far away. It looked as if it had grown straight up out of the water since cliffs surrounded it.

"We are."

"Where will we be docking?" There was probably another set of stairs leading to the top. The thought of climbing more steps made her want to cry.

"There's a cave on the west side." He steered them that way, the open water becoming choppy from the wind.

Sabine held onto the sides tightly while Harta laid on the bottom, whining.

They neared the rocky island. The strong current made it difficult for Rainer to do much. However, the water shoved them right toward the cave and the boat flew inside, hitting something with a jolt.

"It's just a landing area," he said as he jumped out and grabbed the front of the boat, yanking it half out of the water.

Sabine and Harta got out.

After Rainer tied the boat up, he went over to the side and opened a wooden door built right into the rocks.

Sabine groaned, not having the strength to climb up a single set of stairs.

"Hurry up," Rainer said, waving her over to the door.

The thought of an assassin pursuing them was enough for her to run through the doorway. She skidded to a halt, finding herself in a three-foot by three-foot room. Rainer and the dog joined her, making the space a tight fit.

A cord hung next to the door. Rainer grabbed it, pulling it hard three times before closing the door. The three of them stood there in darkness.

"Is something supposed to happen?" she whispered, reaching down and petting Harta's head.

"Yes. In a minute. Have a little patience."

She shook her head and sighed. A low rumbling noise echoed through the room and then it began shaking. It felt as if they were moving. "What's happening?"

"This is a box on pulleys."

"Pulleys?" she said, stunned. "As in ropes are lifting this room?"

"Yes."

Which meant she wouldn't have to climb any more stairs, but her life hung on a couple of ropes that she sincerely hoped were strong enough to withstand the weight.

"Just try not to move too much," Rainer said. "It's hard to turn the lever at the top if the weight shifts or is unbalanced."

"Someone is up there?" She thought they were going to be alone on the island.

"I have three trusted servants that live here full time. When I decided we were coming, my steward raised a yellow flag. The staff here knows that when it's raised, I'm on my way."

The small room abruptly came to a halt. The door opened and Sabine stepped out and onto the top of the island, gawking at the amazing sight before her. Straight ahead was the mainland she'd been on. She squinted, trying to see the palace, but it was too far away. The wind whipped around her body, tossing her hair about. She breathed in the salty air, loving the freshness of it.

"Come inside," Rainer said.

She was standing on a breezeway that connected the box she'd just been in to the castle. "It looks as if the place was birthed from the island itself."

"It sort of was," he replied. "The island is so hard and rocky, most of the exterior was carved right from it."

They had to be forty feet above the ocean. She followed Rainer, Harta right behind her.

Inside the castle, chilly air engulfed her along with dim lighting. This place didn't have the open airy archways that the palace did. While there were several windows along the left wall, they were all closed. The ceiling and walls were made from stone, and the floor was dark wood. "It's vastly different from the palace." And it seemed much older.

"I don't ever entertain here," he said as he strode across the room. Large sofas and low tables were situated on an area rug. An empty hearth was to the right. "Lance," Rainer called out. "We're inside."

A shuffling noise came from a nearby room, and then an elderly man entered. "Your Majesty," the man smiled as he bowed. "It's good to see you. I finished setting up your bedchamber and was just about to light the fire in here."

"It's good to see you as well," Rainer said. "Where's Mika?"

"Mika is closing off the lift. He'll remain there, guarding the entrance." The elderly man peered over at Sabine, his brows raising.

"Lance, this is my fiancée, Princess Sabine Ludwig."

"My future queen." Lance bowed.

"It's a pleasure to meet you."

"Lance runs this place for me," Rainer explained. "He lives here along with his wife, Cassie, and their son, Mika."

Lance reached forward, so Sabine removed her bag, handing it to him.

"I'll have Cassie prepare you something to eat," Lance said. "I'll also make sure that the dog is taken care of. Will you be needing anything else?"

Rainer glanced at Sabine, eyeing her. "We may be needing a marriage binder."

"Whatever for?" she asked.

Rainer rubbed his face. "I think I know who hired the assassin," he said, suddenly looking anywhere but at her. "If we're married and you're queen, it changes things. To stop this person, we need to marry."

"Now?" Shock filled her and her brain tried processing what he was saying.

"Unless you want to give the assassin another go?"

"No, I'd rather not." She'd already agreed to marry him. It made no difference if it was today or three weeks from now.

"Then we need to marry and crown you as soon as possible."

"What about the Avoni delegation? And the approval from the League?"

His shoulders rose and fell. "Those are two complications I'll deal with once I know you're safe."

Chapter Seventeen

The second the door to her bedchamber closed, Sabine sank to the floor. The weight of the day crashed upon her. Someone had tried killing her. If it hadn't been for her brother teaching her a few basic things, she'd be dead right now.

Memories of Alina inundated her. She squeezed her eyes shut, trying to keep the images at bay to no avail. The two of them playing hide and seek as children, running through the fields chasing their brothers, riding horses together, fighting over a piece of jewelry. And then, the last time they danced together. Her dear, sweet sister. Murdered.

Sabine glanced down at her hand—the one that had dried blood on it. It had to be the blood of her attacker, possibly the man who'd killed Alina. She scrambled to her feet and ran over to the wash basin, scrubbing her hands clean.

In her current state, she didn't want to be alone and was thankful she at least had Harta at her side. Every noise she heard startled her. She feared the assassin would burst out from behind a closet door or from under the bed to try to stab her.

She splashed water on her face, trying to calm herself. Her stomach ached with nausea. She needed to pull it together. She was going to be the queen of Lynk. It would not be good for anyone—even servants—to see her behaving so emotionally.

Going over to the large canopy bed that reminded her of her mother's bed, she climbed on top of it, Harta jumping up alongside her. She curled on her side, her arms around the dog, and fell fast asleep.

She awoke, the room bathed in warm sunlight from the windows. She sat up, and Harta licked her face. Her stomach growled and she realized she didn't have anything to eat last night before she fell asleep.

"We need to go and find food," she mumbled to Harta, scratching her side.

A soft knock resounded on her door. She called out for the person to enter.

An older woman came in carrying a tray of food, a smile on her face.

"You must be Cassie, Lance's wife," Sabine said.

"Yes, Your Highness." She curtseyed. "I brought you something to eat. I will take the dog downstairs with me where we have something prepared for her as well."

Sabine slid out of bed and stretched. "Thank you."

"While I'm here, I am to get the late queen's wedding dress from the closet for you."

"I'm going to wear King Rainer's mother's wedding dress?"

"Yes. She kept it here and I think it'll fit you beautifully." She went inside the dressing closet and emerged a few moments later with an off-white dress.

Sabine went over and took it, surprised by its weight. She'd assumed she would be wearing a flimsy dress based on the current Lynk fashion. However, if this one was made before Rainer was born, then that would explain why it was so different. This dress had an abundance of pearls covering the bodice and there were yards and yards of fabric for the skirt. "It's beautiful." She went over to the canopy bed, laying the dress on it. It was even more gorgeous when spread out on the bed. "Why is it here and not at the palace?"

"Her Majesty preferred this castle over the one on the mainland. She always felt like she was on display there. Here, she could be herself."

The admission surprised Sabine. Not only did it shock her that Cassie was being so forthright, but she found this tidbit about the queen to be interesting. She wondered at which residence the queen spent most of her time. "This castle does feel a bit like home," she admitted. "I like it here." There was something comforting about the stone walls and floors, the dark wooden beams along the ceilings, the curtains hanging at each window, and the thick glass windows. Sabine blinked, realizing it reminded her of her own home in Bakley.

The woman smiled. "I'm glad. The king wishes for you to get ready. He left early this morning. Oh, I almost forgot." She reached into her pocket and withdrew a letter. "He left this for you." She handed it to Sabine.

Opening the letter, she quickly read it. Rainer said he'd gone to the mainland to get a marriage binder and would be back later this afternoon for the wedding. An odd sensation jolted through her. It seemed she was getting married today.

"Would you like my help dressing?" Cassie asked.

"I'd like to get ready on my own. If I need help, I'll come and find you." In other words, she needed to be alone to process everything.

Cassie smiled. "Of course, Your Highness." She bowed

and left with Harta trotting along after her.

Knowing this was the queen's room and that the queen preferred this residence to the palace, Sabine observed the quarters with fresh eyes. This room was the opposite of the one in the palace. It had a canopy bed with heavy blankets. Even the rugs covering the floors contained deep, rich colors instead of whites and tans. She meandered over to the dressing closet, wondering what all it contained. Opening the door, she found it filled with dresses. She went into the room, browsing the large selection of clothing; some in Lynk fashion, others more along the lines of what people in Bakley typically wore.

She turned to exit the room when her shoulder bumped one of the dresses, making a clinking sound. Curious as to what made the noise, she shook the dress and felt it hitting something. Reaching back behind the dress, her fingers came across a sword. She wondered why it was there and who it belonged to. She shoved several of the dresses aside, trying to see the weapon. With the clothing out of the way, the back wall was on full display revealing daggers, knives, arrows, and swords.

While Sabine knew nothing about the previous queen, these weapons indicated that she had to have some sort of formal training. However, she couldn't fathom why the weapons were hidden unless at one point in time, being a female warrior had been frowned upon. After sliding the clothing back into place, concealing the weapons once again, she exited the dressing closet.

She eyed the wedding dress on the bed. It seemed odd to be doing something so momentous, so important, in a private ceremony. An odd sensation filled her—a feeling of wrongness. Shaking her head, she shoved her feelings aside. Instead of fretting over getting married, she should be getting ready.

Her bag had been placed on the chair across the room. Someone must have put it there last night after she'd fallen asleep. Going over to it, she picked it up and looked around the room. Spotting an armoire, she went over and opened the doors. She began taking her stuff out of her bag and putting her things inside the armoire. She pulled out Harta's ball, placing it on the bottom shelf. The ball rolled out, bouncing on the floor. She lifted her foot to stop it but ended up kicking the ball under the armoire instead. Groaning with frustration, she knelt on the floor and reached underneath, grabbing the ball. As she pulled it out, she noticed something hanging from beneath the armoire.

Reaching up, her fingers came across something hard. She yanked it out, discovering a book of some sort. She stood and opened it, the cover creaking as she did so. Inside, the pages were covered with elegant writing that had faded from time. Each page had a day and date. This wasn't a book but a personal journal. Sabine traced her fingers over the pages, reading them. The person talked about being a mother and her concerns for her child that had yet to be born. This had to belong to the late queen. As to why it had been hidden under the armoire, she didn't know. She flipped through it, wanting to learn more about Rainer's family.

The late queen talked about the violence of the military and her husband's obsession with training the people of Lynk to be bloodthirsty soldiers. Then the queen went on to mention the king's valet and how she'd begun talking to him. Sabine turned a few pages, discovering the queen's relationship with the valet turned into something more than mere friendship. She wondered if he was the father of the twins.

Flipping through a few more pages, Sabine noticed the writing became jolted and several words were smeared, as if from drops of water or tears. The queen expressed her hatred for her husband who'd killed his valet when he learned of her affair. She'd yet to tell him she was pregnant. The queen went on to write that her husband had begun hitting her where no one could see.

Sabine turned a few more pages. The queen wrote about having weapons hidden around her room in case the king tried to do something more sinister. The thought of being in such a relationship seemed unimaginable. She turned to the last page that had writing on it.

I fear the king intends to kill me. He's managed to keep the secret of the twins from most at the palace though there are some who suspect. Now that I am pregnant with the king's second child, he's stopped hurting me. But I see the look in his eyes and the twitch of his hands as if he wants to strangle me. It's as if he's just waiting for me to deliver this baby. Once I do, he'll have two heirs and no need for me. I pray he doesn't hurt the twins. I've put certain precautions in place to try to ensure their safety. I hope it works. I fear that once this child is born, my life will be over.

Sabine closed the journal, holding it against her chest. She'd had no idea the previous king had been a violent man. When she had more time, she wanted to read through the entire journal. There was a reason the late queen wrote it. Sabine decided to put it back where she'd found it. Since it had remained hidden there for so long, it seemed the best place.

Once the journal was safely concealed, she stood and closed the armoire's doors.

As she headed over to the bed, she looked at the wedding dress differently. Instead of beautiful fabric, she saw a cage. Once Sabine married, her life would be in Rainer's hands. While she didn't think he was a violent man like his father, she didn't know him that well. When she saw him fight in the training facility, another side of him had been unleashed. As to how much he was able to keep that side of him under control, she didn't know.

She rubbed her eyes. Yesterday, when he admitted to having an idea of who hired the assassin, she assumed he'd tell her when the two of them were alone. However, she'd gone to her room and had fallen asleep before they had the chance to talk. Once he returned with the marriage binder, he'd probably share his suspicions with her.

Now that she was awake and thinking clearly, something occurred to her—if the assassin had exited the palace the same way they had, how did he know about the escape route? And if he was savvy enough to know that, he probably knew about this castle as well. That knowledge could only be known by a select few people. Which meant she needed a list of everyone who knew about it.

Several times she'd wondered if Heather could be responsible for hiring the assassin. Since Heather had an intimate relationship with Rainer, she could know about the escape route. If so, she could have told the assassin. If Rainer suspected Heather, that could be why he hadn't shared it with Sabine. The mounting stress made her feel ill.

Glancing back at the armoire, she considered the journal. It could hold a clue to this family or her sister's murder. She rushed over and reached underneath, grabbed it, and shoved it into her bag. Needing to conceal it, she took her clothing back out of the armoire and put it on top of the journal. Her hands shook. She wasn't stealing, so she didn't know why it felt as if she were doing something wrong. The late queen had written her story and left it here for someone to find. That someone happened to be Sabine.

She hurried to the bed, quickly undressed, and pulled the wedding gown on. After tying it as best she could, she went over to the free-standing mirror in the corner of the room to look at herself. The cream-colored dress hugged Sabine's curves, but it wasn't too tight. The previous queen must have been rather petite. She turned, liking how the dress swayed around her legs as she moved. The long sleeves stopped just shy of her shoulders, cutting straight across her chest.

She decided to pull her hair back into a simple braid, draping it over her right shoulder. At the vanity table, she found some dusting powder and she applied it to her face. Satisfied with her appearance, she went into the queen's dressing closet, peering at the hidden weapons. One of the sheathes had a strap attached. Lifting her dress, she exposed her thigh. She took a knife, slid it in the sheath, and then adjusted the strap around her leg, finding that it fit nice and snug just above her knee. She stood, testing it out. While she could feel the weapon and wouldn't forget it was there, it didn't bother her.

Taking a deep breath, she went over to the door and exited the bedchamber. She wandered through the old castle, wanting to get a better sense of the man who owned it. The place had an odd feeling to it, one she couldn't pinpoint but felt, nonetheless. The wind howled outside, rattling some of the windows.

"There you are, Your Highness," Lance said from behind Sabine, making her jump. "King Rainer has returned and is requesting your presence in the sitting room."

"Please show me the way," she said, forcing a smile on her face. Not having her dog at her side made her uneasy as well. She hadn't realized how used to having Harta with her she'd become.

The elderly man nodded before leading her through the castle, up two flights of stairs, and to a door. "He's in there." Lance bowed then left.

Sabine opened the door and stepped into a grand sitting room. A fire roared in the hearth on one wall, bookshelves lined another wall, and several portraits were hung on the third. The fourth wall contained several windows revealing the turbulent ocean below.

"Princess Sabine," Rainer said. "You look stunning."

"Thank you." Sabine walked over to the windows, gazing outside. He looked the same as before and had not prepared for the wedding ceremony. Perhaps something had changed. "Is the plan for us to still marry today?" she asked, not looking his way and instead, trying to see his image reflected in the glass.

He folded his hands behind his back. "Yes. But I want to speak with you first on a delicate matter."

At that, she turned around, leaning on the window ledge. This had to be about the assassin.

His dark eyes bore into hers. "I don't know how to ask this of you, so I'm just going to come out and say it." He took a step closer. "After we marry in private, you will be crowned queen of Lynk." He took another step closer. "However, I do not wish for my subjects to know we are married or that you're their queen until we have a public ceremony."

She raised a single eyebrow. "When will the public ceremony be held?"

"After the Avoni delegation arrives."

"And the reason for this?" It had to have something to do with the assassin, and she wanted to know what he wasn't telling her.

He took another step closer to her, now standing only a foot away. His eyes remained focused on hers, as if searching for something.

She refused to flinch or even blink.

After an uncomfortable minute of silence, he finally said, "I believe someone in my inner circle is trying to kill you to prevent me from maintaining my position as king. To keep you safe, we will marry, securing my position." His voice was soft, louder than a whisper but not loud enough to carry outside the room.

An answer that only led her to more questions. And he hadn't explained why the need for secrecy or who he specifically suspected. If he wanted to convince her to go through with this, then he needed to tell her everything. She folded her arms and tilted her head, looking up at him, waiting for him to explain.

He sighed and then came to lean against the window ledge beside her. "After we legally marry and you're crowned," he said, "I will inform my inner circle of your status. The marriage binder will have a record of our marriage and your coronation thus ensuring you remain safe."

When she realized he wouldn't elaborate, she asked, "Why keep it from the kingdom?" She wanted to know who in his inner circle wanted him to lose his crown. At first, she'd suspected Heather of hiring the assassin. However, she didn't think Heather wanted to hurt Rainer or take the throne from him. It had to be someone else then. Maybe he didn't specifically know who it was. If he did, he would have already arrested the person.

"We must keep it a secret because we still don't have permission. That's why we're waiting for the Avoni delegation. If they give their approval, we can legally marry without any repercussions from the other kingdoms."

"What you're saying is that we are going to marry to secure your throne and keep me alive."

"Yes."

"But it will be done in secret."

"Yes."

"And once the League approves, then we can publicly marry?"

"Yes."

She pushed away from the window ledge and started walking around the room, thinking. "What if we don't get their approval? Then what?"

He stood. "Let's hope it doesn't come to that."

"Because if it does?"

"We'll most likely be facing a war."

Dread filled her. All she'd wanted to do was take her sister's place to save her kingdom. And now Rainer was talking about a possible war. "What will happen to Bakley?"

"It will fall under my protection. I promise."

"You swear?" she asked, wanting to be clear.

"Yes. You have my word."

She nodded. "Very well." She'd marry in private so long as she had his reassurance that Bakley would be safe.

"I must go and prepare myself for our wedding." He bowed and then left the room.

Staring at the door he'd just exited through, she contemplated who Rainer considered to be in his inner circle and why one of his close confidants wouldn't want him on the throne. Once he knew for certain who either killed her sister or hired the assassin to do so, Rainer had better have it in him to bring the person to justice. Otherwise, Sabine would do it for him.

A man in his late forties entered the room donning a long robe the color of sapphire. "Princess Sabine," he said by way of greeting.

"I suppose you're the marriage binder?" she asked.

"I am. My name is Herold." He withdrew a golden crown from beneath his robe. "And I'm here to make you a queen."

Sabine stood in the antechamber to the throne room where she'd been instructed to wait until the doors opened. So much had happened leading her to this moment. She couldn't believe she was about to be married and crowned queen—especially in secret. Her hands shook from a combination of excitement and fright.

The doors swung open revealing a thirty-foot marble pathway leading to a raised dais where two golden high-backed chairs were perched atop the platform, Rainer standing between them. When he saw Sabine, he descended the steps and moved to the side, waiting for her to join him. He wore ivory pants and a form fitting shirt buttoned up to his neck. A gold crown adorned with emeralds, rubies, and pearls sat on his head, making his eyes appear brighter than usual.

If Sabine had to describe the king in one word, it would be breathtaking. She'd never seen such a handsome man before.

As she slowly made her way down the aisle, she noticed Lance and Cassie at the front of the room, off to the right. Their son Mika wasn't there. To the left were Prince Anton and Markis, surprising Sabine with their presence. They must have come with Rainer and the marriage binder to serve as court witnesses to the ceremony. When she reached Rainer, they remained side-by-side and faced the dais.

The marriage binder moved to stand on the steps before them. "First, we will unite these two in marriage," he declared.

Rainer knelt on the first step, so Sabine followed suit and did the same.

"The marriage alliance between Lynk and Bakley is noted in the contract behind me." Herold gestured to a table containing two writing quills and several sheets of paper. "Before me I have King Rainer Manfred and Princess Sabine Ludwig. Once the marriage is consummated, nothing shall tear it apart." He lifted his staff, gently tapping Rainer's right shoulder and then Sabine's. "Repeat after me." He then went on to say a series of declarations about duty, respect, and honoring one's partner. Once each had repeated the necessary decrees, the binder ordered them to stand.

The two of them stood and faced one another. Rainer pulled two rings out of his pocket. Sabine lifted the larger of the two, then slid it on Rainer's ring finger. He then took the last one and put it on her finger.

"King Rainer, you may kiss your bride."

Sabine peered up into Rainer's eyes and found him watching her intently. She had no idea what he was thinking or whether he even wanted to kiss her. The thought of what lay ahead tonight on their wedding night lingered in the back of her mind, but she refused to acknowledge or think about it right now. She had to make it through this kiss first.

Rainer slowly lowered his head, his lips hovering near the corner of hers for a moment before he gently pressed his lips to hers in what she considered to be a warm, chaste kiss. And then it was over.

"Even if Princess Sabine is childless, this marriage cannot be dissolved," Herold announced. "After tonight, it is done." He moved to the side.

Rainer and Sabine joined hands and walked up the steps to the top of the dais.

"The marriage ceremony has concluded."

The irony of the situation was that Sabine had never

expected to be a queen or hold such an important position; however, she did imagine marrying in a small, intimate ceremony such as this one. Though, she had pictured marrying someone she loved. While she could see loving Rainer one day, she didn't know him well enough to care for him that way. Strange that the marriage ceremony was complete in a matter of minutes.

"Now for the coronation. King Rainer, you will take your place on the throne chair," Herold stated. He stood off to the side still holding his staff, reminding Sabine of a sheep herder.

She turned and faced those present in the small throne room.

"Repeat after me," Herold said, his voice echoing in the room. "I, state your name, do hereby swear to uphold the laws of the great kingdom of Lynk."

"I, Sabine Manfred, do hereby swear to uphold the laws of the great kingdom of Lynk." It felt strange and foreign to say her new name. It didn't feel or seem right.

"I will govern, guide, and help my people in any way I can."

Sabine repeated the words, meaning each one she said.

"I will do what is in my kingdom's best interest, I will keep our kingdom strong, and I will not yield to other kingdoms."

Sabine said the words though she found them a little odd. She'd expected there to be something more along the lines of protecting her people and not so much about keeping Lynk strong. Then again, this kingdom was known for being focused on its military.

Herold came and stood before her. He tapped each of her shoulders with his staff while chanting a few words she didn't understand. Then he took a step back, turned, and went over to the table where a box had been set on the shelf beneath it. After putting his staff aside, he pulled out the box, opened it, and then lifted the crown out that he'd shown her before. The crown matched Rainer's, but it was slightly more petite and delicate. He carried it as if it were the most precious thing in the world, setting it atop Sabine's head.

After adjusting it to be sure it wouldn't topple off her head, she moved to the throne chair, taking her seat beside her husband.

"I now pronounce you Queen Sabine Manfred of Lynk."

Hearing her new name and title sent a jolt through her. Within the last thirty minutes, she went from a princess of Bakley to not only the queen of Lynk but now a wife. She belonged to the Manfred family and not the Ludwig family. An unexpected sadness filled her.

Those present lined up before her. One by one, they knelt, took her hand, and swore their fealty to her. Even Markis came up to her, swearing his allegiance to her new title. Once they finished, Rainer stood, holding his hand out to Sabine. She stood and slid her hand into his. They went over to the table, each of them signing the contract for their marriage.

Sabine traced her finger over her father's signature. She missed him dearly.

"Now that the ceremony has concluded," Rainer announced to those in the room, "we must consummate our marriage."

A chill slid over Sabine's skin. She thought she'd have more time before she had to face Rainer in the bedroom. While her mother had told her what would transpire and she'd seen enough animals procreate, the thought of being with Rainer both thrilled and terrified her.

The doors burst open, and Mika ran in. He stopped half-way down the aisle and bent over, panting. "The delegation from Avoni just arrived."

Chapter Eighteen

Rainer cursed. "Is the delegation at the palace?"

"No," Mika answered as he straightened. "They've just started disembarking from their boat."

"We have to beat them to the palace." Rainer placed his large hand on the small of Sabine's back, ushering her down the aisle and toward the doors.

Sabine assumed he was leading her to the bedchamber to consummate their marriage as quickly as possible so they could return to the palace. She tried to mentally prepare herself for what was to come.

Out in the hallway, he said, "I need to find Harta." He dropped his hand from her back as he strode down the corridor at a brisk pace.

Not knowing what else to do, Sabine hurried after him, trying to keep up.

"Change and get your things. Meet me in the sitting room in ten minutes." He glanced behind her. "Markis, don't leave her side. Anton, you're with me."

She hadn't even realized they were being followed.

Instead of responding, she turned down the hallway to the left, going to the queen's bedchamber. *Her* bedchamber. If they were trying to beat the delegation to the palace, that gave her some time before she had to worry about sharing Rainer's bed. She took a deep breath, trying to relax.

"What are you doing here?" Sabine asked Markis.

"I came to serve as a witness for the kingdom of Bakley."

That made sense. She lowered her voice and said, "I didn't realize you'd swear fealty to me under Lynk's banner."

He shrugged. "I've already sworn to protect you. It makes no difference to me whether it's on Lynk or Bakley's behalf. Besides, I wanted to make the declaration in front of King Rainer. I'm hoping he'll keep me on a bit longer."

She remembered Rainer saying something about only letting Markis stay in Lynk until the marriage took place. "While I want you to remain until the assassin has been brought to justice, I know you have family back home."

They arrived at the bedchamber. "I won't leave until you're ready for me to. My loyalty is to you."

Reaching out, she took his hand and squeezed it. "Thank you."

In her room, she quickly changed while Markis waited out in the hallway. Not wanting to leave the crown, she shoved it in the bottom of her bag, next to the journal, and then made sure it was covered with her clothing. After cinching the bag closed, she exited the room.

"Are you ready?" Markis asked.

"I need you to do something for me," she whispered so her voice wouldn't carry down the corridors. While she didn't see anyone else close by, she couldn't risk anyone overhearing.

"Anything."

She handed him her bag. "Keep hold of this. See that it makes it to my chambers in the palace but put it somewhere out of sight." She didn't want Rainer to see it and be tempted to look through it and discover the hidden journal. Since she could be spending the night with him, she needed to take precautions.

He took the bag, slinging the strap over his shoulder. "Is everything all right?"

She nodded.

"When I heard there was an attempt on your life, I ran to see you. But you were already on your way to this location. I didn't know where you were being taken or with whom. No one could tell me anything."

Not once had she thought about letting Markis know what was going on. She'd done whatever Rainer said without question. "We'll have to make sure to rectify that situation for future incidents."

They began walking. "Let's hope there aren't any more. I've had about all the excitement I can handle for a lifetime."

She laughed. "I agree."

"I need to ask you something," he said, lowering his voice to a whisper. "Do you know why you married today in a private ceremony instead of as planned in public?"

She quickly reiterated everything Rainer had told her.

Markis ran a hand over his face. "So the king knows who hired an assassin to kill you." It wasn't a question.

"He thinks he knows. And he obviously feels I'm still in danger which is why we married. The person has to be in the palace if he's in Rainer's inner circle."

"I agree," Markis mumbled. "I need to think all this through and come up with a plan. He really didn't tell you who he suspects?"

"Not yet. I plan to ask him though."

"I doubt he'll tell you."

"Why is that?" she asked.

"Because if he planned to tell you, he would have done it by now."

They entered the sitting room where Rainer stood with Anton and Harta on either side of him. He'd changed into black pants and a dark blue tunic.

"Move your wedding ring to your right hand," Rainer commanded.

She did as he instructed, noticing her hands were shaking.

"Make sure you keep that ring on at all times. It's the queen's ring and will give you the protection you need."

Sabine nodded, wanting to demand to know who it would give her protection from. However, she knew she couldn't ask with others around. If she had any hope of getting him to talk to her, to confide in and trust her, she needed to have that conversation with him in private.

The marriage binder joined them.

"Now that we're all here, let's go." Rainer led the way to the small room that lowered down to the boat. They split into two groups to make it easier on Mika since he had to manually control the pulleys.

Rainer went first with Anton and Herold.

Sabine went second with Markis and Harta.

As they were being lowered, Markis leaned closer to her. "Something feels off."

"I agree." Ever since Rainer had brought her here, she'd had a feeling of wrongness that she couldn't explain or pinpoint.

"Do you have a weapon on you?"

"Yes." She'd left the knife strapped to her thigh.

"Good. Be extra vigilant."

When Sabine exited the room, she noticed this boat was much larger than the one they'd rowed over on.

Rainer sat at the front with Anton, Sabine and Harta took the middle bench, while Markis and Herold sat at the other end. The men all took up an oar. Rainer gave instructions and the four of them started rowing the boat out of the cave.

"You're sure it's safe for me to return?" Sabine asked no one in particular. Somehow the ring on her finger didn't feel like enough to protect her from a skilled killer.

"We have no choice," Rainer answered. "If we're not there to greet the delegation, it'll be seen as an affront. I can't afford to make such a blunder so early on after taking up the crown."

The boat made its way across the open ocean and toward the shore. The sun was high above them, indicating early afternoon. The wind rushed around them, making Sabine cold, so she cuddled into Harta, trying to steal the dog's warmth.

The boat headed directly toward the rocky shore.

"I don't see the cave," Sabine commented. And she had no desire to smash against the rocks, especially since she wasn't the best at swimming.

"That's because we're not going there," Rainer replied. "This boat is too big for the cave so we're landing at a beach just past those rocks."

The men steered the boat to the right, parallel to the shore for a few minutes, and then they turned, heading around a peak and into a small alcove that hadn't been visible before. Sabine wouldn't call where they were headed a beach since there was barely any sand, but at least it didn't have nearly as many rocks to smash against.

When the boat hit bottom, Rainer and Anton jumped out, pulling the boat up onto land where everyone else disembarked.

Rainer led them to a dirt path that cut up the side of the cliff.

Since the path was so narrow, Sabine kept a hand on the rocky side to maintain her sense of balance. Thankfully it wasn't as bad as she'd imagined, and they reached the top within a few minutes. Straight ahead, she spotted the palace perched atop the mountain. They just had to cross the valley to get there. Harta barked and ran ahead, apparently knowing where to go. The dog really was well trained.

The five of them traveled at a brisk pace and after fifteen minutes, reached the base of the mountain next to the palace. Instead of heading up as she thought they'd do, Rainer led them over to a grouping of trees where a wooden home was situated, Harta sitting at the front step.

Rainer knocked on the door.

Sabine didn't see any lights or smoke, so she didn't think anyone was home.

Rainer knocked again.

A minute later, a small, hunched over woman answered. "Your Majesty," she said, her voice raspy. "The donkeys are in the back." She bowed her head and closed the door.

Sabine had so many questions but knew now was not the time to voice any of them. At the back of the house, she didn't see any donkeys or even a pen for them. Rainer went another twenty feet or so to where the jungle started. He ducked between two bushes and disappeared. A moment later he returned, leading two donkeys. He handed one to Sabine and he took the other.

"There are three more in there," Rainer pointed behind him. "The two of us are going to set out." He mounted the donkey and Sabine did the same. "There's a fairly wide path," he assured her. "It's different from the one you took on your journey here. We're taking that to the top. Let the donkey lead; it knows the way and has done this hundreds of times."

Too terrified to argue, Sabine grabbed the animal's harness and held on for dear life as the donkeys made their way to the base of the cliff.

Harta trotted behind them like a good doggie. Markis,

Anton, and Herold joined them a few minutes later. The five of them gradually made their way up the side of the cliff, each on a donkey. Sabine assumed they were on the quickest route since they were trying to beat the Avoni delegation to the palace. As to which way the delegation would be going, she had no idea.

As Rainer told her it would be, the path they traveled on was fairly wide—at least ten feet. Regardless, the donkeys hugged the side closest to the cliff. This had to be the route people took when bringing supplies up the mountain since it was large enough to accommodate a wagon.

At the top, they left the donkeys in a pen near another wooden house. Then the five of them hurried through the town, taking side streets as they made their way to the palace. When they reached the end of the main road, a loud groan shuddered as both sides of the bridge lowered. They hurried across it, the wind starting to pick up.

Safely on the other side, a handful of soldiers surrounded the five of them as they made their way into the palace. Rainer started barking out orders, none of which Sabine paid any attention to.

"Princess," Markis said, the word sounding clipped. "This way."

Sabine followed him and two additional soldiers as they escorted her to her bedchamber, Harta diligently at her side. When she opened her door, she found Claire coming out of the closet holding an outfit.

"What happened to your hair?" Claire asked, her eyes wide.

Sabine reached up, feeling it sticking out in several different directions. "I suppose I should comb it out." It had been quite windy when they rowed across the ocean.

"Dunk yourself in the bathtub. When you're done, I'll run some oil through your hair to detangle it."

Sabine gladly peeled her clothes off and climbed into the warm bath. While under the water, she unbraided her hair. When she got out, she sat at her vanity table while Claire put the oil in her hair and easily combed through it.

"King Rainer wants you dressed and ready to greet the delegation as soon as possible," Claire said, pointing to the bed. "Put that on."

Sabine stood and slid the blue dress on, assuming she'd be matching Rainer. As far as outfits went, this was one of the prettier ones she'd worn in Lynk. The silky fabric attached around her neck and then hung straight down to the floor, flowing loosely around her. Claire came over and attached a braided belt, cinching it around her waist.

"My shoulders and arms feel oddly exposed," Sabine said. "Should I wear a bracelet?"

"No," Claire said. "I like the coloring of your skin against the dress. The contrast is beautiful. Jewelry will only take away from the elegance of it."

"Very well. And my hair?"

"Let's leave it down," Claire said as she took a step back, examining Sabine. "It's hot enough that it'll dry quickly."

Someone knocked on the door.

"The delegation must have arrived," Claire said. "Your guards will escort you to the room you'll receive them in. Good luck."

"Thank you." Sabine kissed the top of Harta's head before leaving the room. Since no one was supposed to know she'd married the king, she wondered if she'd have to share his bed tonight. Their marriage wouldn't be official until they consummated it, so Rainer would probably want to do so. Other than the guard at the door leading to the royal suite, the only other person she'd ever seen in there was Gunther—and even he had to sleep at night. If they dismissed Gunther and the guard, then no one would know. However, that could be a problem in and of itself as someone needed to verify the deed was done. Sabine decided she'd worry about it later. Right now, she needed to focus on the delegation and ensuring she and Rainer received approval to marry.

After her guards formed a tight circle around her, they led the way to a small room downstairs that she'd never been in before. Rainer and his three siblings stood inside, waiting for her.

Rainer instructed her guards to wait outside.

The second the door clicked shut, Lottie said, "My brother told us something extraordinary." She came and stood before Sabine, folding her arms across her chest. "He said he went and married you in a private ceremony." She lifted her eyebrows, awaiting confirmation.

Sabine didn't respond since she didn't know what Rainer had told them.

Lottie reached forward and took hold of Sabine's hands, examining them until she spotted the queen's ring. "It's true." Her voice held a hint of shock to it. She released Sabine and turned toward her brother. "How dare you get married and not have me there to see it." She whacked Rainer's shoulder.

"Anton was there," he said, as if that explained everything.

Lottie rolled her eyes. "And Anton won't tell me a single thing about it. At least Axel would give me details if you'd allowed him to be present."

Rainer, wearing the same shade of blue as Sabine, moved to stand beside her. He wore the traditional loose fitted pants and long-sleeved jacket unbuttoned up the front, leaving his toned chest on full display. Tonight, she'd probably be running her hands over that bare chest. Her face warmed just thinking about it.

Axel chuckled, shaking his head, but he didn't say

anything as he slid his hands in his pockets and turned away from them just as the door swung open.

"It's time," Rainer mumbled.

Sabine heard the royal family being announced.

Lottie went first, followed by the twins.

"We'll go together," Rainer said as he placed his hand on the small of her back, ushering her toward the door.

It would have been nice if he'd told her what to expect and if there were any Lynk customs she should be aware of. However, she'd been to a hundred of these in Bakley, so she held her head high as she glided into a large wall-less room unlike anything Sabine had ever seen before. A dozen or so pillars supported the domed-shaped ceiling. The only wall was a small section around the door that they'd just walked through. The sun began to set, lighting the space in a soft orange, making the mountains in the distance appear as if they were glowing. On each pillar in the room, an oil lamp burned. Hanging from the ceiling, hundreds of candles twinkled like stars.

"Are you okay?" Rainer whispered in her ear.

"This is beautiful," she replied. Like something out of a fairytale.

"There's so much of Lynk you haven't seen," he said, smiling down at her. "I hope to take you on a tour once things have settled down."

"I'd like that." Then she could meet the commoners and understand their needs better, see the land, and gain a new perspective of Lynk.

They joined the three siblings, Anton and Axel on one side, Lottie on the other. The five of them stood on a low platform, facing the crowd that had gathered.

Rainer welcomed the Avoni delegation before thanking his subjects for coming to greet their esteemed guests.

Sabine tuned him out and began surveying those before

her. Hundreds of people were in attendance—probably every single person staying at the palace had shown up. A group of about two dozen stood at the front of the crowd, directly in her line of sight, wearing dark clothing covering every part of their bodies except for their faces. They even wore gloves. They must be the Avoni delegation. Given the warm air and the fact that this room was open, these people had to be hot. Granted, what they wore would keep them warm in a boat out on the open ocean.

Most of the people in the delegation were men; she only spotted two women. Like the men, the women wore pants. The Avoni people all had paler skin. Several had lighter hair as well. One even had dark red hair with freckles on his skin.

"Again, the kingdom of Lynk welcomes you," Rainer's voice boomed.

One of the Avoni men stepped forward. "Thank you, King Rainer." He bowed. "I would like to request a meeting tomorrow with you and your intended to discuss some pertinent matters."

"My steward will arrange everything," Rainer responded. And with that, he headed back to the door through which he'd entered the room.

Sabine took off after him while the princes and princess followed her. She thought there would have been more to the welcoming than that.

Alone in the antechamber with the door closed, Rainer said, "Was the League member with them?"

"Yes," Anton replied. "And he didn't look happy. He kept glaring at Sabine."

Rainer rubbed his face. "That's to be expected."

"They're not going to allow you and Sabine to marry."

"Which is why we already have," Rainer snapped.

Sabine thought they'd married to keep her alive since the assassin was in Rainer's inner circle.

"Is it worth going to war over?" Anton asked. "Because that's the direction this is headed with you not heeding their concerns."

Axel chuckled. "We all told you this was a bad idea."

Rainer stormed from the room.

"I don't understand," Sabine said.

"Of course you don't," Axel responded. "You're not supposed to." With that, he winked and left the room.

Sabine huffed before turning to face Anton, hoping he'd explain the situation to her.

"My first loyalty is to the League," he muttered before leaving the room as well.

"That was entertaining," Lottie said, crossing her arms. "My brothers can be a bit dramatic if you ask me. Want to go to the tavern for a drink?"

Sabine blinked. "No." She did not care for a drink. She needed to figure out how to ensure her marriage didn't fall apart so she could secure troops to send to Bakley.

She left the room and her guards immediately surrounded her, escorting her back to her bedchamber. When she arrived, she found a letter from her mother sitting on her desk. She immediately broke the seal, reading its contents. Her mother had written using an old code she'd learned as a child, so it took her a few moments to decipher the message.

When she finished, she set the letter aside, an uneasy feeling taking hold. Her mother urged her to use caution saying Rolf had discovered conflicting evidence and he believed games were afoot. Her mother also said she feared for Sabine's life and questioned if they'd agreed to her marrying too hastily.

Sabine rubbed her temple. It was a little late to second-guess the marriage now that the contract had already been signed and the ceremony had taken place. If Rolf had discovered something important, her mother should have told her what it was. Since Sabine was alone in a foreign kingdom, keeping information from her could be detrimental. Making decisions not knowing everything could mean the difference between saving her kingdom or dooming it.

It felt as if the walls of her room began closing in on her, suffocating her. Rushing out onto the balcony, she sucked in the fresh air, trying to calm down. Standing at the railing, she reveled in the feel of the wind against her skin as it tossed her hair about. The wind felt uncontrolled—like her life. She'd mistakenly believed she could come here, find her sister's murderer, and save her kingdom. What a naive fool she'd been.

"What are you doing out there?" Claire asked.

Sabine jumped. She hadn't heard anyone enter her room. "I'm just getting some fresh air."

"I feel a storm coming. You should come inside so you don't catch a cold."

Sabine headed back into her bedchamber. "I can get myself ready for bed." She felt like being alone.

"The king asked me to remain with you this evening." Claire went into the dressing closet to get Sabine's nightdress.

Sabine pursed her lips. "Very well." She quickly removed her clothing. If Claire was with her this evening, then that meant the king wouldn't be visiting her bed to consummate the marriage—which was just fine by her.

After dressing, she climbed into bed. Harta jumped up, curling into a ball next to Sabine.

Claire snuffed out the candles, then sat in a chair near the door.

"Tell me," Sabine whispered, "why are you really here?"

"The king wants someone inside your bedchamber to ensure your safety," Claire revealed.

"Are you trained to handle an intruder?"

"In a way." Claire sighed.

"I don't understand."

"I'm here to get in his way so you can escape."

"Even if it means your death?" Sabine asked.

"Yes."

Silence hung in the air. Sabine didn't know what to say to that.

A thought occurred to her. Maybe it was because of her mother's letter, but it was there, nonetheless. "Claire, can I ask you something?"

"Of course."

"Why is Lynk in need of food?"

"Everyone needs food," she said as if talking to a child.

"No. Why do you need Bakley's grain? Do you not have farmers?" On her way here, she hadn't seen any large fields for planting and the land seemed mostly inhospitable. Regardless, they'd been managing to provide food for their people for centuries so something must have changed.

"I'm not well versed in politics, Your Highness."

Sabine's heart pounded at Claire's use of her title, making her wonder if she was lying or hiding something. She'd have to investigate this issue in more detail when she had the chance.

Claire settled on the chair a few feet away.

Sabine wished Markis could be in the room instead of Claire. His strong presence would make her feel safer. Besides, Markis could fight and protect Sabine without having to sacrifice himself to do so. However, Rainer would never concede to a male guard being in her room.

At least she had Harta with her. Rolling onto her side, she wrapped her arm around the dog, thankful for its warmth and protection.

The wind blew into her room, sending a chill over it. She could feel the storm coming, too.

Sabine entered the royal dining hall for breakfast and found not only the entire royal family in attendance but the Avoni delegation as well. Like last night, the Avoni people wore clothing covering almost every inch of skin except for their faces. It appeared the material was mostly leather and consisted of entirely dark colors. Dressed like that, they had to be hot in this humid climate.

Once Sabine took her seat, the food was brought in, and people began eating. Conversations picked up between various individuals. Since no one seemed to pay her any heed, she relaxed, thankful she could just sit there and eat, not having to worry about paying attention since everyone seemed to be doing their own thing.

Last night, she hadn't slept well. The wind had been howling and every little noise made her jump. She kept imagining her door opening and the assassin creeping into her room to hold her mouth open and pour poison into her body, killing her. All the while Harta and Claire slept peacefully, with no idea of what was really happening.

"It looks like rain, does it not, Princess Sabine?" the Avoni man sitting to her left said.

Dark clouds filled the sky, concealing the sun. "It does." She took a bite of her toast, hoping he wouldn't ask her anything else. It was too early, and she didn't feel fully awake. She rubbed her temples, wishing Harta was by her side instead of being forced to wait out in the hallway for her.

"We arrived just in time," the man said. "Sailing over rough waters isn't fun."

"No, I imagine it wouldn't be. However, I've never been on a ship before." She'd been on small boats, but never a large one like the one they must have sailed on.

"Do you find Lynk vastly different from Bakley?" he asked, not formally introducing himself or offering his name.

"I do." This was why she usually had breakfast in her bedchamber—it was more peaceful and quieter there. She wasn't much of a morning person, and she hated making meaningless chit chat.

"Why did you decide to take your sister's place?" the Avoni man asked. He took a bite of food, waiting for her answer.

He was testing her. Perhaps this man was part of the League and would decide her fate. If she wanted to save her kingdom, she had to convince him her marriage was vital to the success of Bakley. "I did it to help my people. Isn't that what a dedicated princess does?" She twisted to face him.

"How is marrying the king of Lynk helping your kingdom?" He also turned to face her.

"Lynk needs food. Bakley can provide that to them, so people don't starve. In Bakley's border towns, children are being stolen. Since we have no army, we can't save our people. King Rainer will send some soldiers to assist our kingdom."

The man's eyes narrowed. "Is that what you've been told?"

Chapter Nineteen

"I know for a fact that if our marriage doesn't happen, there will be war across all our lands," Sabine said, choosing her words carefully. "Carlon will invade Bakley, fighting will break out, people will die, and Bakley will cease to exist. People in Lynk will begin to starve. Desperate people do desperate things. We are in a position to help people, are we not? It is my duty to protect those who need protection. I hope that fully answers your question as to why I'm here." So much tension filled the room that Sabine could feel it tingling her skin. "Now tell me, why is Avoni here?"

The man took a drink of his milk, stalling. "We're here to hash out a few things with King Rainer," he said. "Like you, our intentions are honorable."

"Excellent. Then our kingdoms and people can benefit."

"King Rainer," one of the other men from the delegation said, "I'd like to have that meeting with you and the princess after breakfast."

Sabine took a deep breath, thankful the conversation was shifting away from her.

"How about we let the princess prepare for her wedding while I meet with you," Rainer said. "After all, she is young and naive. There's nothing she can contribute."

His words stung. Sabine realized she must have said something Rainer didn't agree with. Peering over at him, he wasn't even looking her way. She glanced at Axel who was diligently using his fork to move the food around on his plate, not looking at anyone, with a small smile on his lips. If she didn't know better, she'd say he was on the verge of laughter.

"Very well," the man said.

For the remainder of breakfast, Sabine simply sat there, not paying attention to the conversations going on around her. Instead, she kept trying to figure out what she'd said that had upset Rainer. The other possibility could be that he didn't want her in the meeting because there was something he didn't want her to know. Either case was not acceptable.

She feared that once she was announced as the official queen of Lynk, Rainer would still treat her the same way. He wouldn't confide in her or ask for her opinion. She had a feeling that it wouldn't change with time, that it was the way things were here in this kingdom. Not only that, but she was an outsider and didn't understand their ways. The entire time she'd been here, she'd been trying to wear Lynk clothing, do things the Lynk way, and assimilate as much as she could so she'd be accepted. Welcomed. Valued. However, she was coming to understand she was simply a means to an end. Rainer needed to secure his throne, and that could only be done by marrying and producing an heir. She was simply a horse to be bred, nothing more.

No longer hungry, she shoved her plate away. She sat there sipping her tea with honey, the only one drinking the warm beverage in a kingdom where tea wasn't a tradition like it was in Bakley. She didn't know who had asked for it to be brought to her every day, but it was. And she was the only one who had a cup of tea leaves in front of her.

It was time she started paying more attention to the things going on around her. She knew not all was as it seemed.

People started leaving one by one.

Sabine remained there, sipping her tea, a plan starting to form in her mind as she realized she wasn't there to take her sister's place any longer. She was there to ensure the survival of her family and of Bakley.

The last person stood to leave. He was one of the men from the delegation. On his way from the room, he paused next to Sabine. "Why did you really take your sister's place?" he asked, his voice a whisper in the empty room.

She knew this was a loaded question. That the words spoken meant more than what was asked on the surface. For some reason, her gut told her to answer as honestly as possible. She looked up at him and said, "To save the children in my kingdom." Even though Bakley was no longer her kingdom. Lynk was. Her loyalty remained with her native kingdom and always would.

The man's brows drew together. "From being kidnapped, is that correct?"

"Yes. I thought I already explained this about twenty minutes ago?" There had to be something he either didn't understand or agree with. For some reason, this issue felt vital. As if everything hung on what she said.

"Do you know who's kidnapping them?" he asked.

She tilted her head back farther so she could look directly into his clear eyes. "Carlon." She'd already said this, so why was he asking her again?

"What proof do you have that it is Carlon?"

"They've been raiding our towns. They attacked me on the way here."

"I thought you were power hungry," the Avoni man whispered. "I can see I was wrong. It's not you who we need to be concerning ourselves with. Like your sister, you're simply a victim." He bowed his head and then left the room.

Stunned, Sabine replayed the conversation over again in her head, considering everything the man had—and hadn't—said.

Rounding the corner, Sabine spotted Lottie and Anton in the courtyard on her right, their heads bent toward one other, talking quietly so their voices didn't carry. She decided to cut through the courtyard to see what the two of them were up to. When Anton noticed her approaching, he straightened and said something to Lottie, who turned to look at Sabine.

When Sabine reached the siblings, she patted the side of her leg once—the command for Harta to sit and wait. "Do I even want to know what the two of you are gossiping about?" she asked, trying to keep her voice light. The new plan she was putting into action involved keeping up the appearance that she was indeed young and naive. Unfortunately, it also included putting her sister's killer second on her list of things to do. Her priority was now figuring out why Rainer had chosen Alina to marry in the first place. Once she understood what was really going on, she suspected she'd find the assassin.

Lottie smiled. "We were just discussing the Avoni delegation and their awful clothing."

For the first time since meeting Lottie, Sabine realized she wasn't being sincere. Lottie's smile didn't reach her eyes, her words felt forced, and her fingers kept twitching as if nervous. That, coupled with the fact that this was Anton

Lottie was speaking to—not Axel—told Sabine that Lottie was lying.

Whatever it was the two of them were discussing, they didn't want Sabine to know. "I'll leave you alone then." Sabine forced her own smile on her lips. She was just about to pat the side of her leg twice—the command for Harta to follow her—when Lottie reached down, turning her hand out.

Harta went over to Lottie and sat in front of her, lifting her right paw.

"I didn't know she'd listen to you," Sabine said. "And Rainer didn't teach me that command."

"Oh," Lottie said, looking down at Harta. "I work with all the dogs. I help to train them. Sometimes I give a command without even realizing it."

"What command did you just do?" Sabine asked.

"That told Harta she did something well and I have a treat for her." She knelt. "I'm sorry, girl. I don't have anything to give you." She scratched behind the dog's ears and made kissing sounds. "This will have to be enough."

Sabine stood there watching the entire exchange as something clicked into place. She'd been here for weeks and had no idea who any of these siblings really were. They'd only shared with her what part of them they wanted her to see.

"Well then," Sabine said, still smiling though she wanted to scream, "I'll leave you two alone to continue your riveting conversation." Neither seemed to notice the sarcastic tone to her words. "Let's go, Harta." She strolled away, the dog and her guards trailing after her.

Back in the palace, she turned and asked one of her guards to take her to the library. Without questioning her desire to go there, they simply led the way. At the entrance, her guards remained out in the hallway with Harta.

Sabine stepped inside, surprised at how vastly different it

was from the library in her castle back home. As with everything in Lynk, it felt half-naked. Most of the bookshelves weren't even full. The walls were white instead of covered with dark wood. One of the walls was entirely covered with windows, allowing light to cascade through it. The light would ruin the books. At least there were windows instead of archways leading to the outside. Half the books were covered with dust since it seemed as if no one ever came in this room.

Sighing, she meandered through the library—if it could even be called that. She perused the shelves, looking for anything about the League of Rulers. She didn't know why, but she felt like a lot of what was going on had to do with this League. If she could learn more about it, it might help her understand everything. In one of the rows, she found books with maps, in another row she spotted several stories, and another row contained some books on Lynk's history. With her hands on her hips, she shook her head. This was not a proper library. There needed to be more books. Lots more books. What would she read in the winter? This was simply unacceptable.

"Princess Sabine," Markis's voice rang out.

"I'm over here," she said so he could easily find her.

Footsteps pounded and then he rounded the corner of the bookshelf. His eyes were tight and something about his energy felt off.

"Is there a problem?" she asked, reaching down to pat the dagger strapped to her thigh.

Skidding to a halt before her, he bowed. "Your Highness." He held a letter in his hand. "I need to speak with you," he whispered. Then loudly he said, "A letter arrived from your father. I knew you'd want to read it right away." He handed her the envelope.

She hoped his odd behavior didn't have to do with bad

news from Bakley. With shaking fingers, she opened the envelope and found a blank piece of paper. "What's going on?" she whispered, panic starting to build.

"Something's wrong," he replied. "Members from the Avoni delegation have been snooping around your hallway and they've been asking all sorts of questions about you."

Cold fear slithered over her skin. "What sorts of questions?"

Markis glanced over his shoulder to ensure they were still alone. "About the marriage contract, your relationship with the king, whether you came here of your own accord, about the children being kidnapped in Bakley." His shoulders rose and fell. "I know I don't have any evidence, but something's amiss. I'm certain of it."

"I agree with you." Like Markis, she didn't have anything concrete other than a feeling. "Out of curiosity, do you know if the king thinks anything is wrong?" He'd acted oddly at breakfast this morning.

"I have no idea. He doesn't confide in me."

"And you haven't heard anything among the other guards?"

He shook his head.

"What do you know about the League of Rulers?" she asked.

He glanced over his shoulder again. "Only that each kingdom has a single representative in the League."

She nodded. That made sense. "I've been trying to find a book on the League, but this library doesn't have a single one."

"Do you know who Lynk's representative is?" Markis raised his eyebrows, expecting her to draw her own conclusions.

"I do. Perhaps it's time for me to go and speak with my brother-in-law on the matter."

"I'm going to guess Anton?"

"Correct."

"I…" Markis trailed off.

"You what?"

"What do you know about Avoni?" he asked.

"Not much." Her studies rarely included the other kingdoms, especially since her parents saw no need since she was sixth in line for the throne. When she had children, she would make sure they learned all they could about the other kingdoms so none of them ended up in a situation like this one.

"They are quite wealthy," Markis said.

"What from?" She'd never heard of any special goods coming from that kingdom.

Markis shifted his weight. "They're known for being assassins."

A chill spread over her body. Why had nobody mentioned this vital piece of information before now? Rainer had said the assassin came from Carlon. If Avoni was known for having those skilled in the art of killing, and they had a lot of money from being employed, why would someone hire one from Carlon? It didn't make any sense.

"During the Great War, Avoni had quite the reputation. They came out unscathed not because of a large army, but because of a few assassins who were able to change the tide of events by murdering their enemies."

"Do you think they murdered Alina?" Rainer had told her it was someone from his inner circle who'd hired the assassin.

"I don't know. It seems the obvious choice, especially since poison was involved." He reached out, taking hold of her upper arms and looking her in the eyes. "I want you to be extra careful while they're here."

She nodded.

He released her. "I fear there is more going on than either of us is privy to. See if you can get the king to confide in you. Now that you're married, you may have more sway with him."

"I fear the king is immune to my charms." He was far older than her and vastly more experienced. It made all her dalliances seem like child's play.

"No one is immune to your charms."

"I'll talk to him." It was time she confronted Rainer about who he suspected.

"And don't trust anyone right now."

"I won't."

After Markis left, Sabine started pacing in the aisle, considering her next move.

A soft thump came from behind her, making her jump. "Hello?" she called out as she hurried along the aisle, eager to find a guard, when she bumped into someone.

Stumbling back, she looked up and found Axel with his hands out as if to grab and steady her.

"Are you going somewhere?" he asked, amusement coloring his words.

"You scared me." She placed her right hand over her chest, trying to steady her breathing.

"Seeing as how only the royal family is allowed in here, I don't know how I could have startled you. There are half a dozen guards at the entrance; I think you're safe." He stepped around her and reached up, plucking a book off the shelf.

"I didn't know you read."

He raised a single eyebrow. "I believe all members of a royal family can read—even the bastard ones."

Her careless words had upset him. She'd have to keep that in mind for the future. It was good information to know what set him off or could be used against him. "I'm sorry, I meant I didn't realize you *enjoyed* reading." She pointed to the book he'd tucked under his arm.

"Who says I enjoy it?"

She rolled her eyes and started to walk away.

Chuckling from behind her, he said, "I'm only teasing you. You don't have to run away."

She stopped and folded her arms, giving him a chance to honestly respond—if he could.

He sighed. "With the Avoni people lurking around the palace, I thought I'd hide in my chambers with a book." He came to her side. "What are you doing here, *Princess* Sabine?"

"The same as you," she lied. "I'm looking for a book to read as a distraction." Axel could have grabbed any book, but he'd taken the one he had for a reason. She tried to read its title, but he'd placed it in such a way she couldn't see the spine or its cover. The more she was around him, the more she understood how he always spoke in riddles. Said one thing but meant another. Not lying necessarily, but not being completely truthful either.

"Let's walk together." He tilted his head toward the doors.

As they exited the library, her guards formed a loose circle around them, giving them a bit of space for privacy. Sabine decided not to be the one to speak first. Axel had suggested this walk, so she needed to let him lead the conversation.

After they rounded a corner, he said, "Have you heard that my brother is throwing a masquerade for the Avoni delegation?"

"No." Rainer hadn't mentioned anything to her. "I've been told the wedding is scheduled to take place in a couple of days. Why bother with an elaborate party right before the wedding?" Especially one in which people wore masks. It didn't seem like something the Avoni people would enjoy. But maybe that was the point.

"I think Rainer wants to keep the Avonis occupied so they don't snoop around." He winked.

She wondered if he'd heard that the delegation had been asking questions about her. "When is the masquerade?"

"Tomorrow night. You'll need to get a mask before then."

The idea of having a special outfit made and wearing a mask sounded intriguing. Like something she would love to plan back home with Alina. Pain gripped her chest. She hated when she was reminded she no longer had a sister.

"Are you okay?" Axel asked.

"I'm fine." She forced a smile on her face. "What are you going to be?"

"I'm going to wear an eagle mask." He nudged her shoulder with his. "But don't tell anyone. It's supposed to be a surprise."

An interesting choice that revealed a little something about Axel. "I think maybe I'll wear a bird mask as well." Like a peacock or a dove. Since the ball was tomorrow, that didn't give her much time to put one together.

"Oh, I'm sure my brother will pick something out for you to wear. He always does."

She wanted to argue; however, he was right. Not only did Claire pick out what Sabine would wear each day, but Rainer had supplied her with her entire wardrobe. She'd assumed it was because she needed to look fashionable and that it wasn't a form of control as Axel had implied. Since Rainer was king, he had an image to protect. Sabine was part of that image.

"I'm this way." Axel pointed to the corridor on the right. "You might want to take a detour on the way back to your room. The northern courtyard seemed particularly crowded the last time I went by it. You should see what's going on." He started whistling as he strolled away.

Sabine watched him retreat for a minute before she

resumed walking. Even though she didn't want to simply because Axel had suggested it, she headed toward the courtyard, wondering if he was being helpful or sending her to the wolves. Really, she could see it going either way.

When she reached the courtyard, she spotted Lady Regina along with Duchess Cassandra, Lady Karmen, and Duchess Marin gathered before a rose bush as if discussing one of the flowers on it. Something was definitely up, and she needed to find out what. Sabine entered the courtyard and headed toward them, her soldiers taking up guard at the various entrances to give her some privacy.

"Princess Sabine," Cassandra said, her voice sounding pleasantly surprised to see her.

When Sabine stopped before them, the women all bowed.

"We're admiring the flowers," Karmen said. "Aren't they beautiful, especially at this time of year?" She looked up at the clouds and cringed.

"They are quite exquisite, though I haven't been in Lynk long enough to know if them being in bloom is unusual or not." She wondered if they were really talking about flowers. She kept her face neutral and waited for the women to get to the point. If there was one.

"The bright colors of the well-tended gardens here are a stark contrast to our visitors," Regina stated to no one in particular.

The women all nodded in agreement.

This had something to do with the Avoni people being here. "Has a delegation ever visited the palace before?" Sabine asked, suddenly curious if any kingdom had sent people here in the past. In Bakley, they had the dukes and landowners visit frequently, but not often did dignitaries come from other kingdoms. Her father did meet with kings and queens, but usually at a neutral, convenient location and not at their home.

"No," Marin answered.

"They're taking a great risk being here, aren't they?" Sabine thought out loud as she stepped closer to her ladies. "Trusting us to protect them while they're here, in our palace." Especially given Lynk's reputation as a kingdom of brutal soldiers.

"They are," Regina answered.

"Tell me, has your husband been busy preparing his soldiers for this visit?" Sabine asked.

Regina held her gaze. "As far as I'm aware, his duties have not changed."

Given everything Rainer had told her, it didn't seem right that he'd allow a delegation to come into his home without additional guards and protection in place. Especially knowing that Avoni trained assassins. For all they knew, they could have a dozen assassins in the palace just waiting to strike. Needing to change the subject, she said, "Did you know we're hosting a masquerade tomorrow evening?"

"I received my invitation about an hour ago," Regina said.

"Do you think the Avoni people will even dress up?" Cassandra asked. "They seem like a boring lot."

The women all chuckled. Surely others had to be aware of Avoni's tie to assassins. However, based upon these women's easy demeanor, she wasn't certain.

Karmen looked pointedly at Sabine. "I'm wondering why throw a party at all, especially with the wedding so close."

Sabine had been wondering the same thing.

Regina sighed. "It's clear none of you have husbands in the military." She shook her head. "The party is clearly a distraction." Her attention turned to the guards at the perimeter, probably making sure they were far enough away and hadn't overheard her.

"What does the king want to distract the Avoni delegation for?" Karmen asked.

It felt as if they all took a step forward, toward one another, tightening their circle.

"I have no idea." Regina shrugged.

"If you had to guess?" Sabine said.

She glanced about the courtyard before answering. "I'd say something is probably going on tomorrow night. The king must want to ensure the Avoni people are at the party and accounted for, so they don't discover whatever it is he plans on doing." Her hands kept fidgeting with the cane she leaned on. "Now, if you'll excuse me, Your Highness, I must take my leave."

"Thank you, Lady Regina," Sabine said, her voice louder than it needed to be. "Your knowledge on this rose is quite insightful."

Regina bowed her head and then made her way out of the courtyard.

"What do you think is going on?" Sabine asked softly, feigning innocence. The more she learned about Rainer, the more she appreciated his ability to control the kingdom, the army, and his people. He seemed to have a keen understanding of what needed to be done. If he was planning something tomorrow, then it had to be because he wanted to investigate the Avoni people.

"The king can't harm the delegation while they're here in his palace," Cassandra mused. "It would cause a war if he did."

And Rainer wasn't stupid—he'd never harm a person, let alone a delegation, visiting his palace.

"If he wants them in one place and accounted for, do you think it's so he can search their rooms?" Marin asked.

"What would he be looking for?" Cassandra asked.

"Surely no one would have brought something incriminating with them," Sabine said. No one would be that stupid.

"Didn't they come by boat?" Karmen asked.

"Yes," Sabine answered.

"Then that's it," Karmen said. "King Rainer is going to search their boat while everyone is here dancing."

"What does he hope to find?" Sabine asked, trying to come up with something that made sense.

"He must suspect something," Karmen said.

Sabine happened to agree with her, although she couldn't imagine what.

"If they catch him, it'll start a war," Marin said.

"Maybe they're responsible for Princess Alina's death," Karmen said. "Maybe the king is looking for evidence."

Sabine knew he suspected one of his own. But what if he intended on planting evidence? She shoved the thought away. That didn't make any sense.

"If we go to war," Marin said, "will Bakley stand with Lynk?"

"Of course," Sabine replied. As the words left her lips, she realized that was why the other kingdoms were objecting to her marrying Rainer in the first place. She needed to be alone so she could think this through. "I must go. I have a costume to plan for tomorrow." She turned and started to head toward the exit.

"A war will cost thousands of lives," Cassandra said from behind her. "It's better to use diplomacy rather than swords."

Sabine happened to agree with her. However, she needed to figure out what was going on, so she could stop it in the first place.

Walking out onto the balcony where about two dozen guests had assembled for an impromptu gathering in honor of the Avoni delegation, Sabine easily spotted Rainer and his siblings among those in attendance. Taking a deep breath, she forced her temper under control. She'd been trying to speak with the king all day, but he hadn't had time for her since he'd been too busy playing host.

A servant handed Sabine a drink. She took the goblet and headed over to Lady Regina.

"I advise you to use this opportunity to speak with someone far more interesting than me," Regina said. Then lowering her voice, she whispered, "I'm trying to get closer to that man over there. I think he's a commander in the Avoni military."

Sabine took a sip and peered at the man in question.

"The woman to my right is an adviser to the king and queen of Avoni. She knows a great many things." Regina gave a slight nod and then headed toward the man she'd mentioned previously.

Sabine smiled at those present while moving closer to the woman Regina had pointed out. When the woman was finally alone, Sabine moved in. "It's a nice evening out," she said by way of greeting.

"Princess Sabine." The woman's assessing eyes scanned Sabine from head to toe.

"Lynk's fashion takes some getting used to," Sabine said. "I've tried embracing all I can, even if I feel ridiculous."

The woman chuckled, clasping her hands behind her back.

"However," Sabine continued, "let's not let appearances get in the way of what really matters."

"And what really matters, Princess Sabine?"

"Duty, family, loyalty."

The woman—who still hadn't introduced herself—sucked in a deep breath, scanning the balcony before focusing back on Sabine. "I think it was brave of you to volunteer to take your sister's place and marry King Rainer." The woman's dark blonde hair had been pulled back into a bun, highlighting her narrow cheekbones. She appeared to be around thirty years old, the average age for a prominent advisor to the king and queen.

Sabine mulled over her words. The one that stuck out was the word *volunteer*. Not many knew she'd offered to go in Alina's place. Most people assumed her father had sent her to save the alliance. "I didn't really have a choice," she replied. "Since children are being stolen from my kingdom, I had an obligation to do something. Our borders are not secure. We have no standing army. I did what I had to do to protect my people." She took another sip of her wine.

"I can't imagine many being brave enough to do as you did." She raised her eyebrows, awaiting Sabine's response.

She was being tested; she was sure of it. As to why or what for, she had no idea. "I'm sure anyone in my position would have done the same." She didn't smile because it would have been fake. And for some reason, the need to be authentic with this woman seemed imperative.

"Perhaps."

"What's your name?" Sabine asked, wanting to get to the point.

"Josie."

No last name. No title. "Forgive my bluntness, but I need to ask, is Avoni involved in my sister's death in any way?"

"No." Josie glanced to her right, at one of her companions, the one with the strange dark red hair. She gave him a single nod.

"You understand why I had to ask."

"I understand, though I don't agree."

"Why not?" Sabine asked before she could stop herself, curiosity winning out over decorum.

"If there is a scuffle, do you blame Lynk because it is a kingdom of soldiers? Or if there is a famine, do you blame

Bakley since it's a kingdom of farmers? Or what about a lumber shortage for building homes? Do you blame Nisk since they're known for lumber? Or if you don't have coal to heat your home, do you blame Carlon since they produce the most coal?"

"Well, when you put it that way," Sabine said, not finishing her sentence.

Josie turned to face her. "I can see why Lynk and Bakley feel the need to unite. I understand Bakley has no army and Lynk certainly seems to be suffering from a lack of food." She pointedly looked at Sabine. "You all appear to be starving here."

When she put it like that, Sabine realized Josie was right. Bakley had an army; it just wasn't a large one. Lynk had food, just not a lot of grain for bread and things of that nature. And just because Avoni had assassins didn't mean one of them was responsible for killing Alina. "How did Avoni become known for having assassins?" she asked, trying to steer the conversation to a less heated topic.

A servant walked by, handing Josie a goblet.

Josie took a drink of wine before answering. "I'm surprised you didn't learn this in your studies." She paused, as if waiting for Sabine to respond.

"I probably did," she mumbled. "That's what I get for not paying attention to my tutor. I was always more interested in being outside than learning something I never thought I'd use."

Josie chuckled. "No, I suppose as the sixth child you wouldn't think you'd be in the position you're in." She tilted her head to the side and walked over to the railing.

Sabine followed her. The sun was setting over the mountain, turning the sky a brilliant orange. The two of them leaned on the railing, observing the sight before them.

"A hundred or so years ago, there were two families vying

for the Avoni crown," Josie said, her voice soft. "Each family tried killing the other one by more and more...shall we say creative means? Until only one family survived, and they became the royal line. To this day, the royal family believes in teaching certain skills to keep themselves alive should another rival family decide to try to overthrow them."

That sounded rather intense. Sabine played with the stem of her goblet, lost in thought. "Can I ask you another question?"

"You can ask." Josie took a sip of wine.

"Why is Avoni really here?"

Josie looked sidelong at Sabine. "Since your sister's death, things have changed."

"I don't understand."

"New information has come to light."

"Are you implying that you no longer approve of my marriage to King Rainer?"

"Not necessarily," she answered. "But there are some who feel it needs further consideration."

"Princess Sabine," Axel said as he strolled over and joined them.

When Sabine turned to ask Josie another question, the woman had moved away, already engrossed in a conversation with someone else. A chill slid over Sabine. She couldn't shake the feeling that Axel had interrupted her for a reason.

Chapter Twenty

Walking through the palace, Sabine was eager to return to her room to see Harta. Since nothing else was scheduled for the evening, she planned on curling up in bed with her dog and writing a letter to her family.

Her guards took her down the corridor to the right, which led to the staircase at the back. They didn't usually go this way, but perhaps they wanted to change things up in case her movements were being watched. Her guards suddenly stopped.

Sabine peered around them and saw Heather standing in front of them, blocking the way.

"Your Highness," Heather said. "May I please have a moment of your time?"

"Did you arrange for my guards to bring me this way?" Sabine demanded.

"I simply asked them which way they'd be taking you to your room." Heather remained standing where she was, not coming any closer to Sabine. "I wish to speak privately with you."

Sabine told her guards to remain where they were while she stepped around them and joined Heather. "Now that you have me alone, talk." She folded her arms, waiting for Heather to get to the point.

"I'd prefer a conversation in which no one can overhear." Heather slid a hand over her stomach in a way Sabine had seen her two eldest brothers' wives do when pregnant. "Not even your guards."

The reminder of the woman's condition—knowing it was her husband's child that Heather carried—left an uneasy feeling in her stomach. "Why didn't you just send me a letter requesting to meet privately?"

"I don't want anyone to know about this conversation." Heather glanced at the nearby guards.

Sabine took Heather's arm, pulling her farther down the hallway, away from the soldiers on duty. "What's going on?"

"As you know, Rainer must marry and have a child before he turns twenty-five to maintain his throne. He's running out of time."

Sabine stared into Heather's eyes, trying to figure out where this conversation was going.

"He's asked me to marry and then leave with Cutler before the end of the week. I'm to remain at Cutler's family's residence until after I've delivered."

Nausea rolled through Sabine. She knew where this was going. Standing there, she forced her face to remain neutral.

Heather's eyes filled with tears. "My child will serve as a backup in case you don't get pregnant or deliver a healthy child in time."

"Why did you feel the need to tell me this?" Sabine asked. "Rainer is perfectly capable of speaking on his own behalf." It felt strange to use Rainer's name and no title. It was too informal and personal.

She shrugged, her delicate shoulders rising and falling. "I

wasn't sure if he'd tell you," she whispered. She wiped her eyes, her fingers shaking. "I'm already losing Rainer. If my child is taken away from me as well…"

Sabine reached out, patting Heather's arm. "I understand." There was nothing Sabine could do about it. Rainer was the king and what he said was law. If Sabine didn't get pregnant in time and Rainer decided to pass off Heather's child as Sabine's, they had no choice. Heather understood that and had come here to speak to Sabine as a mother, fearful for her unborn child. However, Sabine couldn't offer any sort of assurance. "It is my intention to give him a child and heir for this great kingdom." It couldn't be that difficult. People got pregnant all the time. Hopefully she'd only have to share Rainer's bed once or twice and then she'd be with child.

Heather flinched.

This was about more than just the child, Sabine realized. It had to do with Sabine sharing the king's bed. Heather still loved Rainer. "I think it is best if you leave with Cutler as soon as possible. Being here and having to see the king with another woman can't be easy." She almost apologized but stopped herself from doing so. As a princess and queen, it wasn't her job to apologize. "I'm here to make Lynk stronger. To secure a bright future." Not deal with a jilted lover.

Heather nodded. "Rainer wants me to return after I have the baby."

Sabine curled her fingers in, forming two fists, trying to figure out if Heather was implying that she'd resume her relationship with Rainer as his consort. Rainer had told Sabine he would not be taking a lover, but she didn't know him well enough to know if he'd been telling the truth or not. Perhaps things had changed since that conversation.

"He still loves me," Heather added. "I know he does."

"My marriage to the king is not about love," Sabine said.

"It is about providing for Lynk and Bakley. I am a royal. And as such, I have a duty to the thousands of people in my kingdom. I know you are concerned about yourself and your unborn child. But I am concerned about thousands of people and thousands of unborn children. I will do what's best for everyone involved. I don't have the luxury of doing what I want or what's in my best interest." With that, she turned and walked away, her arms shaking.

Her guards fell in line behind her. Once she turned the corner, she spun around, facing them. "If any one of you ever pull something like that again, I'll be sure the king knows of it. Unless I'm queen when it happens. Then I'll have you all killed for treason."

"Your Highness," the guard to her right said. "We were told she needed to speak with you. We assumed you'd be amiable to the meeting."

"Don't ever assume anything about me ever again," she said, her voice a tad deeper than she'd intended. From rage or on the verge of crying, she couldn't be sure. But her emotions raged within her. She longed for home and the comfort of her family.

"My apologies. It won't happen again."

Sabine resumed walking. "Thank you."

They went up a flight of stairs and along another hallway, the left side containing several archways revealing the courtyard below. Glancing down, she noticed movement, so she slowed to get a better look. Axel had a woman at his side. He kissed her, and they embraced.

The palace seemed to be abuzz with activity this evening.

The day of the masquerade ball arrived. Late last night, she'd sent a note to the king since she hadn't been able to speak with him privately, asking if they'd be wearing matching masks this evening. She was pleased to find his response when she awoke stating that she was free to wear whatever she wanted.

Originally, she'd planned to dress as a peacock or some form of elegant bird. However, in her dream last night, she danced with hundreds of beautiful butterflies. Unable to get the image out of her head, she quickly drew one on a piece of paper, deciding that she simply had to be a butterfly for the ball. She sent the drawing to the royal seamstress asking the woman to design a mask.

After dressing for the day, she went out onto her balcony. A light mist covered the nearby mountains like a soft, fuzzy blanket. Even though the sky was light, the sun had not yet risen high enough to see it. She breathed in the fresh air, reveling in the crispness of it. No heavy wheat or animal smells here in Lynk.

"Excuse me, Your Highness," a deep voice said from behind her.

Her heart pounded as she jumped from fright, a yelp escaping her mouth. She spun around and saw a man dressed head to toe in black blocking the archway leading to her room. His legs were slightly bent as if he'd just jumped onto her balcony from up above.

"Forgive the intrusion," he said, his gloved hands facing out in a placating gesture, "but I need to speak with you." The only things visible were his pale green eyes.

She took a step back, away from him, hitting the railing.

He reached up, pulling his mask down, revealing his entire face.

Sabine recognized him as one of the men from the Avoni delegation. He was the youngest of the group and the one with the dark red hair. "Are you here to kill me?" she whispered, unable to speak any louder since she was so stunned. She couldn't even scream for help.

His brows drew together in confusion. "Kill you?"

She nodded.

"If I wanted to kill you, you'd be dead instead of standing here talking to me."

She slid her hand down her side, reaching for her dagger and not finding it strapped to her leg like it was supposed to be. Panicking, she glanced into her room and spotted Harta sneaking up behind him.

The man's eyes narrowed and then he slowly sat on the ground, his hands out on either side of him, revealing he wasn't armed. "I mean you no harm," he said. "I've been trying to get a meeting with you, but the king refused."

Twisting her hand so her palm faced down, she gave the silent command for Harta to freeze. The dog immediately stopped advancing. "You should have tried knocking. I would have admitted you."

"I did try. Your guards turned me away."

"Sneaking into my room doesn't foster good relations between our kingdoms."

"I agree. However, I need to make sure you are not being held here against your will."

She smiled. "Not unless you are preventing me from leaving?"

"I am not."

"If someone finds you in here, you'll be killed."

"I know."

She tilted her head to the side, trying to understand this strange man before her.

"Is someone here in the palace holding you here against your will?" the man asked again, as if it really mattered.

"No." She folded her arms across her chest as if that would protect her. "Why does Avoni care anyway?"

"There is a powerful organization that does not want you and King Rainer to marry."

"The League of Rulers?" she asked, her interest suddenly piqued.

"You know of the League?"

"A little." She wished her father had told her about them, so she'd have a better idea of what she was dealing with. "Can you explain why they oppose my marrying the king, but it was okay for my sister?" What she really wanted to know was if the League hadn't approved of Alina's wedding either. If that were the case, then they could be behind her death.

There was a long pause before the man answered. "New information has been revealed that changes things."

"My father only made one small alteration in the contract. That can be easily fixed."

"That's not it."

"Who, exactly, are you?" Sabine asked. "And how do you know all of this?" He could just be trying to scare her.

"I'm from Avoni. We intercepted a letter that gives us reason to believe something devious is in the works. I was sent here simply to make sure you are not being held in Lynk against your will."

Unable to fathom who in Lynk would be holding her here against her will, she said, "If there's anyone I need to be afraid of, it's someone like you. Someone from Avoni. You're the ones known for being assassins."

The young man's eyes narrowed. "Sometimes there are things worse than death. I suggest you consider what role you play here in this pretty little palace. Not all is as it seems." He slowly stood and moved to his left until he reached the railing, glancing over the side.

"You're not going to jump, are you?"

He peered at her. "If you're here of your own free will, then my job here is done." He climbed up onto the railing and then scaled the wall, going up. He disappeared over the roof.

Sabine rushed over to the wall, feeling it. It wasn't as smooth as she'd thought it was. Several of the stones jutted out, making climbing it feasible.

Hurrying into her room, she found Harta still sitting where she'd told her to sit. She released her, giving her a big hug. Harta licked her face, making her smile.

"There really should be doors on these archways," Sabine said to the dog. "Doors that lock."

She stood and started pacing in her room, trying to decide what to do. The idea of screaming and alerting her guards didn't seem like the best course of action. She had no idea why, but her gut told her to keep this encounter to herself. The man had meant her no physical harm. Like he'd said, if he had, she'd be dead. Which meant he'd either been there to warn her or to scare her. The question became why he would do either one of those things.

Going over to her desk, she found her mother's letter and read it again, trying to see if there was anything she'd missed the first time. The part about Rolf discovering conflicting evidence and being fearful of something going on they weren't aware of concerned her. Especially since the man she'd just encountered had said something eerily similar.

Could the Avoni delegation be trusted or not? She resumed pacing. Were they friends or foes? Yesterday when she'd spoken to her lady friends in the courtyard, they'd wondered if the masquerade was a distraction so the king could have the Avoni ship searched. If Rainer was doing something so extreme, he had to have reason to suspect the Avoni delegation of treachery.

If they were harboring something terrible, the best place to hide it would be in the palace. The king couldn't have their rooms searched without causing a major incident. But she could accidentally stumble into the Avoni delegation's rooms and look around them herself. Everyone would be at the masquerade, and no one would suspect her of doing something like that. If she was caught, she could claim ignorance and say she simply wanted to speak to the red-haired man.

By the time the night was over, she'd have her answer regarding Avoni. As to whether Rainer or Sabine would be the one to discover it, she didn't know. But either way, this cat and mouse game was going to end.

Claire entered Sabine's bedchamber carrying something wrapped in a blanket along with a box.

As soon as Sabine saw the items, excitement filled her. "Is that my outfit for this evening?" Despite the huge task ahead of her tonight, dressing up and attending the ball would be fun.

"It is." Claire placed everything on the bed. "The seamstress didn't even let me sneak a peek. I'm curious to see what you chose."

"Let's hope it turned out half as good as I imagined." She removed her clothes and then slipped the outfit on. Turning slowly before the full-length mirror, she couldn't help but marvel at how it had turned out. "I love it."

"It is rather striking. No one will have anything like it in the palace, I'm sure."

Sabine didn't know if that was a jab aimed at her or not, but she didn't care. Granted, the outfit wasn't in the traditional Lynk style. However, since it was a masquerade, she thought it highly appropriate. The dress was form-fitting on top while loose and flowing on the bottom. The skirt and sleeves were made from a sheer fabric—the sleeves see-through while the skirt had layer upon layer of pale pink and a soft blue material. The bodice was etched with gold, and to top it off, the shoulders had butterfly wings attached to them. It went perfectly with her mask which covered the portion of her face near her eyes; each side a butterfly wing encrusted with jewels. She twirled, watching the layers of the skirt float with the movement.

"Am I to arrive with the king?" she asked. She hadn't seen him all day and had no idea what he'd been up to. Probably planning his clandestine trip to the Avoni ship this evening.

"Yes. He's waiting for you in his room. You are to join him once you're ready."

Taking one last look in the mirror, she smiled, ready to get on with the evening.

After kissing Harta's snout, she went over to the door connecting her room to the king's and knocked.

It opened a moment later, and Gunther ushered her inside. "You can wait here for the king. I'll let him know you're ready." He bowed then left.

Watching his retreating form, Sabine realized she needed to try harder to get the steward to trust her a bit more. It seemed he still kept her at arm's length and his unfaltering loyalty was clearly to the king.

Meandering over to the sitting room, she decided to remain standing so she wouldn't mess up her dress.

The king joined her a moment later. "I did not expect so delicate a partner this evening," he said by way of greeting.

"And I did not expect you to be so majestic tonight." The golden mask the king wore looked as if it had been molded to his face. Perhaps it was. On each side, large antlers stuck out. "Are you a deer?"

"Elk," he said with a grin. "I find it difficult to move my head."

She would imagine so. "Is the entire mask made of gold?" It had to weigh a lot.

"It is. I'm not sure how long I'll keep it on." He wore brown pants and a long-sleeved brown tunic that was buttoned closed. The mask covered his face from his nose up, hiding his eyes.

If she hadn't heard Rainer's voice, she wouldn't know it was the king standing before her. Maybe that was the point. If two men wore the exact same outfit, or switched outfits, no one would know.

"Is everything all right?" he asked.

She nodded. What she found disconcerting was not seeing his eyes. With the mask on, the part of Rainer that she found appealing had been stripped away. It was easier to keep her wits about her and not be sucked into the essence of him.

"Let's be on our way," the king said, holding out his hand for her to take.

Sabine slid her hand into his, and they exited the king's chambers. Their guards surrounded them and then they headed through the palace.

"I assume we're going to the ballroom?" she asked, wanting to make polite conversation. Since their marriage, they'd barely spent any time together.

"No. Tonight, we are in the throne room. I thought it would be better since it's more open and would help set the mood."

That surprised her. "And what mood is that?" She wondered why she hadn't been consulted when planning the masquerade. Her mother usually planned events like this back home. It was surprising Rainer had bothered to make these sorts of decisions. Unless, as she suspected, there was more going on tonight than he wanted her to know.

He leaned in and whispered, "Seductive." Then he

straightened and said in a regular voice, "Too bad your outfit isn't more appropriate for the evening."

His words stung. She thought he liked it since he'd made that comment earlier. He'd said she looked *delicate*. He'd chosen that word for a reason. Maybe he didn't want someone delicate by his side since he was a warrior king. He wanted—needed—a warrior queen. She'd chosen to dress the way she wanted tonight, not taking his or Lynk's needs into account. It went against everything she believed by having to tailor herself to fit a mold. Yet, she was the king's wife and the queen of Lynk. If they needed her to play a part in strengthening the kingdom, she would. When she was alone, she could be herself. But not at social gatherings such as this. Lesson learned.

They reached the ante chamber of the throne room.

"Your siblings aren't here?" she asked.

"No. They're already at the ball. We will enter separately from them."

Somehow the act felt important but before she could ask him about it, Rainer went over and knocked on the door.

A voice on the other side announced, "Lords and Ladies, esteemed guests, may I present His Majesty, King Rainer Manfred, and Her Highness, Princess Sabine Ludwig."

The doors opened.

Rainer took her hand and led her into the throne room.

Chapter Twenty-One

Like the last time Sabine had been in the throne room, thousands of candles hung from the domed ceiling, casting the area in a soft glow. Warm air floated in since there weren't any walls. A group of musicians were situated off to the side. A couple hundred guests were in attendance. Most wore brightly colored outfits. Many of the men wore loose fitting pants, vests open in the front, and their masks covered their eyes and foreheads. Sabine spotted several bear, wolf, and deer masks. The women wore sleeveless dresses with high slits revealing their legs. Their masks tended to cover less of their faces and were mostly flowers or exotic plants.

As Sabine stood there holding Rainer's hand, she easily spotted members from the Avoni delegation since they wore dark colors, a stark contrast to everyone else in the room. The Avoni men had what Sabine considered proper tunics and pants, fully covering their bodies. The women wore floor length dresses with long sleeves. Their masks tended to be a single color covering their lips up to their foreheads, none of them representing an animal.

After Rainer said a few words to the guests, he led Sabine to the center of the room for a dance, everyone parting to make way for them. The musicians began playing a soft, haunting tune that Sabine considered an odd choice. A joyful, fast-paced tune would have been preferable. However, the slow song allowed Rainer to easily lead Sabine around the dance floor without her getting tripped up. The skirts of her dress swayed, almost matching the music.

As they turned, she saw a maskless face behind Rainer amongst the crowd of people watching them. She blinked, and he was gone. How strange to have seen a single face among a sea of masks. Especially a face she thought she recognized. A face she'd seen before—the red-haired man from her balcony.

"We haven't trained in a couple of days," Rainer said. "Let's meet tomorrow before breakfast."

"That's a good idea." Not only did she want to practice, but it would give her the chance to speak with him privately on a few pressing matters.

"I'll admit to being disappointed in your attire this evening. Next time, I will make sure to have Claire take care of your clothing."

It was a good thing she'd spent years learning how to conceal her emotions. Anger and hurt warred within. "I understand my error," she said. "It will not happen again. I apologize." She wished she could see around his eyes to determine his reaction.

"At least you're a quick learner." He dragged his right hand up her back, over her shoulder, and along her arm, shaking his head. "Every single time I touch you, I should be able to feel your skin." As the song came to an end, Rainer leaned forward, placing a kiss on her bare neck.

Sabine shivered, not having expected the intimate gesture.

He released her and the two of them faced the guests, everyone clapping.

"I believe you know the drill," Rainer mumbled.

"I do." She spotted Regina standing with her husband, Felix, not far away. Felix stepped forward, and Rainer handed her over to the commander. It was the first time she'd seen him not in uniform. Rainer took Regina's hand just as the music started back up.

"Commander Felix," Sabine said as the man placed his free hand on her back.

"Princess," he replied.

"I see you've come as a wolf this evening." She honestly wouldn't have recognized him had he not been standing with Regina.

"I thought it a fitting creature for the commander of the army."

"I agree." She glanced about the room. Everyone else had returned to dancing now that the king had completed his first dance. "Tell me, have Cutler and Heather married yet?"

He slowed the pace, almost stopping in the middle of the dance floor. "Are you implying you won't be attending their wedding?"

"Not at all," she said with a forced smile. "In my kingdom, the royal family doesn't go to many weddings. I did not realize it was the custom here." She was making one blunder after another tonight.

He grunted, barely moving to the music. She wondered how someone so capable with a sword could be so lacking on the dance floor.

"My wife tells me you will make a good queen," he said, peering at her. "I will admit, I've had my doubts. But she has spent time with you; I have not. Plus, King Rainer seems to think you are what this kingdom needs."

Sabine kept her mouth shut. She wasn't sure where he was going with this.

"As the commander of the Lynk army, I serve the king... and the queen. I will be first in line to pledge my loyalty to you during the coronation."

Shock rippled through her. She hadn't expected him to make such a declaration. "Thank you. When I'm crowned queen, you have my word that I will always put Lynk first. Everything I do will be for this kingdom." She hoped he heard the sincerity in her words.

He nodded. "I'm glad to hear it."

The song came to an end.

"Thank you for the honor of the dance," Felix said with a bow.

The night wore on. Sabine danced with one person after another. Since everyone wore masks, she often had no idea who she was dancing with. These functions had been much more fun in Bakley when she didn't have an important role to play. She could dance with whomever she wanted and sneak away to a dark corner for some gossip.

As the night wore on, she became parched. Fearful she'd never have a break to get a drink, she excused herself from her current partner before the song ended and hurried over to the drink table situated off to the side. It was filled with wine and ale. Needing some water, she left the throne room, finding her guards just outside of it.

"Your Highness," one of the guards said, "is something the matter?"

"I am in need of a drink of water."

"I will go directly to the kitchen myself to fetch it. Please wait here." He bowed and then hurried away.

Thankful for the break, she leaned against the nearby wall, just out of sight in case anyone exited the throne room or came this way. The last thing she wanted was someone dragging her back in there for another dance. However, she made sure to remain in full view of her guards.

Closing her eyes, she took a deep breath, letting it out slowly. It was quiet out here in the hallway. Peaceful.

"Princess, your water."

She opened her eyes and took the cup. "Thank you."

The guard turned and joined her other guards not far away.

Movement caught her attention, and she glanced down toward the other end of the hallway. A man dressed in black walked past, his cape floating behind him. He turned his head and grinned—his smile the only thing visible with his mask on. He had to be one of the guests at the ball. And then he stepped out of sight.

Goosebumps covered her skin, though the air remained warm.

Needing to make another appearance at the ball, she finished off her water and handed the cup to one of her guards. She'd go back in, dance to a few songs, and then slip away, unnoticed. She just needed an hour or so to search the rooms the Avoni delegation was staying in. That should be more than enough time to snoop around to see if she could learn anything of importance.

When she returned to the throne room, a man immediately stepped in front of her, requesting the next dance. Based upon his black outfit and simple mask, he had to be from Avoni.

Sabine agreed, and the man gently took her hand. They began dancing. Even with the mask on, she could tell he was an older man, in his forties, based upon the lines around his mouth and the dark spots on his hands.

"How are you liking Lynk?" she asked, wanting to make some polite conversation.

"It is too hot and humid for my taste," he replied, guiding

her toward the edge of the room, on the fringe of those dancing.

"It is rather humid here," she agreed. "I'm sorry, I didn't catch your name."

The corners of his lips rose. "That is because I didn't give one."

"Do you have a title I can use?" His evasiveness made her uneasy. Not only that, but she was a princess and outranked him. When she asked for a name, he needed to give it.

He peered around before leaning closer to her and whispering, "If it's money your family needs, there are other kingdoms with the means to assist you."

It was a good thing no one was nearby to overhear this conversation. When she'd first agreed to dance with the man, she'd hoped to learn a thing or two about Avoni. Not once did she consider it going this way.

"My family does not need money," she replied. "Besides, the contract has been signed. It cannot be broken." Although, thinking it over, if Bakley had more money, they could afford to fund a larger army. But her father had never seen the need. Regardless, at a time like this, having extra resources would help.

"The contract is meaningless."

She opened her mouth to argue.

"New information has come to light," he said.

"What information?" she asked. They'd stopped dancing altogether.

"You don't know?"

She shook her head.

He glanced about. "How can you even be in this palace knowing your sister died here?"

Her hand tightened around his. "My kingdom's children are being kidnapped." She would do whatever necessary to stop the kidnappings and protect the Bakley children.

Being careful not to make eye contact or garner anyone's attention, she stepped out into the hallway.

"Princess?" a guard said. He wasn't one of her personal guards but rather, one of the many stationed throughout the surrounding corridors for security this evening.

She stepped closer to him and said in a soft voice, "I'm feeling dizzy. Can you please escort me to a nearby guest room? I want to lie down for a few minutes to catch my breath."

He shifted his weight from foot to foot.

"I know this is terribly untoward, but I am embarrassed and don't want the king to see me like this. Your assistance won't be forgotten once I'm queen."

He nodded. "Of course, Your Highness. This way."

Relief filled her as he led her down the hallway, away from the throne room.

The Avonis were staying in the east wing. From what she understood, they had a joined sitting room with individual bedchambers off it. She should be able to scour the sitting room and maybe one or two bedchambers if time permitted.

Her hands began to sweat. The problem with her outfit was that if anyone saw a glimpse of it, they would know it was hers. She should have worn something inconspicuous.

They turned down another corridor. Something sounded behind her, so she glanced back. The same man that she'd seen earlier, the one dressed all in black with a cape, passed by the intersection, heading the other way.

"Princess?" the guard in front of her said.

She realized she'd stopped.

"Is everything all right?" he asked.

"Did you see that man?"

"I did not. Shall we go and get additional guards?"

"That won't be necessary. I was simply going to ask his name." She forced a smile on her face. "Let's be on our way."

They entered the west wing. The guard stopped at the third door on the right. "Wait here," he said as he opened the door and stepped inside. He returned a moment later. "The room is empty."

"Excellent. I am going to take a short nap. Do not disturb me. When I awake, I will let you know, and you can escort me back to the throne room at that time." Without waiting for his reply, she closed the door, leaving him out in the hallway.

The only light came from the moon shining in through the window. Sabine went over to the bed and shoved two of the pillows under the blankets, making it look like a body was lying there sleeping. Satisfied that if the guard peaked in, he'd believe her to be asleep, she went over to the corner of the room where she thought the servants' entrance would be. When she'd asked Gunther about the servants' passageways, he'd told her they didn't connect to the royal wing for security reasons. However, each guest room or suite had a door leading to the network of passageways known only by the most trusted servants.

Sabine squatted and put her hand beneath the door, pulling it toward her. It opened. She stood and stepped inside the passageway, gently closing the door behind her. Oil lamps lit the space in a soft glow every fifty feet or so. They seemed to be positioned away from the doors so as not to shine beneath them. It was just enough light for her to see along the corridor. She'd been told there were five single rooms on either side and then the suites began. The Avoni delegation was staying in the first set of suites. Since she'd been in the third room on the right, she needed to go three more doors until she reached the correct location.

Not having a lot of time, she needed to get moving. She hurried to the third door and slowly pushed it open, peering inside. The room was dark. She didn't hear anything or see any movement, so she pushed the door open farther and stepped inside. She found herself in a large sitting room with two short hallways jutting off either side of it. On the low table between the four sofas, a handful of papers had been scattered about. She went over and looked at them, not recognizing a single word. They had to be written in another language. Moving a few, she checked the papers below the ones on top, not finding anything she could read.

Frustrated, she went to the hallway on the right. It had six doors off it, three on either side, leading to bedchambers. Pressing her ear against the first door, she listened, not hearing anything. She opened the door an inch and peered inside. It was empty, so she pushed the door open and went in. The bed had been neatly made and a bag sat on top of it. She went over and opened the bag. It was filled with clothes. As if the person had packed and was ready to leave. She closed it and left the room, going to the one across from it. Inside, she also found the room tidy, and a bag packed.

As far as she knew, the delegation wasn't supposed to leave any time soon. She was just about to exit the room when she heard a doorknob jiggle. Pressing her body against the wall, she kept the door cracked open and listened. If someone had returned early from the masquerade, she'd have to sneak out of here once that person went to his or her room since the guest suite only had an entrance to the servants' passageways in the sitting room. Her heart thudded and panic set it. What if the person stayed in the sitting room and more of the delegation returned? She'd need to come up with another way out of the suite. Maybe she could hide under the bed and then once everyone went to sleep, she could sneak out. However, by then someone would realize she was missing, and a search would be carried out for her. Everything seemed to be going wrong tonight.

"She can't be touched now that she's been crowned," someone whispered. "At least not by anyone here in Lynk."

They were talking about her—and not many knew she'd been crowned. She leaned closer to the door, straining to hear the people whispering.

"No one knows she's the queen. I can still arrange for her to be killed in a way that can't be traced back to you. I promise."

"It was supposed to be done the first time."

"Technically it was when we took care of her sister. When you hired me, it was one person, not two. The fact that things have changed is not my fault. Besides, if you'd let me handle her death the way I wanted to, the mess in the sewing room wouldn't have happened. That's on you."

Red filled the corners of Sabine's vision as rage inundated her. She had to force herself to breathe slowly, trying to calm herself down, so she didn't do something stupid like run out there and confront the murderers. If these were people from Avoni, they'd enter their rooms soon and she wouldn't get another chance to see their faces. She had to look so she could identify them.

"Why did you want to meet me here?" the one whispered.

"To arrange a new deal," the other answered. "I will plant evidence here that Avoni is responsible for her death."

A ruffling noise sounded, though Sabine had no idea what it was.

A low chuckle filled the room. "Oh, that is good. I can see why your services are so valued. Yes, right there is perfect."

"I want double my payment."

"Done."

"And now that this has been put in the room, we can go. I'll take care of Sabine tonight."

If Sabine didn't look now, she'd never get the chance. She

pulled the door toward her more, leaning her head out into the hallway.

She caught a glimpse of long, dark brown hair. The woman wore a navy-blue dress with a matching mask covered with feathers. The man at her side wore traditional Lynk clothing. The two of them exited the suite.

The second the door clicked shut, Sabine hurried from the room. She scanned the sitting area, looking for whatever had been left behind and not seeing anything. Not having time to lose, she turned, about to leave, when she spotted something on the floor, sticking out from under one of the sofas. She knelt and picked up the paper. It was a letter and written in her language. Not wanting to take the time to read it now, she shoved it in her dress and hurried from the room.

She used the servants' passageway, counting the doors until she reached hers. She opened it and went inside. If an assassin was coming for her, she needed to return to the party and let Rainer know. She had to tell him everything she'd overheard. Not bothering to fix the bed, she exited the room and found her guard across the hallway, sitting on the floor beside a different door, slouched over. Sabine knelt and examined him. He had odd spots on his skin and his eyes were lifeless.

Bile rose in her throat. He was dead. The assassin must have killed him on his way to the guest suite. Thankfully the guard wasn't at the door to the room she'd been in. However, that didn't mean she was safe. The assassin could be searching the passageways right now. And Sabine was all alone.

She stood and ran. She had to get back to the masquerade and find Rainer.

The palace seemed oddly empty at this hour. She sprinted past the library, down another corridor, and then turned down the hallway leading to the throne room. The sound of music filled the air, and she spotted several sentries up ahead, putting her at ease.

She forced herself to slow.

"Princess," one of the guards said, "is everything all right?"

Holding her head high, she assured him that it was.

"Princess Sabine," Lottie said from behind her. "I was just looking for you."

Relief filled her at Lottie's presence. Together they could find Rainer and tell him what was going on. She wasn't alone in this.

She turned around, about to tell Lottie everything, when she froze, unable to utter a single word.

Lottie was wearing a navy-blue dress and a mask covered with feathers. She was the woman with the assassin from the guest suite.

Chapter Twenty-Two

Sabine forced herself to maintain a smile as she faced the woman responsible for her sister's death. Her entire body shook as she tried to grasp the fact that Lottie had hired an assassin to kill Alina. Questions swirled in her mind as to how and why. Then she remembered learning that Lottie was next in line for the throne. She had to find Rainer and tell him his sister was trying to overthrow him. And then another unwelcome realization hit her. Rainer already knew it was Lottie. That was why he'd secretly married Sabine. It felt as if her world tilted to the side.

"Are you all right?" Lottie asked.

"I'm perfectly fine," she lied.

A couple exited the throne room, arms linked together, laughing. "Princess Lottie!" the woman cooed.

Sabine used the distraction to step past them. She entered the throne room, scanning the sea of faces. Perfume, ale, and laughter filled the air. With everyone wearing a mask, she didn't see anyone she recognized. If Rainer was searching the Avoni ship, he wouldn't even be here. Panic filled her.

A man approached. "May I have this dance?" he asked.

"I must speak with King Rainer. It's of the utmost importance. Have you seen him?"

He shook his head.

She walked out among the dancers, searching for Rainer.

People bumped into her, laughing, too drunk to apologize for touching someone of her rank.

She spotted Lottie on the other side of the room, talking to someone and laughing as if she didn't have a care in the world. Their eyes locked and Sabine had to look away.

The music seemed too loud; the room too hot.

"Princess, a dance?" another person asked.

She ignored him, pushing past people to find the king.

The man she'd seen before, the one dressed all in black with a cape, stood ten feet away. A couple spun before her, and she lost sight of him. Standing still, she turned in a slow circle, looking for Rainer while keeping an eye out for the mysterious man. The assassin she'd seen in the guest suite hadn't had a cape on, so she didn't think it was the same person. However, she couldn't be certain at this point.

She never would have suspected Lottie would be behind her sister's death.

Now that she was looking at those around her, she realized no one from Avoni was here. They must have all left. Not finding the king, she headed to the other side of the room. Perhaps he was out on the balcony. At the edge of the dance floor, she glanced at the balcony, finding it empty.

"Princess," a deep voice said from right next to her left shoulder. Something was shoved against her mouth and nose for a brief second and then it was removed.

Shocked, she spun to face the person, just as a potent smell hit her—one she recognized immediately.

Images of back home flashed before her eyes. Sitting at the dining table with her mother, several bowls before them. Queen Elsa instructed Sabine on how to memorize the various poisons by associating their smell with something. The one bowl contained a most dangerous poison.

"Giplig," she whispered as she looked up into a masked face. It was the man in black. The one with the cape.

He lowered his hand, which had a black handkerchief against his palm. "Yes," he whispered, seemingly surprised.

Her senses started to dull. She tried speaking, but no words came out. She knew she had less than a minute until she blacked out.

The man held her as if dancing. He glided them closer to the edge of the room and then out onto the balcony.

She hoped he didn't toss her over the side, letting her plummet to her death. Although, it would be a fitting death considering how stupid she'd been. She knew her sister's killer, she knew about the poison giplig, and yet here she was. She reached down, fumbling through the fabric of her dress until she found her dagger. She withdrew it, and it fell from her limp fingers, clinking onto the stone floor.

Her world went black.

Sabine felt as if her body were swaying up and down in a gentle rocking motion. Was she falling to her death? No, she didn't think so. She'd be dead by now if that were the case. Breathing in, she smelled salt and wood. A strange combination.

She peeled her eyelids open. Everything was blurry. She blinked several times, clearing the haze from her eyes. A low wooden ceiling was above her, and she was lying on a narrow bed.

"You're awake," a male voice said.

She turned her head to the side, toward the voice, and saw a man dressed all in black. He'd removed his mask revealing a face she recognized. "You're the man from my balcony." The one with red hair.

"Yes," he said.

"You're from Avoni." He was the youngest in the delegation. Sabine guessed his age to be close to hers.

"I am." He was sitting on a chair next to the bed, his elbows resting on his thighs with his hands clasped together.

It dawned on her that he was the one who'd drugged her. "Have you...kidnapped me?" she asked in disbelief.

"Yes."

The word sounded loud in the small room.

Terror gripped her. "Where are we?" she demanded, pushing herself to a sitting position in order to better observe her surroundings. She didn't see a weapon anywhere.

"I'm sorry, but I couldn't let the marriage happen."

Her mind continued to clear. Now that she was sitting, she could feel the rocking motion. "We're on a boat."

He nodded.

"Where are you taking me?"

He obviously hadn't killed her yet for a reason. Which meant he not only wanted to prevent the marriage, but he wanted her alive for something. She did not want to be held hostage for ransom or used as a bargaining chip. Her mother had told her being kidnapped was a fate worse than death.

"The League of Rulers did not sanction your marriage to the king of Lynk."

"They sanctioned my sister's."

"And you are not your sister."

"No." Because she was dead. The memories of her last moments before being drugged bombarded her. She dropped her face into her hands. Rainer's own sister had killed hers. She rubbed her temples, her head starting to pound.

"Here." The young man reached for a cup of water and

handed it to her. "It'll help clear the poison out of your system."

The poison *he'd* given her. She eyed the water, wondering if it contained another poison. However, she knew if he'd wanted her dead, she'd be dead. She took the cup and drank it all.

"I'm really sorry about this," he said. "If you married King Rainer, it would have given him too much power. I had to stop it from happening."

"*You* had to stop it from happening? Or the *League* had to stop it? Or *Avoni*?" Who was he and who was he working for?

"All three."

She set the cup down. "It's a shame you're too late."

"Too late?" His brows drew together. "What do you mean?"

"I already married the king, and I wear the queen's crown."

OTHER BOOKS BY JENNIFER ANNE DAVIS

True Reign:

The Key

Red

War

Reign of Secrets:

Cage of Deceit

Cage of Darkness

Cage of Destiny

Oath of Deception

Oath of Destruction

Knights of the Realm:

Realm of Knights

Shadow Knights

Hidden Knights

Reigning Kingdoms

Sword of Rage

Sword of Desire

League of Rulers

The Queen's Crown

The King's Sword

The Royal Throne

The Order of the Krigers:

Rise

Burning Shadows

Conquering Fate

Single Titles:

Evil Lurks Beneath

The Voice

The Power to See

ABOUT THE AUTHOR

Jennifer Anne Davis graduated from the University of San Diego with a degree in English and a teaching credential. She is currently a full-time writer and mother of three kids. She is happily married to her high school sweetheart and lives in the San Diego area.

Jennifer is the recipient of the San Diego Book Awards Best Published Young Adult Novel (2013), winner of the Kindle Book Awards (2018), a finalist in the USA Best Book Awards (2014), and a finalist in the Next Generation Indie Book Awards (2014).

Visit Jennifer at:
www.JenniferAnneDavis.com

facebook.com/AuthorJenniferAnneDavis

x.com/authorjennifer

instagram.com/authorjennifer

bookbub.com/authors/jennifer-anne-davis

goodreads.com/jenniferannedavis

pinterest.com/authorjennifer

tiktok.com/@authorjenniferannedavis